THE ROAD TO GLORY

Lawrence Brooks

Rush to Glory Publishing House

Ottawa, On

Lawrence Brooks

Cover designed by Greg Boileau

This book is a work of fiction. Names, characters, places, and incidents either are products of the author's imagination or are used fictitiously. Any resemblance to actual persons, living or dead, events, or locales is entirely coincidental.

Lawrence Brooks
Visit my website at www.rushtoglory.com

Printed in North America

First Printing: March 2018
Rush to Glory Publishing House

ISBN-978-1-7752488-0-4

Preface

He crossed the finish line hollow, isolated, and drenched in sweat. The media swarmed him. Chaos was everywhere as microphones and cell phones were shoved into the young man's face. Reporters surrounded him, shouting to gain his attention. Roars from the fans dampened his sensations, making him lightheaded. His body was limp, and tears began to stream down his face. His soigneur sensibly concealed it with a damp sponge.

Minutes before, his heart rate had been beating just shy of two hundred. He'd struggled for position in the high-speed peloton that stretched across the Champs Élysées, pushing and shoving to stay upright. He was shaking, choking in anticipation of this moment. The hardened cobbles leading up to the Arc de Triomphe had jolted his bones and numbed his body. He thought of the tomb of the Unknown Soldier buried deep beneath the concrete, the 660 names engraved inside the wall of the monument. Had these three weeks defined his eternal existence?

Race officials were trying their best to escort him to the media tent, but his lycra jersey was being tugged in multiple directions by fans. He knew his next move should be to smile; find the strength to stretch his lips from cheek to cheek, turn his bike around and search for those who had helped him. He should seek out his teammates; not all, but a few. He should grab his close friends on the team and participate in the customary embrace and celebratory fist-pumping; all for the media, of course—the Media! But instead, his eyes moved back and forth scanning the crowd for his fiancée, Emma Blake. He was trembling and felt like vomiting. He needed her.

At one point during the Tour de France, physical and mental exhaustion had bullied him. He would never have imagined being part of the final, magical stage of the most significant annual sporting affair in the world, the mammoth competition that inspired hardened athletes to conquer the harshest external elements while battling one another. Like every cyclist, he had dreamt of growing up and winning the Tour de France, the pinnacle of the sport. He spent countless hours on and off his bike fantasizing of competing in the Tour, wearing the coveted Maillot Jaune, and standing on the top spot of the podium on the final day on the Champs Élysées. Had he prevailed?

He continued searching the crowd for Emma, doing his best to deal with the incessant questioning coming at him from the media. He became frustrated and began waving his hands frantically at the reporters to move out of his way. The constant attention was overwhelming, and he was desperate to see that familiar smile that would melt his heart, his savior. She was the type of woman people noticed; tall and blonde with beautiful, big emerald eyes; the picture of Hollywood. She shouldn't be difficult to pick out of a crowd, but he couldn't make contact.

He looked out into the distance, ignoring the incessant voices screaming in his ear, taking a moment to reflect on the first time he'd laid eyes on her. They met in their hometown, Ottawa, Ontario (Canada's National Capital), three years ago. They'd come across each other at Bridgehead, a free-trade, organic cafe located in Westboro—a hip neighborhood, with an abundant number of excellent eateries, quality java shops, yoga studios, and natural and environmentally responsible retail outlets.

On the weekends, this popular community would become home to cyclists. They'd converge on the patio of every coffee shop for their pre-event pick-me-up espresso, and tables and chairs would quickly disappear. Bikes would be scattered everywhere, propped up against the walls of shops, lamp posts, and newspaper stands. Serving lines would swell in size and locals would be left with no place to sit. Westboro was known to be the place for the free-spirited, ambitious dreamers who wanted to conquer the world. It was a place for people like him.

He recalls sitting at Bridgehead Coffee Shop, sipping an Americano, decked out in his full professional cycling kit. His presence hadn't escaped the attention of every recreational cyclist, and a commotion began building around him. Amid the ruckus, he saw her. She walked by to wipe down a table. They made eye contact for just a moment, and he was nearly floored by her radiant smile.

An older gentleman caught the exchange between Emma and the young cyclist and waved her over. "Do you know him?" he asked.

"No idea. Should I?"

"Of course, you should. He's going to race in the Tour de France someday."

"But will he win it?"

At this very moment, it was a question even the young cyclist was unable to answer, as he searched the sea of screaming fans for his Emma on the Champs Élysées. The media had herded him into the steel barriers like a trapped animal, probing him for answers he couldn't provide. At last, he spotted Emma alongside his parent's and broke free from the media scrum.

He rode up to her an aged man, reaching out with his lifeless arms. He wobbled as his flimsy, narrow tire lost contact with the pavement. Emma grabbed him as his balance deserted him, saving him from an embarrassing crash. With unwavering determination, he brought her close to him and whispered in her ear, "I'm fucking done in every way. I hate this sport. They made me hate it."

CHAPTER 1

Monaco

The Tour Prologue

Monaco at 6:30 a.m. was nothing short of vibrant and breathtaking. The sunrise was effervescent with powerful rays of light bouncing off super anchored yachts in Monte Carlo's Harbor. The sky was void of clouds; a deep, vibrant blue that mirrored the Mediterranean Sea. The air was fresh and crisp. And, as magnificent as the scene was, Nick Carney was not there for the view.

The young cyclist was swaying back and forth in his seat of the Mercedes AMG: a powerful vehicle with an ample amount of torque and acceleration that threw its passengers back and forth. At the wheel was the cycling team's Assistant Director, Willie Lotz. The two were accompanied by the Team Director Tomas Christenson and Team Leader, Jack Bomber. The roads were empty, and the motor of the AMG rumbled triumphantly; an echoing sound that threatened to wake all the sleeping tourist in the many high-rise hotels that lined the roads. By 11 a.m., the streets of Monaco would be littered with close to a quarter of a million die-hard cycling fans waving Tour de France paraphernalia.

The pending crowds and excitement should've been the reason Nick was feeling uneasy since getting into the car earlier this morning, but it wasn't. He was confused as to why he'd been invited on this pre-course recon with Tom and Jack. His hands were wet and shaky, and he wasn't sure what to do with them. His invite didn't sit well with some of his more seasoned teammates. They teased him at breakfast, making the already anxious young man more tense and nervous. He could barely get his food down, forcefully shoving spoonsful of oatmeal into his mouth, and then gagging. His invite seemed to go against the well-established etiquette ingrained within the professional peloton. You had to earn that type of respect. What had Nick done to deserve this invitation?

At twenty-three, Nick was making his debut at the Tour de France. Not many cyclists at his age were presented with this type of opportunity, and Nick knew it. He was confident that over the past few days he'd spotted a few grey hairs that sprouted out of nowhere, giving his dark chocolate-like hair some additional highlights. He was riding for the biggest team in the sport of cycling, and now he was in the car alongside Jack Bomber, two-time champion and the potential winner for this year. What made Nick significant enough to be in the company of one of the greatest cyclists of this era? Nick didn't know. He was perplexed and in awe, and trying to contain his excitement was difficult. His stomach turned in anticipation of being under the spotlight. He was scared—scared as hell.

It was the day of the Prologue of Tour de France. It was a technical course; one that had Willie screeching the AMG through narrow and twisty turns during this recon. Every corner had Nick covering his mouth with his hand. He was positive breakfast was going to make an appearance. He wasn't sure how that would go over with the other men in the car. Thankfully, Tom excitedly rattled off the dangers and challenges of the route. "You'll need to lean the bike hard here. Keep your line. No braking allowed. It must be full speed. We're looking for seconds, guys."

Tom's enthusiasm for the seemingly impossible was almost contagious, but Nick still had his doubts. He fidgeted in the back seat, trying to make room for his long skinny legs. "No braking, Tom? It's a 180-degree turn. Are you sure? I'm not positive I can do it." Bomber looked over at Nick and gave him a wink.

"He's not literal, kid. Relax." Tom softened his tone, realizing he was worrying Nick. "Yes, minimal braking, of course."

The men stopped talking, the car became eerily silent, and Nick became absorbed with Jack's demeanor. It was an authoritative and chiseled face set in stone-cold concentration, taking in the whole course. His deep brown eyes were fixated on mapping out every corner—every marker and piece of road was meaningful, every meter had a purpose. Nick believed he could envision Bomber's thoughts along with the racer; go hard, hold the heart rate close to max, breathe deeply and keep the arms relaxed, head down to break the wind and remain aero, keep the cadence high no matter how badly the legs are screaming to stop. Every second counts. Don't back down. *Goddamn it—are you backing down? DON'T!!*

They approached the finish line, and Nick was clearly lost deep in his thoughts as he observed Bomber. Tom waved his hands fervently back and forth trying to gain Nick's attention.

"Did you hear me, kid?" Tom shouted. But Nick hadn't. He was too focused on taking in every moment. He was engulfed in his thoughts, trying to figure out what would be required to win today. He couldn't admit to not hearing the boss. It would be too embarrassing. What would Tom think of him?

"Yeah, yeah I did, I did," replied Nick.

"So, you'll ride naked with only a helmet on to attain the best aero advantage?" Tom laughed. Nick gave an embarrassed chuckle at himself. He realized he wouldn't be able to bullshit any further. "Oh yeah, no. I guess I'm kind of off in my own world."

"Well, get the fuck out of your head if you plan on doing well today. Details matter, kid. They need to be understood and perfected. We've given you an opportunity seven other guys on the team would kill for. Do you think you're that good you don't need to listen to your Director?"

Nick felt uneasy. He respected Tom, but at that moment Tom had made him feel like he'd stolen an opportunity from his teammates, and it weighed heavily on his mind. Nick wasn't daydreaming about trivial matters, he was focused on winning the race. Why couldn't Tom see that? Nick was sure the man would understand. Instead, Nick wondered if he'd disappointed Jack and Tom.

These two men had become the most prominent figures in the world of cycling over the last few years. Tom, the Danish Director, a former teammate of Bomber, had been given a World Tour Team to manage. He had wasted no time recruiting Jack Bomber. He knew the man well and knew his talents were being lost at his former team. Their Management had Bomber racing everything from the beginning of the year until the end. The racer seemed to possess an innate talent for suffering and could get consistent top results all year long in every event he entered. It didn't matter if it was a one-day race, a week-long stage race, or a grand tour. He was gracing more podiums than any other rider of his era. Jack possessed so much more; he should have been winning the biggest races in the world, but instead, he was garnering a reputation as a bridesmaid, an also-ran.

That was until the Dane, Tom Christenson came to the rescue. The hardened man, with his strong jaw, dirty blonde hair and piercing blue eyes had a soft and gentle soul. He was kinder than his exterior portrayed, and he knew what Jack needed to be successful. He gave the athlete permission to rest, putting aside his maniacal work ethic—work that was too demanding, too fatiguing and took away from the athlete's actual ability. Bomber learned how to relax, and began to win the biggest race in the sport—the Tour de France. Once he became the boss, the patron of the peloton, everything changed for the two men. They became a force to be reckoned with, a duo to fear, and Nick Carney could feel their presence throughout the car. To fail in front of these two men would mean certain dismissal. He knew he had to stay more focused on what Tom was saying. He'd have time later to visualize his race.

Tom pointed to the Tour officials placing gates along Boulevard Albert, a barrier to keep rowdy or absent-minded fans from interfering with oncoming racers. "The finish line is going to be tight and narrow, and the road surface is rather bumpy. You're going to be at your limit. You'll be in utter agony with your brain turned off, and I don't want you looking out at the Mediterranean Sea daydreaming about girls in bikinis. You got that, Nick?"

"Got it, Tom. Thanks."

Nick held his apologetic smile in place outwardly, but inside he was cringing. His uncertainty of being on this recon was growing tenfold, and his thoughts were turning to anger. *What was he doing here?* It gnawed at him relentlessly, and he squirmed in his seat while attempting to remain outwardly calm, and not merely glare at Tom's head. But, his mind started to race with angered thoughts, and it didn't stop. *You bring me along, and I'm privileged, but your tone is so fucking condescending. I'm concentrating on what I need to do for Christ's sake. Naked on a bike. Daydreaming about girls in bikinis. Who do you think I am? Fuck you, Tom. Fuck you!*

Meanwhile, Jack Bomber gazed at the young cyclist sitting alongside him. Unlike his tiny muscular frame, this kid was a giant—

a gangly young man standing 6'5—an anomaly in the cycling world. He was young, too young to be at the Tour as far as Jack was concerned, but Tom had insisted he come. The kid had taken up cycling at age 8 in his hometown of Ottawa, and by 15 he was dominating men twice his age at the national level. By 16 Nick was winning World Junior titles, and at 18 he had already been given a pro contract with a French Continental Pro Team in France. Jack had wanted him on the team as soon as he'd learned of the phenom, but he wanted him for selfish reasons. He didn't want him going to an opposing team and becoming a threat to him. It was smart to keep your potential enemies as close as possible. In the past, before Nick signed with Team Apex, Jack had been put under intense physical pressure in early season races trying to keep up with the wonder kid. He knew what Nick was—a raw talent, with a natural ability to win races—even if he didn't realize it himself. Nick was gifted.

While cyclists with talent often have a physical advantage, their brains are typically weak and penetrable, according to Bomber. It's why he liked surrounding himself with young talent. He could exploit their physical power to help him win races while guiding them at will—maneuvering them like helpless pawns in a chess match. Jack's only concern now, as he sized up the kid, was that Nick might become a problem. He hadn't yet decided what to think about the young cyclist, and that's partly why he wanted Nick here, on this recon.

They arrived back at the hotel, and Willie jerked the AMG back into the parking lot. Nick was quick to get out of the car. He anticipated a showdown with Tom, perhaps a patronizing comment about how he got out of the vehicle. *Maybe he jumped out too fast. Didn't he know he should save his energy for later? What was he doing moving at a blistering pace before the biggest race of his life?* Nick couldn't shake the hostility brewing deep within him. His thoughts couldn't stop. They were like a bike going downhill without brakes.

Tom nodded in Nick's direction. "Go relax. Be down here at nine with your bike. Then be ready for a pre-ride course with the boys. " Nick may have been happy, and a bit worried to be alone with Tom and Jack, but now he was fuming and glad to be leaving their presence. The pre-course recon had proven to be too much for him. He was overwhelmed and looking forward to going back to his room and talking with his roommate. He didn't know him well but needed to vent.

Nick was rooming with his Belgian teammate, Didier Van Welte, a well-built muscular gentleman with dark hair and dark features. He excelled in the early spring classics, the monuments, but was not a winner. He was calm and humble, here to shelter and guide Bomber through the flat and windy stages of the Tour, grab water bottles from the team car, and keep morale high. At thirty-eight, his years of experience in the pro peloton made him a *superdomestic*. He was waiting at the edge of his bed when Nick arrived back in the room.

"How does the course look?" asked Welte.

"Technical, with lots of corners, but there are some solid, long stretches to grind a big gear and hit it hard."

Welte nodded but seemed dismissive. The conversation ended as quickly as it started. The Belgian wasn't much of a talker, and Nick found it disheartening. He would need to find strength and comfort in silence, not something he was used to. Nick loved to socialize, to burn off his anger and nervous energy. It was therapeutic, and even at a young age, he understood the value of dealing with his emotions. He wanted to talk about what happened in the car earlier, the course, the effort required to do well, and how both men may be feeling about today; what their expectations were. More than anything he wanted to connect. And, today of all days, he really didn't know how to feel or what to think. He wanted the veteran cyclist to provide him with guidance and be the mentor he'd hoped Jack would've been today.

Maybe he was asking for too much, maybe having a mentor at the World Tour level was out of the question, but Nick didn't believe talking should be.

Since his days as a junior cyclist, Nick had always felt the need to talk to fellow teammates extensively before races. He wasn't a gibbering idiot, projecting empty content. Speaking about his feelings and his chances at success calmed him and provided him with motivation. His strategy would be to talk negatively about the hardest parts of the course, or a fierce headwind that would require massive physical effort. His demeanor and language portrayed an insurmountable challenge, not achievable by mere mortals, while internally his thoughts were electrified with overcoming all obstacles like a champion.

Four years earlier, before the start of the Junior World Time Trial Championships in Italy, Nick went on and on about the challenging course, much to the annoyance of his coaches and fellow Canadian teammates. They were faced with a torrential downpour and howling winds that day. Everyone was worried; a sharp turn with a slick manhole cover awaited the riders at the end of a fast descent. The sky was dark, and the air thick and humid. Nick began his pre-race rant. *That rain and wind are non-stop. There's no way anyone is going to average over forty kilometers per hour today on that course. Wheels are going to be slipping. Are you ready for some meaningful road rash? The winner is going to be the guy who jumps back on his bike as quickly as possible after crashing. We' re all losing skin today, folks. The winner is going to be something special because with this course the conditions are epic in every way.* At the end of the day, Nick was on the top step of the podium, adorned with the rainbow jersey, listening to the Canadian anthem while happily smiling for the cameras.

Nick's cell phone buzzed. It was time to head out. Beyond their initial exchange of words, nothing more was said over the next hour between Welte and Nick. Welte had read Jacques Anquetil's biography—discovering that the 5 time Tour de France Legend had conceived a daughter with his stepdaughter and a son with his step daughter-in-law—Nick caught up on Instagram. But now it was time to go. The two men grabbed their gearboxes—a fashionable container for their helmets, shoes, and cycling apparel. They headed down to the lobby to meet up with the rest of the team.

It would be a quick drive to the starting area of the Prologue, where the team bus was parked. Along the side of the bus would be every rider' s time trial bike, set up on a trainer with a turbo fan in front to cool them down while they warmed up. No other sport in the world allows their fans to get as close to their heroes as cycling, which meant a thin layer of yellow caution tape would be placed around the warm-up area. This was required to protect the racers from adoring fans seeking autographs and selfies.

The Prologue was an individual time trial event—rider against the clock, with the fastest rider crowned the winner. The first rider started at 11 a.m., with each rider starting one minute apart. Nick would be getting underway at 1 p.m. The current time was 9:30 a.m. Nick entered the team bus and changed into his cycling kit. He grabbed his road bike and headed out to do another quick recon of the time trial course.

People were gathering along the streets of Monaco to cheer the riders warming up; the onlookers packed behind the barriers Nick had seen being assembled earlier. Nick had competed in world championships, the monuments of cycling, but this was entirely different. The energy was contagious, and Nick's trepidation bubbled beneath his skin, vibrating his bones. It was overwhelming. His stomach was churning, but his mind was racing with thoughts of winning. They shouldn't have been. He wasn't a proven rider who needed to bear this type of responsibility, but he'd been born with an internal pressure to win. Ever since he was little, he'd wanted to be perfect in everything that he put his heart and soul into. If he'd desired to be good at something, he often found himself being the best after a brief period of time. People called him gifted or talented, but Nick resented those labels. For him, they seemed to negate the demanding work he put forth—work that was created from fear of failure.

Nick became tense on the bike, and a slick sewer grate caused his wheels to wobble. In wet conditions the tires would have lost contact, throwing Nick to the ground. It would have been a recipe for road rash or a broken bone. Thankfully, the dry conditions ensured he stayed upright, but it'd been too close for comfort. Nick didn't like feeling out of control. He never did. His whole life Nick managed every scenario he could, planning intensely for every possible outcome—some would call it worrying, unproductive thinking. Bike racing was different; he couldn't control it. Maybe, that's what made him fall in love with the sport. He could manage his training, preparation, and mental outlook, but he couldn't control the 180 other racers he was competing against, the weather and the other teams' strategies. He had to let go freely at times—relenting all thought so his mind could go empty—producing the effort needed to win.

Nick chose to end his recon early and find safety on the bus, away from the noise, the fans, and the external physical forces that were being thrust upon him, rattling his mental preparation. Now wasn't the time to lose control, nor was it time to be dealing with potential crashes, and worrisome thoughts.

Nick flopped down in his La-Z-Boy-style assigned seat in the bus, sucked back an energy gel, and made sure to enjoy his electrolyte drink. He felt good. This was everything Nick imagined it to be. He looked out the window watching the crowd of fans surrounding the bus, chanting and waving flags. This was their Super Bowl, and he could feel their energy. Welte was beside him and still in no mood to talk. Bomber was yet to arrive at the starting area, and the rest of the team was either riding the course or outside on their trainers warming up.

Nick obviously wanted to chat but settled for his iPhone, earphones, and his pre-race playlist. Now was the time for Nick to get focused. He remembered the early course recon with Jack and Tom and began visualizing the entire course over and over. Nick fidgeted in his seat, unable to control the excitement. He pictured the course and the tight turns, swaying back and forth with his arms stretched out in front of his face as if he were on his tri bars. He was feeling the tight turns and preparing himself for any adverse outcomes. He wanted to ensure he took each corner with the right amount of speed. The course was short, and he couldn't afford any mistakes if he were to win. The imagery of him on his bike caused his feet to move up and down, shaking his legs endlessly. He couldn't control or expel the increased energy coursing through his body. He would have to wait until he was on his bike, racing through the streets of Monaco.

At 12:20 p.m., forty minutes before Nick's start he mounted his time trial bike and began warming up on the trainer. Fans were waving and shouting his name, but Nick couldn't hear any of them. His ears were too busy being filled with hard pumping hip-hop; the classics from Drake, The Weekend, and Kendrick Lamar. His ice vest was on, and his turbofan was blowing at max to keep his core body temperature down. He was about to begin an intensive interval when he peeked to his right and observed Tom and Jack entering the warmup area. They were smiling, laughing, and looking chummy. This display of comradery irritated Nick. At that moment he felt like an outsider wanting to be in that elusive club. He tasted exclusivity this morning when invited for the pre-course ride, and now he wanted more. He wasn't sure why it's not as if he'd felt comfortable in their presence. Maybe it was because they were essential to the team, the men he looked up too and the reason he joined Team Apex. He wasn't sure, but he knew he had to put it aside and begin hitting his warm-up intervals.

Nick's muscles had to be primed and ready to fire, his mind free to focus on enduring a broad spectrum of thoughts and emotions. This was his time to become one with himself, before the start, and he didn't need to be consumed about Jack Bomber and Tom Christenson.

The starting ramp of the prologue beckoned Nick. He was ready. He climbed the stairs leading up to the ramp, straddled his bike and looked out beyond the crowd. His face was relaxed, with no hint of a smile to be found. His time trial visor hid his eyes from the media, giving him the appearance of being stone cold. Leading up to races, Nick could be consumed with anxious thoughts, but moments before a race those thoughts melted away. He was empty, like what death may feel like.

The commissaire counted down. *Five, four, three, two* ... Nick took a deep breath, his heart thumping hard against his chest, and began the race of his life. His long and lean legs applied massive force to the pedals as his body swayed back and forth to gain the necessary speed. He folded his long torso over the top of his bike, getting it down and low into a speed-skater tuck. His 6'5 body was now positioned aerodynamically, and he was cutting through the wind like an arrow in flight. After a fair bit of effort, he was hitting over fifty-five kilometers per hour and cruising along. He breathed deeply from his belly, drawing in copious quantities of air. His heart pounded, rattling his rib cage, and his legs moved fast and deliberately. In a short while, his legs would feel as if someone took a sledgehammer and pummeled his quads.

In the first half of his race, Nick was detached, his mind desolate. He focused entirely on the action necessary to propel his bike forward with speed. Nick crushed the first-time check, coming in first, and began thinking about winning. His legs responded to his positive thoughts, and he moved them in perfect harmony. But, with good thoughts come bad, and in the second half, his mind was cracking from the unrelenting pain. A voice echoed from a deep abyss he thought he'd destroyed long ago. At first, it was a faint whisper, but soon it was growing, gaining speed and looking to penetrate the surface. If it emerged, it would put an end to Nick's pursuit.

He fought hard, thinking about her, and his legs found the suppleness needed to turn a big gear. The pain was no longer interfering with his movement, even though he was working at his maximum. He crossed the finish line shaking with exhaustion, unable to stay upright.

Forget winning. Would Nick's time be respectable? He wasn't sure.

CHAPTER 2

Stage One

The Sprinter

Nick gazed through the hotel window, contemplating the day's monstrous two-hundred-and-twenty-kilometer stage. The first official stage of the Tour welcomed the riders with luminous rays of sunlight and winds full of dry, potent heat; the kind that suffocated the riders. The sky was endlessly blue, not a single cloud in sight. Monaco was serene, and the Mediterranean Sea calm.

It would be a day for the sprinters and their teams. A day in the Tour where the fastest men in the final meters of a flat race showcase their talent. Charlie Spitz from Great Britain was the pre-race favorite. He was tough as nails and showed no fear in the last three hundred meters of a race. Spitz was methodical, hunting down his competitors like prey. He possessed a formidable team of flat-landers and lead-out men; riders that could drive the pace to startling speeds more than fifty kilometers an hour, topping out at sixty, and launching Spitz to the win. He was also skilled at winning sprints without his team. He could bike surf from one wheel to the next, displacing riders with his aggression, to maintain his position and take the sprint victory.

Spitz was an entertainer on and off the bike. The media loved him. He was blessed with having captured fifteen Tour stage victories in the last five Tours, but he wasn't a threat for overall victory, to Team Apex-Colnago (Nick and Bomber's Team), and he wouldn't be a threat in overtaking Nick today. Nick knew him a bit, but they weren't on the best of terms. Earlier in the year, Nick found himself at the front of the peloton in the closing meters of a small race in Belgium. He got excited and thought he could challenge the sprinter for victory. It went wrong, horrible actually. Nick's long and emaciated body, designed entirely for climbing couldn't generate the powerful kick needed to propel him over the finish line first. Instead, his front wheel slipped, causing him to veer off his path. Riders were forced to react quickly and dart around him. In the process, Nick's elbow had swung out to help him maintain his balance, and it ended up hitting Spitz in the rib cage. The great sprinter almost crashed and was robbed of victory.

Since then, Spitz won't have anything to do with Nick. He's taken verbal shots at him on Twitter and other forms of social media; calling the young cyclist a threat to the peloton, a menace with limited bike handling skills. It has frustrated Nick knowing how it all went down. He respects the sprinter but can't understand why Spitz won't let it go and move on.

Nick stopped gazing out the window and instead turned his attention to his roommate. Welte was sleeping, tucked away beneath his cozy sheets. He looked at peace, and Nick wondered if his sleep had been restful and whether the big Belgian would wake up refreshed. For Nick, it had been a night full of restless sleep that contained an endless dream after endless dream. He fell asleep in his new jersey, something he'd wanted to do since childhood. Most of his dreams that evening had been filled with triumph, but one contained a dark shadow that sought to strangle the life out of him. The shadow possessed no shape or form. Its only intent was to hurt Nick. And, it worked; jolting him out of his bed, leaving him soaked in a puddle of sweat, gulping for air, tears streaming from his eyes. He desperately searched for his Fiancée, Emma, but knew it was in vain. She was a world away, at home in Canada. In that moment of terror he needed her, and now he was alone, unsure of how to cope. Had he brought this on himself? He wasn't sure.

That evening, before going to bed, Nick fell asleep under a blanket of contention that began within the team and ended with Nick feeling out of control. His prologue had been brilliant. In fact, his finishing time was so good he was crowned the winner, putting him in yellow—the jersey the rider leading the Tour wears. For now, it belonged to Nick, and in his eyes, it meant he was the current leader of his team, but would he get the support from his teammates to keep it?

Following the finish of the prologue, he'd climbed the stage and was presented the yellow jersey by two young women (podium girls) who appeared to be in awe and admiration. Each in heels, but both needing to tippy-toe to reach Nick's babyface to give the customary kisses on his cheeks. Nick looked out into the crowd and saw thousands of people smiling and chanting his name. He had never felt so important in his life. His stomach filled up with butterflies as he hoisted his arms over his body. In one hand, he held a stuffed lion adorned in a yellow jersey and in the other, flowers. He wanted this moment to last forever. He didn't want to move, and even though he was being ushered quickly by the Tour hostess to shake dignitaries' hands, he made sure to soak in every moment. Every handshake felt different, some were strong, and some were soft. What mattered most to Nick was the look in their eyes; he could feel their respect. Since turning sixteen, Nick had been told he would do remarkable things in the sport, including winning the Tour de France, but he was never positive he could do it. What if this was as good as it got? He wanted to savor it, and most of all, he wanted to share his joy with his teammates. After he left the podium, he was given a marker and ordered to quickly sign his name on a dozen replica yellow jerseys, most of which would be given to the dignitaries who were on the podium.

Once the prologue and presentation ceremony had been completed, and the fans in the street slowly disappeared, the riders made their way back to their team buses and hotels. Nick felt like a young child in a candy store, jacked up on sugar and chocolate. He was pumped to see his teammates. This should have been the beginning of what could only be described as the best moment in Nick's young life. But, it would quickly sour. Nick boarded his bus as though his feet were floating. His tanned cheeks were rosy with red and purple lipstick marks. He could barely make it to his seat without his teammate's fist-pumping, hugging and kissing the young superstar. They were clamoring to touch his yellow jersey and be part of Nick's success.

At one point in their lives, they would have all dreamt about being in Nick's position. For some of these riders, this would be the closest they ever got to *'having'* the yellow jersey. A loud whistle came from the rear of the bus interrupting the celebration. Tom stood on a seat. *Here it comes*, thought Nick. He readied himself for his Team Director's praise. *Should I be humble, should I smile, should I show excitement? Okay....Okay, here he goes.* Tom lowered his head slowly until everyone was quiet then snapped it back up and stared directly at Nick. "Guys, remember this is day one, not the fucking Champs Élysées. Let's keep it together. I'm happy you're in yellow Nick, but we're here to win the overall Tour de France with Bomber, not just the fucking prologue."

Nick was shocked and angered and wanted to respond with words, but he couldn't trust his feelings. All he knew for sure was he didn't like the way he was being treated. Nick had just won the prologue of the Tour de France, he was in the midst of a life-changing moment, and this was how his Director responded? Nick was fully aware he was here to support Jack Bomber's quest for overall victory, but Tom's statement didn't feel right. It was bold, inappropriate and seemed unfair at that very moment. Logically Nick understood Tom's message, but he was wearing the yellow jersey. Hadn't he earned some respect and support? He examined the back of the bus and could see Jack Bomber, behind Tom, quietly looking on. There was a small smirk on his face. He hadn't yet congratulated Nick, and his body language suggested he wouldn't be moving any time soon.

Everyone took their seat, and as the bus pulled out, Nick made his way towards Bomber. Nick tried to contain his contempt, "Are you happy? Upset? What's the deal?" asked Nick.

Jack seemed unfazed and remained stoic, "I'm satisfied. It was a demanding course, but a bit too short for my liking," he replied.

Nick was confused by Jack's demeanor and terse, matter-of-fact tone. He felt offended and angered but tried to be friendly and offer encouragement—be a good teammate.

"Still, second place for you and first for me. That's an amazing start for the team, right?"

Bomber spoke slowly and deliberately, choosing his words so Nick could fully understand what he was about to say, "I'm not so sure this is the ideal start for the team, kid. Defending the jersey is demanding work. If we are defending it," Jack slowed his speech to a crawl, nearly spelling out the last word, "with p u r p o s e…"

He didn't finish the sentence. It was simple and to the point. Nick understood what Bomber was implying. Bomber supported Tom's sentiment—winning the prologue wasn't the focus of this team. And, Bomber took it one step further, suggesting that trying to keep the yellow jersey at this point would be detrimental to his chances of winning. Nick felt disappointed, like winning somehow fucked up everything. He tried to reply but found himself unable to find the right words. The best he could conjure up was a, "yeah," and he turned away to take his place on the bus.

Supper that evening caused further issues for Nick. Tom hadn't allowed a customary glass of champagne to accompany the team's meal. Not at this stage in the Tour, he had said. But no speech, no reflection on the team's achievement, or on Nick claiming yellow. It caused the young racer to practically shake with anger; a bomb ready to explode. Nick was prepared to let the incident on the bus pass. He'd spent the past hour lying in bed with his feet propped up against the wall, relaxing and reflecting on Tom and Jack. He felt he had a better understanding of their position. However, it didn't stop him from craving recognition from his boss and his team leader. When it didn't happen, Nick began to wonder, *had I not done enough to gain their respect? Isn't winning what this sport is all about? Talk to me, please.*

It wouldn't happen. The supper table was a dismal sight to witness. Bomber sat at the table in isolation, only chatting with his loyal lieutenants on the team, the Spaniards. He had Miguel Rosas to his right and Joaquin Escartin to his left. The well-renowned climbing specialists were doing an excellent job protecting their leader from Nick's attempt to confront Bomber further. They'd accompanied Jack in his last two consecutive victories, helping him traverse the tricky terrain of the high mountains; setting inferno-like paces that blew up the peloton. They'd do anything to protect their leader. Nick's roommate, Welte sat silently looking at pics of his daughter on his phone. As the oldest rider on the team, he didn't mind not talking. He was happy to eat the wonderfully prepared pasta with light rose sauce, a strip of chicken and grilled vegetables, in peace. The French guys on the team, Antoine Doucette, and Frederic Bouchard spoke loudly in their mother tongue as if no one else was there.

Meanwhile, the British youngsters Bradley Willowfield and Simon Brown surrounded Nick. They were more than happy to gaze at the coveted jersey Nick wore. Like Nick, they'd both dreamt of winning the yellow jersey someday. They knew the odds were against them, but at the moment their dreams felt closer than ever.

Dinner ended without a notable incident. The mechanics left early to wash the team's bikes and prepare them for tomorrow's stage. The soigneurs were next. They needed to shop for goodies that would find their way into the rider's musettes—their mid-race grab-bag used for lunch on the go in tomorrow's stage. The massage therapists were the final staff members to get up and go. They needed to prepare for the last massages of the evening.

Nick had been rubbed down after the stage, before media interviews, but he would receive another massage before bed. As the designated Team Leader, Bomber would enjoy a great massage to ensure his legs were ready to tackle the exhausting two-hundred-and-twenty-kilometer stage tomorrow.

Nick was the first rider to leave. He'd had enough of watching Bomber, the Spaniards, and Tom converse and laugh as though nothing extraordinary had happened today. He felt distraught as he moved quickly towards his last interview. This one was with world-renowned cycling journalist, Robert Saunders. Saunders had written numerous cycling articles for various publications, as well as many non-fiction cycling books on the Giro D'Italia, The Belgian Classics, The Tour de France and the Vuelta. He was here covering the Tour for the New York Times, and he was determined to get an interview with Nick, the future Great North Canadian Hero.

Nick entered the hotel lobby, searching for the prominent reporter. He spotted Saunders waiting for him at the bar, and approached the reporter slowly, less from nerves—Nick was thrilled to be giving such an interview—but because his legs still ached from the race. Robert extended his hand to greet Nick, "I know you're on a tight schedule, so I'll get right down to business."

"Sounds good to me," Nick replied.

"You're in your first Tour, you're twenty-three, and you're in yellow. Can you describe how you're feeling?"

"Amazing. A dream come true. To win the prologue...to be in yellow...the team is very proud and pleased."

"So, no discord between you and the reigning champion, Jack Bomber?"

Nick didn't flinch or hesitate. He stared straight into the eyes of Robert and said, "Absolutely none. We're here for final victory with Jack. Winning the prologue is an unexpected result. I'm here to support Jack. I know my role on the team."

"Will the team defend the jersey tomorrow, defend your position?"

"We may, we may not. Tom will provide instructions for us tomorrow morning. We'll want the sprint teams to take control. There is no point in expending energy this early in the race to defend someone who doesn't have a chance of winning the Tour overall." *Or do I*, Nick thought.

Saunders' passion was interviewing riders, but in the last five years, it'd become increasingly frustrating. With team budgets more than fifteen million euros a year, riders were being molded into well-drilled, programmable media droids. Training camps consisted of classes on how to speak to journalists, even how to convey the right message using appropriate body language. Riders were no longer raw with emotion. *But what about Nick?* Robert eyed the young cyclist thoughtfully. He could see something in the kid. He wasn't quite sure, but he was convinced Nick's eyes were beckoning him to dig deeper.

"Come on, Nick," Robert probed, "you're in yellow. This is totally unexpected. You're an up and coming rider, but this is sensational. You're telling me you wouldn't be happy to stay in the jersey a few more days?"

"Yeah, I'd love to. Who wouldn't," Nick insisted.

Robert pressed further. *Let's see if I can push this kid's button. Let's see where it takes me.* "Well, you're rather blasé about whether you want to keep it or not. Is something going on between you and Bomber?"

Nick held his breath, becoming as still as a statue. One of his hands slowly formed a fist, and he pounded the table. To gain control over his emotions he sighed deeply. He was trained for this type of probing, but he was lost for words. *Jack and Tom did this to me; they put me on edge,* thought Nick. Then he turned his thoughts towards Saunders. *What's this guy's deal with Bomber? Everyone knows he hates him.* Nick's composure was lost, but only for a moment. He unwound his fist and regained the strength to reply curtly, "Nothing is going on within the team. I'm not blasé about anything. I have the yellow jersey, and nobody cares but me. It's late, and I'm tired. I need my sleep, Mr. Saunders. Goodnight."

The interview had ended abruptly, but for the first time in years, Robert had garnered something genuine from a pro rider. There was an explosion of emotion, and Nick's eyes seemed to be covering an authenticity that was bubbling at the surface and pleading to be exposed. *I care, Nick Carney. I care and so will the rest of the world,* thought Saunders.

Nick made his way to bed. He was overcome with feelings of dread about what transpired during his interview. He had a nagging feeling, a consistent pull on his conscience that something was wrong, something the team would find out about and use to isolate him further. The guilt of losing his cool weighed on him, and it was the precursor to his endless unpleasant dreams—the dark shadow.

The morning light finally came, putting an end to Nick's rumination about the events over the last twelve hours. He knew he had to flip the mental switch and put it behind him. Using the rising sun as an alarm clock, he woke up Welte so he could head to breakfast and not be completely alone. There were no other Team Apex riders there yet, which meant Nick would most likely be eating breakfast in silence. He hoped Bradley or Simon would arrive shortly. Chatting with his buddies would get him pumped. With both being in their early twenties and English speaking, these were the two teammates he felt the closest too. He needed their support and their ears. He was desperate to talk about the long day in the saddle ahead. He grabbed his coffee, along with some oatmeal and an egg white veggie omelet, a few pieces of dense whole wheat bread, apricot jelly, and a chocolate croissant--everything prepared by their team chef. Nick would need a sufficient number of calories to make it through today's stage.

Team staff trickled into the breakfast area. Some were joking, while others appeared half asleep—all were making their way towards the nearest coffee pot for their morning caffeine. All were happy to see Nick, and once again congratulate him. They were excited to see him in yellow and looked forward to watching him defend the jersey today.

Thirty minutes later, Nick finished off his chocolate croissant as Tom, and the rest of the riders entered the room. "Good morning, your highness. I suppose now that you're in Yellow, you're too special for early morning team meetings," Tom exclaimed.

Nick almost choked on his croissant. "Wh—wha—what?"

"Calm down kid. He's pulling your chain," Bomber said.

"The Yellow Jersey gets to sleep in. We want to make sure you're well rested today. No need to bore you with team tactics. Your only job today is to ride your bike. Everyone here will take care of everything else," said Tom.

Nick sighed with relief, relaxing into his seat with his coffee in hand. He'd chat with Bradley and Simon, and everything would finally feel right.

Tom tapped Nick on the shoulder. "Come finish your coffee with Bomber and me, please. I need to speak to you about today."

Nick grabbed his coffee mug and made his way to a small table with Tom and Bomber. "Sorry about this morning," began Tom.

"You wanted me to sleep in. I understand."

"Not exactly. I don't want any team tension."

Nick whipped his head back, and his eyes widened. "Why would there be any tension? I don't follow."

"We're going to ride today as we should. You're in yellow, but Bomber and I both agree, we don't want the team to expend any unnecessary energy."

"Okay, that makes sense. I get it," said Nick

"Do you?" interrupted Bomber, looking at Nick suspiciously

Tom noticed the way Bomber was gazing at Nick. There were intensity and authority in his eyes. He tried to defuse the growing hostility.

"This is all about optics. The Tour is like no other cycling event. The media, especially certain reporters, will do whatever they can to make a story out of nothing. If we're not at the front the whole race, riding tempo, people are going to talk. I want you and everyone on the team prepared."

Nick's paranoia from his sleepless night and long day yesterday began to take hold of him. He couldn't help but wonder, *did he just, certain reporters? What the fuck Robert Saunders? I have one wrong moment, and you're off tattling to my Team Director, stirring the pot.*

TEN MINUTES UNTIL THE START OF STAGE ONE and Nick was full of restless energy. Nick had no choice but to let the conversation with Tom and Bomber at breakfast go, at least for now. Fans crowded around Nick for autographs and selfies, and he was more than happy to accommodate them; so much so, that he almost forgot to sign in for today's stage. Like yesterday, he wanted to soak in every moment of being the Yellow Jersey, and he didn't want it to end. A call by the Tour Officials for the multiple Jersey holders could be heard over the speakers. They were being ordered to the front of the peloton for media pictures. Nick made his way over, took his place, and posed with the Polka-dot, Green, and White Jersey riders. He smiled for the cameras but grinded his teeth, squeezing his handlebars, anxious to start. In mere moments, the official red car containing the Chief Commissaries would take off, and the riders would follow. It would be civilized: A controlled and relaxed speed until the flag dropped, and then it would be an all-out war between the cyclists.

As the car rolled out, Nick would take this moment to survey his body and his bike. His legs felt good, and his upper body relaxed, fully recovered from yesterday's prologue. His bike was smooth, no rattling, no chain rubbing the front derailleur. He was ready. The flag went down, the official's car sped up, and the race burst into action. Riders were sprinting aggressively into position, looking to get into the early breakaway. Like a speeding herd of mustangs, Nick was engulfed by a swarm of charging riders. He glanced around for a teammate's wheels. It was not long before Welte was in front of him, guiding him back towards the front and keeping him safe. Bradley and Simon were by his sides and Bomber was behind him.

Teams who didn't boast designated sprinters or overall contenders for victory were pressing hard at the front to keep themselves positioned to make the day's breakaway. It would be one sprint after another, with small groups of riders moving away from the peloton then being brought back by others. The peloton was a picture of chaotic distortion, but it was being controlled by pure eloquent athleticism, each cyclist looking for his moment to shine.

A day in the breakaway could mean several hours of television exposure for team sponsors; crucial for some of the smaller teams with small budgets. After an hour of high-speed, locomotive combat practiced on two wheels, a group of 8 riders moved away from the peloton; the breakaway was established. As was routine, the peloton settled into a sustainable, relaxed tempo. Some riders sought shelter on the side of the road for their early morning nature break, others went back to their team cars for water bottles, while others looked to Team Apex to take control, and set the pace. A few riders came up to Nick to congratulate him, while others approached him to question him about team tactics.

The breakaway continued to push hard, pulling further away from the peloton. Eventually, the breakaway group established a lead with a time gap of eight minutes. The peloton was utterly disorganized. Riders from opposing teams were getting angry with Nick and Team Apex—shouting to get them moving, to take responsibility for setting the tempo. They wanted Team Apex to begin chasing the breakaway, to close the time gap to something more controllable. A smaller time gap would allow the sprinters' teams to take over the chase from Team Apex in the final kilometers; setting up their fast men for the win.

With the pack struggling for leadership and direction, Bomber sprinted out of the peloton. His legs were churning powerfully and rhythmically, and within moments Bomber gained a minute on the peloton. This type of move by an overall contender was unusual. What was Jack Bomber trying to accomplish?

Bomber kept moving further away from the peloton, happy to be taking time out of the chaotic pack of riders. Jack wasn't sure why he chose to bolt out of the peloton. It was unlike the calculated champion. He had nothing to prove at this point in the Tour, but something made him want to stamp his authority on the race. Was it because he wasn't the rider on Team Apex wearing the yellow jersey? He kept turning his legs, staying within his limits but trying to get out as much speed out of his legs as he could to hold his lead. Part of him wanted that yellow jersey, and he wanted it now. He knew what Nick was capable of. He'd seen him in action during their training camps, early season races, and everyone in the world had seen it at the Tour of California. Nick Carney was a genius on the bike—a freak of nature. Jack Bomber knew he couldn't back down now. Every second counted.

The peloton didn't know how to react to Bomber's attack. They knew Team Apex wouldn't chase their own teammate. Nick felt perplexed, wondering why the other General Classification riders hadn't reacted. They had a lot to lose with Jack gaining a minute. Where were they? Where were their teams? Why were they not chasing?

TV announcers and journalist were just as dumbfounded as the riders. They were thrilled with the emerging storyline and the possible headlines:

Defending Tour Champion Seeks Revenge by Attacking Younger Teammate in Yellow!

Robert Saunders' hands were in the air as he shouted, "Are you watching this?!" He was in the media tent, and he didn't care who heard him. "Are you fucking watching this?!"

Legendary TV commentators Phil Ligget and Paul Sherwin watched in amazement, trying their best to ignore Saunders' yelling. They had their own commentary, rife with historical tales about previous battles between protégé and leader. Tweets began to flutter around the internet about the internal battle brewing between Nick Carney and Jack Bomber. The story was going viral, and every network covering the Tour was talking about the developing action.

Meanwhile, Nick's mind was racing with thoughts; his body rife with unrelenting anger. If he weren't on his bike, he'd be on the cusp of throwing an all-out tantrum. His face was twisted, and he wondered what the cameras were picking up. He had to keep it together for everyone's sake.

Bomber kept moving and built a comfortable lead of two minutes on the peloton. Nick couldn't take anymore. His body was shaking, he was losing control; he thought he may be on the verge of crashing his bike. He did everything he could to steady his arms and squeeze his mic on his race radio, "What the fuck is going on Tom?" Nick shouted.

Tom squirmed in the seat of the team's car. He was watching Bomber build his lead, but questioning what his team leader was doing. They'd agreed to do as little work possible today. Going on the offensive was never part of the plan. Tom hesitated before replying to Nick. "Relax. Jack's having some fun. We talked about it in our meeting this morning. Everything is going as discussed."

Nick shook his head in disbelief, and mumbled to himself, *yeah, I remember that fucking meeting. The one I didn't know about and wasn't invited to.* Nick tried to calm himself down. *Why am I freaking out? I am here for Bomber anyways. Why does it suddenly matter?*

As Nick yelled into his mic and tried to contain his anger, the tone of the peloton transformed. Opposing teams' came to the front and began to chase Bomber. There'd be no more playing around. Charlie Spitz rode up to Nick, bumping his shoulder to gain his attention, "Fucking amateurs." Nick was embarrassed. He was the leader of the biggest race in the world, wearing the most prestigious jersey in the sport, and he didn't know what his team was doing.

The sprinters' teams couldn't have cared less about what was going on within Team Apex; they only cared about the win today. They could smell the finish line approaching and decided it was time to put an end to Jack Bomber's charades and haul back the breakaway of 8. They rode hard, increasing their speed with every pedal stroke.

A rider would pull the peloton at maximum effort, swing off and then rely on the next rider to do the same. A pack of men going at maximum effort is faster than one, and it wouldn't be long until they caught a tired Bomber. Further up the road, the breakaway was crumbling. The sprinters' teams were in total control of the race now.

Once Bomber was caught he eased back towards Nick. "That's how we make the other teams work, kid." Nick was too disgusted to respond. He stared ahead, pretending he was consumed with the effort. He recognized he didn't have control over Bomber's action, only his own, and as such he said and did, nothing.

The final meters of the race was thrilling. The earlier tactics employed by Team Apex meant the sprinter's teams couldn't catch the remnants of the breakaway until the final two hundred meters. But, once they did pre-race favorite, Charlie Spitz, battled hard, squeezing his bike and body through small pockets of space between slower riders. He threw his bike to the line and did what he was expected to do—win, and win with panache.

Nick crossed the line with sweat pouring down his face, his anger turning him red. He was mumbling to himself, and he knew if he didn't get to the team bus quickly, he'd blow. No amount of media training had prepared him for what he felt now.

He couldn't talk to the press. Not yet.

CHAPTER 3

A Team is Your Family,

Treat Them Well

Jack Bomber's path to cycling success could not have been more different from those of his peers. He grew up in Boulder, Colorado. A city known for its rich cycling heritage, it had been host to former pro-races, The Red Zinger, Coors Classic and Tour of Colorado. The majestic landscape surrounded by the Rockies was the perfect environment for athletic pursuits and enriching the soul. Boulder streets were lined with designated bike lanes, and every corner had a bike shop. The culture in Boulder valued athletic pursuits over capitalistic endeavors. It was a given that Jack would grow up to become a cyclist, but to be a champion, that had everything to do with how Jack felt about his older brother, Michael. Michael had been a kid with so much talent, but no desire to commit and nurture it over time. He was always jumping from one pursuit to the next. Jack knew real champions were born with a strong work ethic.

Michael excelled at every sport he participated in. During the summer months, he played organized baseball and football. During his spare time, he was maneuvering his skateboard like a young Tony Hawk. During family outings on the weekends, whether it be hiking up Flagstaff or mountain biking around the city's outskirts, Michael was always ahead of the entire Bomber family. In the winter time, Michael competed in downhill skiing events and rarely lost. But in his late teens, Michael would forget about every sport, eventually, go to college and then join a big tech firm.

Jack had worshipped and envied his older brother in his younger days. He wasn't alone. Kids in the neighborhood tried to emulate Michael, and many only became friends with Jack for the opportunity to be close to his older brother. It didn't faze Jack that his brother possessed an innate athletic talent— gifts from their mother, a former NCAA track star at the University of Oregon. Jack was easygoing and rarely competitive. Unlike Michael, he didn't care for organized sports and had often struggled with anything skill-based. He was much more of a free spirit.

In their early teens, their father took up cycling. Jack, surprisingly, was intrigued. After a few months on the bike, his father's physique drastically transformed. Once an overweight software engineer, struggling for air as he climbed the stairs leading up to his office building, he was now lean and flying up mountain passes. Friends and family were in awe of his transformation. In fact, when he met strangers, he stopped introducing himself as a software developer. Instead, saying he was a cyclist.

His new lifestyle and happiness were contagious. Michael and Jack followed in their Father's footsteps and started riding religiously. Michael was barely a month into riding when racing was already on his mind. His sights were set on an up-and-coming race in Boulder later that summer. Jack was fascinated with pushing his body for the first time. The euphoria that accompanied a spirited ride in the mountains was enough to have him hooked. He didn't need racing. He didn't need the competition. He was happy to go out with his father and brother. Spending hours on his bike, in the heat, climbing the legendary passes that surrounded Boulder was enough to fulfill Jack.

In fact, the family's first attempt up the well-known climb, Superflag proved too tricky for Jack. Not the type of failure you would imagine from a future Tour de France Champion. Their approach up Broadway was uneventful, but as the grade steepened around Gregory Canyon, Jack suffered from every turn of his pedals. He watched in disbelief as Michael effortlessly spun ahead of him, his legs moving in a controlled and deliberate manner with no excess movement coming from his upper body. His dad, up ahead, slowed down to check on Jack. "How you doing, kiddo?" he asked. It wasn't his goal to watch his son suffer.

"I'm fine, dad. Go back to Michael," Jack insisted. He didn't want his dad's pity. Jack wanted success, like Michael. At his age, he was too young to understand the anger brewing in his stomach.

In typical Michael fashion, he climbed the full thirteen-kilometer ascent in a respectable thirty-five minutes. Jack crested the climb in a tad over fifty-five minutes; ecstatic to have survived. Their dad treated the two boys to ice cream on Pearl Street before going home for supper. For Jack it didn't get any better than this, work hard and get rewarded.

After only a year in the sport, Michael quit and declared himself retired. He'd won a few races and was on to his next sporting endeavor. Meanwhile, Jack and his father became even more preoccupied and dedicated to their hobby. Jack was racing the under-fifteen category, while his dad raced in the Masters. Weekends were spent traveling the State of Colorado to races, while weeknights were for training and group rides with fellow cyclists.

Cycling didn't come easy to Jack, but he was never deterred by his race results. He wasn't winning—in fact, most races he was dropped and finished near the back, or worst, dead last. It never fazed him, because his dad was always there, encouraging him along the way with an enlightening conversation about challenging work and discipline. After punishing races, his father still awarded Jack with ice cream. Not the cheap stuff from the grocery store, or the soft-serve white crap they served at Dairy Queen. His dad chose nothing but the best, Sweet Cow—the good stuff. It was the type of ice cream that took away the pain and put happiness back into Jack's life.

At some point, in his first year as an over-18 senior racer, it all clicked. Jack grew into his body. His baby fat melted away and was replaced with thick, dense muscles. His previous lack of passion for competitive endeavors turned into an incessant need to win at all costs. He thought back to those days when his brother would ride effortlessly in front of him, urging him to go quicker and not get dropped. This memory pushed him during events to race ahead of seasoned veterans in their late twenties and early thirties. He made the pros look like amateurs.

The easy-going, good-natured kid in him had turned into a man. He no longer worshipped his brother. He despised Michael for his wasted talent. For Jack, every rider in the peloton became a Michael—a talented kid who had it easy, a kid that didn't know what it was like to work hard. Jack's internal dialogue pushed him to punish his competitors, propelling him to the top of his sport.

STAGE THREE, halfway through the team time trial, Bomber was in front of his teammates leading them into a gale-force wind. His muscular legs were applying massive power to the pedals, and he was doing a formidable job protecting his riders, but his teammates were suffering. In a moment, Nick would need to come out of Bomber's draft, pull through and take his turn at the front of the team echelon. He wasn't sure he'd be able to move his legs any faster.

Thanks to Bomber, the pace over the first eighteen-kilometers of this team time trial had been excruciating. Team Apex was down to seven riders after losing their climber, Escartin and the Frenchman, Bouchard. Nick shouted at Bomber, "Jack you're going to hard. I'm not able to pull through."

"You want to keep yellow? You go until you can't, then you go again," he shouted back.

Nick pulled through, but it was agonizingly painful. He managed to maintain the pace Bomber had been setting, but when he glanced at his power meter, he saw it spike over five hundred watts. His mind began spinning faster than the wheels on his bicycle, unraveling like a ball of yarn. *We're going to blow up. This is stupid. The guy's a champion, and he's acting like a first-year junior. You don't go this fast unless you're up to something. Are you up to something, Bomber? Are you?*

Nick finished his pull at the front (breaking the wind), eased off and made his way towards the back of his teammates. "Great pull, kid. We have to stay strong and keep pushing it to the limit. We do that, and we win this thing," roared Bomber. Nick could only nod in acknowledgment. He swerved his bike and took his place in line, behind Bomber. He'd have a few moments of rest before having to do it all over again.

Team radios—the bane of some riders and loyal fans had changed the dynamic of racing. Directors were now able to communicate directly with the riders during races. They played an integral part in team tactics and helped to shape the outcome of races. With small televisions hooked up in team cars, Team Directors could get different vantage points of the race and guide their riders appropriately.

Cruising through the race route directly behind Team Apex were Tom and Willie in the Benz, keeping a close eye on their cyclists. Tom shouted into the radio, "Smooth and steady guys, smooth and steady. We've already lost two guys. Stay calm. Only eighteen kilometers to go."

Bomber squeezed the mic clipped on his ultra-smooth, aerodynamic skinsuit and screamed, "time check."

Tom quickly replied to his leader. He knew Jack needed an update, to pace the team correctly. If they were going to have a chance at winning it was necessary to understand how the competition was doing. "Team Aqua Talon are up on us by twenty-five seconds at the halfway mark but keep it steady. The last part is hilly, and you'll make up time."

Bomber wanted to rip his earpiece out. He didn't like hearing that Team Aqua Talon was leading. His principal rival, Alexi Morkov, was their general classification contender. He was also last year's Tour de France runner-up, Jack's biggest threat.

Bomber knew he had to remain patient and wait for the final five kilometers of the stage when the terrain would tilt upwards and time could be gained. He yelled at his teammates to go harder. He wasn't anxious or eager, only determined to pick up the pace and get the team working towards perfection. He wanted the pulls to be faster and more powerful, and the transitions, smoother. He wanted the riders to be positioned smarter when the gusts of wind hit. He wanted them moving like the highly paid, talented athletes they were.

Bomber crushed his next pull with such ferocity that Nick didn't have the energy to pull through. Bomber's bloodthirstiness for victory had his teammates paying the price for his savage pull. Nick panicked and yelled into his mic, "What the hell, Jack? You're fucking everything up. If you keep pulling like this, I'm going to crack. Brad is already having trouble keeping contact. We can't afford to lose him. Everything is falling apart."

Tom didn't give Bomber a chance to respond. He needed everyone on the same page, "Keep it together, Nick. You need to be going Bomber's pace. He's the team leader. He's got this. Maybe you're on a bad day."

Fuck talking. This guy is acting like a junior—a total amateur, thought Nick. He looked down at his Garmin computer to check his heart rate. He was going a hundred percent and knew he needed to tuck back into the draft of his team. *If I'm almost gone, the rest of the team has to be on the brink of cracking. This whole team is going to implode. Imagine the story Robert Saunders will have then,* wondered Nick.

Welte took his designated pull and moved to the back of the echelon. He should have slipped in behind Nick, but instead, he jumped back into the rotation in front of him. Welte believed it was best for Nick to skip a few rotations, reserve his strength, and make a difference on the gradual climb to the finish. If he was still there. If he didn't become a casualty to the terminal pace Bomber was setting. Welte felt he needed to look out for his young teammate. He'd been around Jack Bomber long enough to know that his leader didn't always understand his own strength. Jack was known to ride like his life depended on it, without any regard for his teammates. Welte may not have known Nick well enough, but he knew the kid didn't hold back his feelings. The kid talked a lot, and that could only mean one thing—trouble.

Earlier, when Nick had screamed into his mic, cursing Bomber, Robert Saunders had been in the media tent watching it on his monitor. He scribbled on his notepad as fast as he could,

Yellow Jersey in trouble.

A team in distress.

A team with conflicting goals.

A divided team.

A scowl had taken hold of Nick Carney's face. His upper lip moved towards his nose, showing his clenched teeth.

His hand squeezed the mic pinned on his jersey, and he screamed something into it. The team car swerved. Not enough to cause obvious concern but given the panic all over Nick's face, it provided intrigue.

Jack Bomber pulled so hard, he pissed off the Yellow Jersey.

Lousy etiquette Jack Bomber, and now I'm going to make sure the entire world knows it!!!

The final climb of the time trial approached, and Team Apex was down to only four riders: Bomber, Nick, Welte, and Bradley. Nick began the climb tapping out a steady, efficient pace just above his physiological threshold. At this point, they couldn't afford to lose any more riders. The time would be taken when the 4th man crossed the line. Nick was careful and methodical with his pacing, but when he pulled off, he could see Bradley was straining and could hear him muttering, "I don't know guys. I don't know. I'm cracking. I'm CRACKING."

Bomber flew to the front and steadied the pace further. "Stay calm, Brad. We'll ease off. We can't drop anyone at this point."

Brad moved around Bomber and took a quick pull before retreating to the back. He wouldn't see the front again—this was his last match. To get the job done would be up to Welte, Bomber, and

Nick—who was in so much discomfort he was begging God to keep him alive. Every breath of air required a full contraction of his rib cage, causing his whole upper body to spasm. His lower back was collapsing with the weight of the pain, and his legs felt utterly empty. He was committed to the effort, but for how much longer—he didn't know.

Bomber was infallible. Every movement was so precise and athletic. It was intoxicating. Nick was desperate to admire what was transpiring on the road today, but couldn't. There was no time to watch Bomber's muscular legs effortlessly propel his bicycle at frightening speeds. No time to appreciate the gracefulness of a mighty champion. There was only emotion, pure bitter emotion—frustration that brought about anger and criticism.

Tom sat in the car, patiently watching his four remaining riders struggle up the final climb. There was complete silence. He was no longer speaking into his radio. The boys were trailing Team Aqua Talon by only two seconds now, and with a strong final push, they could win. He calmly conveyed this message to the team with five hundred meters to go. The stress of watching had him sitting at the edge of his seat, biting his lower lip as he gazed at the clock.

Having worked with Bomber for the past five years, he was cognizant of the fact that Bomber detested Directors who screamed into the rider's radio. In their first Tour together, when Bomber was on the verge of winning an individual time trial, Tom didn't stop yelling words of encouragement into his mic. Bomber's physical form broke, and he lost by ten seconds. After the race, Tom was dumbfounded. Bomber was direct, "I need my peace. Your screaming is the reason I lost. Lesson learned Boss. Lesson learned." Tom had never screamed at Bomber in a race ever again.

With two hundred meters to go, Bomber charged ahead, eager to hit the line first. Nick's legs could no longer move, and he lost contact, freewheeling over the line with his head down. Nick came in three seconds behind. As the fourth remaining rider, the team was given his time.

Tom studied the clock, confirming his riders hadn't done enough to win. Team Aqua Talon took the victory by one second. Nick's tiny gap at the end had cost them the stage win. Bomber's face twisted with anger unable to hide his dissatisfaction with losing. Tom examined his leader and knew the evening would be a delicate one between Jack and the young Carney.

CHAPTER 4

The Beginning of a Rivalry

Tom paced the hallway of the hotel, looking at the checkered carpet, counting his paces and trying to visualize one second. Losing the team trial by so little was disappointing, and he couldn't let it go. Tom kept visually trying to force a different result. If he could only think harder... maybe he could change the day's outcome. He knew it was futile but couldn't stop. His brain was working overtime.

Bomber entered the hallway. He'd just finished his massage and was in good spirits; relaxed, calm and smiling.

"Pissed?" Tom asked.

"Hmm, pissed about what?"

"Jack, don't act stupid. You must be furious."

"It is what it is, Tom."

"Please don't say that. You know that bugs the shit out of me. I can't stand it. We had the win. What happened?"

"Maybe I went a bit too hard. We didn't pace it out the way we should have. I thought we had it, but it was only one second."

Tom thought about it for a moment. "Jack listen, maybe it's not exactly the one second that bothers me. It's the fact that you guys came over together as a team, and Carney came in three seconds later. The team didn't lose this for us, Nick did."

"I don't know, I didn't look at the footage."

"Well, you need to look at it."

"That's your job, Tom. I'm here to race my bike."

Last year, after the team time trial, Bomber had been in yellow and didn't relinquish the jersey for the remainder of the Tour. The team had been utterly dominant in the team time trial, winning it by over a minute. Bomber wasn't exactly happy about this year's outcome, but he didn't like to get too emotionally wrapped up in the past. The stage was over, the result stood, and there was nothing he could do about it. He never understood why people would spend time contemplating a race and visualizing what had transpired. Why couldn't they move on, and apply what they learned towards their next challenge?

Bomber believed emotions led you astray. He had first-hand experience, witnessing it with his brother. Although Bomber's brother had been the gifted athlete in the family, he was too emotional to ever be great. His thirst for challenges always garnered him success, but his lack of discipline and commitment—his emotional weakness, meant he could never stay focused long enough. When the work became too monotonous and seemingly unchallenging, he would move on to a different sport.

On the other hand, Bomber was pragmatic by nature, his matter-of-fact attitude was often mistaken for aloofness. It didn't mean he never thought about the past; he just preferred not to dwell on it. But Tom had him thinking now. *Could the kid be playing games? Do I need to be worried?* Bomber couldn't imagine a world where Nick would have backed off intentionally. *Would he?*

Jack stopped. *Nick had to be fried at the end of the team time trial…*

Nick had indeed been exhausted at the end of the team time trial. He was cross-eyed and looking ahead, unable to hold the speed of Welte. The line was quickly approaching, and his legs were twitching, ready to cramp. They were rebelling, and no amount of pressure to the pedals would get him closer to Welte. It was only a bike length at most, but he knew what it would mean to the team? He gasped for air as if it was his final breath on Earth. His chest and abdomen stretched to their full capacity. Still, it wasn't enough. He looked above at the clock and in an instant his hopes were shattered; they'd finish second, and it was because of him. He nervously wheeled towards Bomber, Bradley, and Welte. They huddled and congratulated one another, but there was a look in Bomber's eyes. It was a look of disappointment, one that fingered Nick as the culprit.

The media was quick to pounce on Team Apex, capturing the riders' grimacing expressions. Nick knew there'd be a photo of that stare between himself and Bomber—the one that identified him as the wrongdoer. What would the headlines look like in tomorrow's papers? What questions would be asked? What story had the TV announcers concocted during the stage? Nick's mind was moving a mile a minute, and there was nowhere to hide. He was the yellow jersey holder, and he had obligations to the media. Journalist surrounded him screaming his name, "Nick! Nick! Can you tell us what happened at the end?" shouted a reporter.

"I had nothing left. A gap opened up."

"You guys had the win. What happened?" yelled another.

Again, Nick replied, "A gap opened up."

"Are you disappointed with the result?"

"Yeah, of course, I am. To lose by a second is annoying. It's not pivotal to the team's overall aspirations, but the victory would have been satisfying."

Robert Saunders moved in and placed his cell phone in front of Nick's face. He sneered then poignantly asked Nick, "Did you back off on purpose?"

Nick was caught off guard and angered. He hadn't forgotten the other night's outburst in front of Saunders. This time he remained calm. He backed away, "No Comment." It was enough for Robert. He had what he came for.

The journalists were crammed into their headquarters filing their reports on the day's aftermath. It would be a simple story—Team Apex loses to Team Aqua Talon in a tight race to the finish. The Tour wouldn't be won or lost today. The Yellow Jersey losing the stage for Team Apex on purpose could be a sensational story if it were the likes of Jack Bomber, but this was a surprise neo-pro in his very first Tour. They had to give Carney a break. Who knew how he was reacting to the pressure of being number one. Nothing to report.

Meanwhile, Saunders believed he recognized what would become the central story of this year's Tour de France, and he felt smug, sensing it well before any of his colleagues. It was time for Saunders to start plotting his intricate sporting tale.

There is a rivalry building between Bomber and Carney, a rivalry like no other. Forget Lemond versus Hinault, or more recently, Wiggins versus Froome. In each of those instances, both Lemond and Froome were ready to win the Tour. This Canadian kid, to the surprise of many, came out of nowhere and is wearing yellow. And now he was seen screaming into his mic midway through the race when

Bomber was at the front pulling. In the end, did he sit up on purpose? Was he sending Jack Bomber a message?

Nick finished his massage and was making his way to the team meeting. He was prepared to be blasted about today's minor mishap, but it gnawed at him; he'd given it a hundred percent. Nick knew the truth. He never let up at the end. Bomber stopped him before entering the room. "Just a heads-up kid, Tom isn't too happy about the loss today."

"Okay, well it was a team effort, right? So..."

"So, be prepared. Tom's looking to blame someone, and I think you're going to be the target."

"I figured," Nick said.

"Just one question Nick. Did you let up at the end? Did you think we had it, or were you just gone?"

Nick knew it was a reasonable and direct question, but he didn't want his team leader thinking he was hurting. Cyclists never want to show weakness to anyone, even their teammates. If he admitted he was physically gone, would the team continue to support him while in yellow? Nick liked being number one on the team and didn't want to be relegated to a helper, fetching bottles for teammates and riding tempo early in stages. He took a moment to think about it, and then tried looking Bomber straight in the eyes before speaking.

"I thought we had it. I just eased up a bit, Jack," replied Nick. He was lying of course. Nick was empty. And yeah, maybe a bit fucking angry, but he wouldn't have thrown the chance of winning another stage.

Bomber stared vacantly beyond where Nick stood, and the two entered the room where the rest of the team had gathered. Nick examined his teammates' faces for clues. He was apprehensive, believing a confrontation was inevitable.

"Thanks for joining us, guys," said Tom.

He nodded at the two of them and didn't appear upset. His body language was complacent and reserved. *Should I be worried?* Thought Nick.

Tom began going on about the stage, how things played out, and where the other Tour contenders were sitting relative to Bomber. There was no finger-pointing. It was direct and straightforward. He began with the day's result. There was hesitation at first among the team, then applause. Tom moved on to discuss Bomber's gains and losses that resulted from the stage. He lost one second to Alexi Morkov, but he was still fifteen seconds ahead of the Russian on the General Classification. Every other leading contender was between thirty to sixty seconds behind.

Bomber was now a solid minute ahead of Italian Fabian Bartoli, who'd finished 5th in last year's Tour after winning the Giro D'Italia. This year he had made the Tour his sole priority, skipping the Giro, and taking flak from the Italian Tifosi. He now sat fifth in the General Classification. He was a superstar in his home country and coming home without a Tour victory wouldn't sit well with his fans.

The French rider, Guillaume Peraud, was thirty-five seconds down on Bomber, but had a reputation for being unpredictable. He finished third in last year's Tour sharing the final podium with Bomber and Morkov, but he's been inconsistent this year. His form was off. He started with brilliant condition early in the season, winning the prestigious one-week Paris-Nice stage race, but hadn't been able to finish any event since. His coach put it down to a new form of training that would see Peraud peak at the Tour. So far, he'd stayed out of trouble, had a superb prologue, and his team was riding well.

British superstar, Ryan Ellington had won the Tour previously but had struggled with form over the last two years. He was riding for the top British cycling team, and this was his last chance to prove he was worthy of being a team leader. Ellington was forty-one seconds down on Bomber, better positioned than last year after the team time trial, and was brimming with confidence. Last year he'd never seemed to find his form. Ellington had been sitting second behind Bomber, looking poised to do something spectacular in the mountains when he lost form and faltered. The year before he had to abandon after the rest day, due to illness.

Finally, there was the prominent Spaniard, Miguel Alvarez, a proven superstar who had won the World Championship and the last four editions of the Vuelta Espana, the Spanish equivalent of the Tour. He'd never had the desire to ride in the Tour but was being forced to by his team. The sponsors wanted more global exposure and believed Alvarez possessed the qualities to win the Grande Boucle. He was thirty-two seconds behind Bomber and spoke confidently with the press about his chances of victory.

Nick left the team meeting satisfied but feeling slightly confused. Tom had been reasonable, no blame had been laid, but the conversation with Bomber before the meeting suggested it should've transpired differently. Nick had come into the meeting expecting a fight and spent the whole meeting waiting for it to happen. He had used up emotional energy he'd need for stage four. Bomber had gotten into his head. He'd manipulated Nick, forcing Nick's concentration away from where it needed to be. Nick made his way upstairs, steaming. *How could I be so fucking stupid? Wait. They're both playing me—Tom and Bomber!*

Stage four had been an uneventful day in the Tour. It'd been a flat, long day, perfect for the sprinters. Charlie Spitz would rack up his second victory, and both Nick and Bomber arrived safely home with the peloton and the rest of the favorites. The biggest news was the headline from the previous day's Team Time Trial.

TOUR DE FRANCE TEAM TIME TRIAL. CARNEY SENDS BOMBER A MESSAGE: NOW WHAT?

Robert Saunders' story had been published in North America, but globally it hadn't generated much noise. It did, however, get Jack Bomber thinking. Originally, he'd placed the team's loss on his shoulders, but Tom had thought Nick sat up, and now the journalist he hated the most in the world, and the journalist who more than likely despised him above all other riders, was questioning Nick Carney's actions. Could Nick be trusted?

It was the early days of the Tour, but sometimes the uneventful days turn out to be the catalyst for fireworks later.

CHAPTER 5

The Crash

Who is Frank Carney?

Frank Carney received a frantic call from his wife Catherine to turn on the television—The Sports Network, pronto. He knew what to expect and couldn't have cared less. For the past five days, the Tour de France had been playing at the Carney household around the clock. His wife was fixated on their youngest child's success.

Frank reached for the remote to his ninety-inch flat screen TV and turned on channel thirty. The announcers were going on about a high-speed wreck. Their voices were hasty, and they were using words like carnage, havoc, mass pile-up. Why did Catherine call him for this?

"It's the Yellow Jersey," shouted one of the announcers.

"Carney is down...he's down, and he's not moving!"

Nick's back wheel had touched a teammate's, and he was down. His bike was broken into pieces and lying on top of him. The pain was radiating from his shoulder down to his wrist. It shouldn't have happened. It never should. It was late in the stage, and he was exhausted.

Frank could only look on and smile. What an embarrassment. His wife had unintentionally made his day. He had expected to see his son being presented with another yellow jersey. More accolades from the TV announcers. More smiles and interviews. Kissing young beautiful podium girls. Instead, he got to see Nick on the ground, broken, and more than likely out of the Tour. At the very least his yellow jersey would be gone. Frank could get back to living peacefully. He could go back to being the King of his Castle.

It wasn't just the past few days that he'd struggled with resentment when it came to Nick. Frank grew up in Rockcliffe Park; the wealthiest neighborhood in Ottawa. His family came from old money, and Frank had built a tech empire in the 90s during the height of the Dot-Com Era. At that time, Canada's Capital was home to tech giants, Nortel, Newbridge, and JDS Uniphase. Ottawa had been labeled Silicon Valley North and money had been poured indiscriminately into tech companies. Frank had made a fortune with a few startups, which he later sold to multinational giants. He was now a motivational speaker getting paid fifteen thousand dollars per event.

Corporations loved Frank Carney, he was animated, well-spoken and funny. He could take a dry subject and get an audience fully engaged. He stood six-foot-four and was well built. His hair was jet black, his eyes green, and he could command any room he entered. He was charming, electric and his smile produced dimples on each cheek. He was the type of man that women adored. He was good-looking, influential and wealthy. He could have made an exceptional salesman had he chosen that profession.

Catherine entered the home with grocery bags in her arm. "Frank, did you see? Did you see Nick?"

"I sure did. It's a tragedy."

Catherine was upset. She had watched every Tour stage live, but with only ten kilometers left today, she decided to get a head start on her chores. She'd been grocery shopping when she received a text from Nick's Fiancée, Emma, letting her know that Nick had crashed. Immediately, she felt the need to let Frank know. Maybe he would care. Perhaps Frank would finally show some interest? But looking at him now as he stood there, silent, barely an expression on his face— it broke her heart.

Catherine was proud of her youngest son. He was the baby of the family, coming seven years after his brother and sister. While her two eldest children were thriving, Nick had always shown the most passion towards life. He was an intense and gifted child both academically and athletically. It didn't seem to matter what she enrolled him in, Nick always succeeded. He reminded her of Frank.

Perhaps it was the age difference between her children, or maybe because it was an accidental pregnancy, but Frank often appeared distant. She compensated by spending substantial amounts of time with Nick. Catherine loved his good-natured humor and his vivid imagination. In his earliest years, she would build elaborate forts with blankets throughout their basement. Lunch would be prepared by their Nanny, and both her and Nick would eat in their secret Labyrinth. He was so polite and gentle at these times. She'd had to resort to these types of home activities because he'd shown strange behaviors towards other children in public settings. Her psychologist had assured her it was a stage, and that Nick would eventually grow out of it.

Catherine worried that her early teenage years had caused her son's behavioral issues. She had grown up in a rough neighborhood in Ottawa and fell prey to drugs and alcohol at the age of fourteen. Catherine was tall, blonde and beautiful, and could have easily been mistaken for sixteen or even eighteen. Boys and men alike pursued her, and she used her womanly assets to her advantage. She could be vulgar at times, hardheaded and threw random fits when she didn't get her own way. Her father was barely present, and her mother was a drug addict. She cared very little for love, stability and the family ties. She had a few close friends, but for the most part, people served only one purpose; to be manipulated.

She first saw Frank when she'd been at a local park, smoking weed and drinking vodka straight from a bottle. He'd been well dressed and surrounded by a group of young boys and girls. As an outsider, she believed Frank to be the leader of this group. There was something special about him, and it wasn't because he was older. She knew the group was passing through the lower end of the city before making their way up the hill to their luxurious homes, and she felt drawn to follow.

When she had first laid eyes on Frank, she felt feelings she hadn't felt before. Her stomach had become fluttery, and she had become overwhelmed with emotion. She hadn't been sure how to cope with her feelings. They were foreign to her. Her reaction was too merely observe. She draped her hoodie over her face, and quietly kept a sufficient distance behind, not to get noticed.

Frank would be the first to reach home. A massive home in the center of Rockcliffe Park. This should have excited her; a young boy with money she could use, but she'd only felt guilt and disgust with herself. She crawled through some bush in the yard and watched as Frank entered his bedroom. She felt enamored with his physical attributes, but it was the way he'd held himself earlier with his group of friends that had impressed her more. All she knew for sure, she wanted more of Frank Carney.

Months later, she would see him again waiting at the bus station, alone and reading a popular science magazine. He had been wearing a school uniform—a blazer and a tie. He looked preppy, studious and, for Catherine, intoxicating. Moments after Catherine spotted him, a group of boys began to harass him. They were equal in size to Frank, but aggressive. They were bullies, and Catherine knew how to handle them. The boys shoved Frank back and forth, ripping the magazine from his hands, tearing it to pieces and throwing it to the ground.

Catherine moved in slowly, strutting with her hips swaying back and forth. She twirled her blonde hair with her right hand and gently placed her left on her hip. "Hey, boys, which one of you wants to walk me to school?" The boys instantly stopped harassing Frank and turned their attention to Catherine. She moved towards Frank. "I choose you," she declared. The others hollered in laughter, snickered and promptly left.

Frank skipped school that day and spent it with his heroine. She was apparently the wrong type of girl; his parents would never approve, but there was immediate chemistry. At the end of the day, the two exchanged numbers and set up a proper date for the coming weekend. That same evening, Catherine made the decision to quit alcohol and drugs. She knew it'd be difficult. Catherine also knew that to gain the love of someone like Frank Carney, she'd need to be clean. And, to win the approval of his parents, she'd have to be the ideal girl-next-door.

The phone rang, and Catherine rushed past Frank hoping to hear Nick's voice. He had called her after every stage, but she hadn't heard from him today. If not Nick, maybe Tom, or someone from the team who could let her know how her baby was doing. She put the phone on speaker so Frank could also listen. It was Emma.

"He's fine. Nothing is broken. Just some road rash and a sore shoulder," said Emma.

Frank was visibly annoyed, then smug, "Boy's out of yellow though. Damn shame."

"Oh no, Frank. He was within three kilometers of the finish."

"What does that mean?"

"It's a rule in cycling. If you crash within the last three kilometers of a flat stage, you get the same time as the leader."

"So, he's still in yellow?" Catherine asked, trying not to sound too excited. She didn't want to annoy Frank, and she didn't want to get her own hopes up that her son was still succeeding.

"Yeah. Still in yellow. No time loss and no broken bones."

Catherine breathed a sigh of relief and felt herself smile. Nick was safe. And, still in the lead.

At that moment those unnerving feelings Frank had struggled with over the last few days; those feelings he had wrestled with since Nick's early years, had returned. The peace he'd felt earlier slowly faded away and was replaced with an inner rage. A rage he would need to suppress while empathizing with Catherine.

CHAPTER 6

Stage 6

I Own Every Kilometer

It was 7:00 a.m. and Nick woke to a knocking on the door. He knew instantly that it was UCI officials; they were here to collect urine and a small blood sample. He'd already had three drug tests since the beginning of the race. He scrambled out of bed and rushed to the door. "Good morning, Mr. Carney. My name is Jacques Giroux from WADA. I'm going to need a urine sample and some blood. May I enter?"

It was a stupid question, and Nick almost rolled his eyed. He didn't have a choice. He had to let the WADA representative come in. Drug testing was part of the race. It was part of being the leader. He grabbed the small plastic container and headed to the bathroom. The door would have to remain open so Jacques would have visibility. Next, a small vial of blood would be needed to ensure his hematocrit level was consistent with previous tests. Those taken from the Tour and those taken throughout his professional career.

Nick was still sore from yesterday's crash and getting woken early and poked for blood didn't help his mood. He made his way down for breakfast and headed straight for the fresh coffee; black, no milk or sugar. Nick began his daily breakfast ritual. He grabbed a bowl and scooped fresh oatmeal into it, sprinkled some brown sugar on it, and topped it with walnuts and raisins. Next, he cut himself four pieces of fresh white bread and layered it with apricot jelly. Lastly, he complimented his breakfast with a six-egg-white omelet for protein and a chocolate croissant for his after-breakfast dessert.

He sat down and picked up the French sports newspaper L'Equipe. His spectacular crash was front page news. The photograph was of him on the ground clutching his bleeding elbow while the Tour doctor attended to him. The actual article about the incident was rather thin, and primarily focused on the Tour contenders escaping the crash. Nick sighed and shook his head. He didn't like the fact that more wasn't written about him. He was the fucking yellow jersey holder, the leader of the race, and he 'd crashed. What could be more newsworthy? Why did they have to focus on his teammate, Bomber, and the riders behind him?

Nick continued to flip through the paper when Tom came by and asked him how he was doing? Tom hadn't been the only one to ask that question. Every team member and staff member had asked him how he was feeling this morning. Even Bomber had graciously stopped by for a quick chat. His phone was filled with text messages from Emma, his mother, and his closest friends. His voicemail was full of good wishes. Even his father had texted him, but he had yet to look. He didn't know if any good would come from reading it. His father never had anything nice to say, and he'd learned from Emma to avoid his father as much as possible. His dad hadn't talked to him once since the Tour started. Perhaps his father was worried about him after the crash, but Nick wasn't convinced.

A year ago, he 'd been in a small race in Italy, grabbing bottles for teammates, fighting his way back to the peloton, drafting behind team vehicles, when the caravan came to a halt and Nick went flying through a team vehicle's windshield. He suffered contusions on his face and a concussion, spending the night in an Italian hospital. While Emma, his mother, and older siblings checked on him—his father did not. His father never texted, called or even spoke to Nick about the incident—even when Nick returned home. So, why would he be texting him now? He had nothing more than a sore elbow. At last, Nick found the courage to look at the text.

I DIDN'T KNOW LEADERS FELL OFF THEIR BIKES!!!

Nick pounded the table. He hated himself for looking. His eyes filled up with tears, and he left the breakfast area at once. He couldn't be seen crying. He would look weak, and leaders needed to be strong. He knew someone like Bomber would never complain. He was a no-nonsense, hard-headed man who would never succumb to a few meaningless words. So, why had he?

Back in Ottawa. It was the middle of the night, but Nick needed to call Emma. He was shaking, his skin tingling, and he was having thoughts of going home. Perhaps someone at breakfast saw the way he reacted after looking at this phone. Maybe they saw through him, saw the guilt and shame he was concealing. He knew if he didn't call Emma now he wouldn't be at the start line in two hours. "Emma, it's Nick."

"Hey, baby. What's up? Are you okay?"

It wasn't the hour in which Nick called that concerned Emma, there was something in his voice. Emma could always tell when there was something wrong with Nick. She gave him space when needed, ensuring he felt secure enough to express his feelings. Nick wasn't afraid of sharing, but he was fearful of being judged. Emma made him feel trusted and valued, and as such, she felt a powerful sense of responsibility and duty towards him. When he spoke, she listened.

"I'm done, baby. I can't keep going. This is all fake. I'm not a born leader like my dad."

Emma knew right away that Frank had been in touch with Nick, and that Nick truly needed her help. Why else would her fiancé be thinking like this? "What did he do? What did he say?"

Nick forwarded Emma the text, and within moments she began blasting Frank for being stupid, jealous, juvenile, and insensitive.

"He's just a bully, baby. Nothing more. You need to let it go."

The two chatted for a solid thirty minutes before Emma was confident that Nick would be okay. He was calm now, and she hoped he would be ready to go. At the very least he'd be on the start line.

STAGE SIX was about to begin, and Nick still found himself a bit out of sorts. He kept looking around wondering how many riders were thinking about him and his crash yesterday. His mind began to race. *Do they think I'm less of rider? Of course not, every rider crashes. It's part of the sport. Stop being so stupid. Do I belong here? Am I a good rider? Should I be wearing Yellow? Fuck. I'm the leader for a reason. Stop this shit!*

The lead car rolled out, and Nick followed, along with the other notable jersey holders and the pack in tow. It wouldn't be long before the day's action began. It would be fast and relentless until a break of riders went, then Nick would sit back within the draft of his team as they rode tempo. Eventually, the sprinter's teams would take up the pace, keeping the speed high until the end, battling to put their fast man into position. It was a routine day at the Tour. No wind was expected, and the weather was perfect. Nothing could go wrong.

At fifty kilometers into the stage, the break was established. The tempo Nick's team was putting down was fast and efficient, but within their draft, he was capable of talking with other riders. American Tyler Smith rode up to Nick. "How you feeling, champ?"

"Not bad. Shoulder and elbow a bit banged up, but I'm good."

"Yeah, it looked pretty serious on TV last night. I was happy to avoid it."

Nick felt annoyed. *What the fuck does he mean by that? Is he for real? Does he think he's fucking better than me?*

"Yeah, no doubt," Nick replied.

Tyler kept talking, but Nick tuned him out. He was focusing on the wheel in front and keeping himself protected from the wind. He kept his answers to Tyler's questions short, hoping he'd get the message and move on. Nick had never been a fan of Tyler. He had been a superstar on the North American circuit before making it to a World Tour Team, but Nick didn't believe he 'd go much further than being a domestique in Europe. He didn't have it. He wasn't in Nick's league.

Tyler wasn't getting the hint. He kept trying to gossip until Nick fed up and exploded, "I'm done talking, Tyler. I don't have time for you today." Nick accelerated, and pull away to position himself further up in the peloton.

Once he was able to calm himself down he shook his head in disgust, *What's my problem? Did I just say that, and say that out loud? What's Tyler going to think of me?* He became entrenched in guilt, believing there was no coming back from his actions. He'd probably never speak to Tyler again.

It was silent now; the only noise was the humming of tires. Nick was composed, positioning himself directly behind his steadfast teammate, Welte. There was nudging towards the feed station as riders jockeyed for position. The feed zone can be chaotic: Team personnel standing on the side of the road with bottles of water and small bags filled with food, trying to hand them to the riders as they whip by at fifty kilometers an hour. Nick, wasn't concerned about missing a feed, he was worried about crashing again.

As the peloton entered the feed zone, Nick detected a shoulder going into his left rib area, then a handlebar hit his seat on the right. There was a wobble, and Nick felt himself almost falling off his bike. He gasped, pushing forward, and grabbing his musette. He swung it over his shoulder and began examining the contents; a ham and cheese sandwich on white bread, a power bar, a few jelly chews, a gel, and a bottle filled with carbs and electrolytes.

Bomber rode up to Nick. "Good job staying upright."

Nick almost lost it. *Nobody thinks I can ride a damn bike now. What the fuck!*

"Thanks," said Nick

"What's for lunch?" asked Bomber.

"Ham and cheese sandwich, and the usual race food."

"Ham and cheese!?" Bomber was shocked that such a young athlete would choose real food over a manufactured sponsored bar. He also thought Nick might be living out some 80's cycling fantasy. *Did he honestly think eating this was a smart choice?* Nick could tell Bomber didn't look impressed with his nutritional decision.

"Yeah, I'm a bit old school. I asked the chef to prepare it for me today. I woke up with a craving. What can I say?"

"If it works, it works, kid."

Nick devoured his sandwich in haste, feeling nothing but guilt and hatred. He was annoyed with Tyler. He was annoyed with Bomber. In fact, he was annoyed with every rider in the race. He hated the Team Directors, the spectators, and anyone involved in today's proceedings. He was just plain angry, and the sandwich wasn't making him feel any better.

The end was approaching, and the Peloton was moving at a terminally exhausting speed. The sprinter's teams were coming to the front, while the teams looking to win the overall Tour (General Classification or GC teams) did their best to keep their leaders at the front and out of trouble.

For the past few years, sprinters such as Spitz had been making a stink about GC teams riding at the front near the end. While Spitz understood the need for GC teams to keep their leaders protected, he believed their involvement at the end of the race impeded the finish. He felt it was detrimental, dangerous, and caused unnecessary havoc. He wanted better rules in place that allowed GC teams to back off well before the last five to ten kilometers of a flat day to ensure a safe and proper sprint finale.

Today, Charlie Spitz was expected to win his third stage. His Tour success had made him vocal in the pack, and he was doing whatever it took to stay near the front. He was shoving when needed, headbutting when necessary and screaming when frustrated.

With three kilometers to the finish, Nick found himself slightly behind Bomber. Team Apex was at the front, drilling the pace and not showing any signs of letting up. Spitz was annoyed and started screaming at Nick, "You guys are fucking done, Carney. You're within three kilometers to the finish. Pull your men off." *These aren't my riders*, thought Nick. *This is Bomber's team.* He ignored Spitz and kept riding, trying to stay focused. Spitz was infuriated. "Get your fucking guys out of here. Do you even know how to race a bike, Crashfest?"

Spitz was to the right of Nick, screaming at him. Nick lost it. First, he punched Spitz hard in the thigh, then the arm then grabbed his jersey. He brought him close and shouted in his face, "This is Jack Bomber's team, Charlie. You have a problem. He's right there. Fucking talk to him."

The incident had been caught on film and broadcasted live throughout the World. TV announcers from every country began speculating on what was transpiring between the Yellow Jersey and sprinting mega star Charlie Spitz. How many euros would Team Apex be penalized for Nick Carney's behavior?

The finish line beckoned the riders, and the German Sprinter, Hans Ulrich, crossed the line first. Spitz came in a disappointing fifth; looking a bit shaken up.

Media scrums were quickly formed and converged around both Nick and Spitz. Spitz was the epitome of professionalism. He showed signs of disappointment, frustration with the incident and the day's result, but did so respectably. Nick, meanwhile, did not. He held it together for the first five minutes, but as the questions continued, he lost it again, "Fucking guy thinks he owns the last three kilometers of every flat stage. He needs a reality check. Look around Charlie Spitz...Nick Carney is in Yellow, and he owns every fucking kilometer of this race."

CHAPTER 7

Emma Watches in Disbelief

Emma watched and listened in disbelief. This wasn't her Nick. The pressure was getting to him, and she was overwhelmed with guilt. Before the Tour, Emma had secured a full-time position with Business Development Canada; a career with a crown corporation—her first full-time job. This was a far cry from serving coffee at Bridgehead, where she had worked to put herself through University. The place she and Nick had met for the first time. Before getting this job, Emma had every intention of being in France for Nick during the Tour, even if she would not have been welcomed by the Team Management. She had mapped out hotels close to where he and the team were staying and had planned on being at the start and finish for every stage. She would be there when allowed, just to mellow Nick out.

It would be an adventure for the twenty-three-year-old beauty who had never been to France. She'd heard from Nick that the taste of croissants, baguette, coffee, and wine was significantly different than in North America. The sky was bluer, the sun hotter, the scenery more exquisite. The mountains were majestic, the small villages in the southwest appeared ancient, and the roads twisted and wrapped themselves around luscious vineyards. Certain parts of France were littered with castles or ruins of castles; historical battlegrounds of forgotten civilizations. Then there was Paris. Who wouldn't want to go to Paris?

Sadly, she had received the job offer two weeks before the start of the Tour and had to begin straightaway. She was too scared to ask her new boss for time off. What would he think? Now, after sneaking a peek at stage six on her work computer and listening to Nick tell the world that he owned every kilometer of the Tour, she knew she needed to find the courage to speak to her boss.

Emma walked down the hall to the corner office where her boss, George Breckon, was working away on his computer. She knocked on his door to gain his attention and smiled through the glass window. George waved her in. "What can I do for you, Emma?"

Emma didn't waste any time. "George, I know I just started here, but I need time off. Would that be a problem?"

"Umm, well it could be."

Emma became flustered and her eyes began to water. George feared the worst.

"Is it a death in the family, Emma?"

"No, God no. I'm sorry, George. I suppose some context will help…" Part of the reason George hired Emma was her direct responses to his questions during her job interview. She didn't sugar coat her answers, or fill them with fluff, but at that moment, he needed more than she was providing.

"I need to go to the Tour de France," blurted Emma.

George rolled his eyes and shook his head. He was confused George wondered if this was a practical joke. Did she actually just say she needs to go to the Tour de France? Did his buddy Jake Epson down in sales put Emma up to this?

Everyone in the office knew George was a cycling nut. He was the guy who owned the ultra-expensive road bike that retailed for thousands of dollars, potentially costing more than a car. He was passionate about cycling. His evenings were filled with solo training rides, while his weekends were dominated by group rides, mimicking the pros, he watched on TV.

George decided to play along with Emma. "So, you're a big Tour fan, are you?"

"Well, not exactly. I just...well, I had planned on going before starting this job."

At that point, George was convinced it was a joke. Emma was fidgeting, barely talking, and her eyes kept drifting. "Okay," said George. "I'm going to ask you a series of Tour de France questions. You answer them correctly, and I will let you go. Fair?"

Emma was shocked and felt she needed to explain further. She knew she had failed to communicate appropriately. George began to rattle off questions, and Emma found herself unable to squeeze a word in, "Who is leading the Tour?"

"Nick Carney."

"Okay, that was easy. Nick's local, and he's all over the news. Who won the Tour last year?"

"Jack Bomber."

"Damn, yeah. Another easy one. Hmmm. How many stages is the Tour?"

"Twenty-One."

"Name each Jersey and their relevance."

"Yellow—Leader. Green—Points, Polka-dot—King of the Mountains, and White—best young rider."

"Well, Emma Blake, it looks like you're going to the Tour."

Emma could tell by the way George was speaking that something had been lost in translation. The stupid quiz…the ease at which he said she could go…it didn't add up. "George, I really need to go, but I don't think I've done a decent job explaining—"

"No need to. You passed the quiz. Make sure to bring me back a yellow jersey from the Tour. When can we expect you back, my dear?"

"George, stop! Listen….please! My fiancé is Nick Carney. He's having a rough time now. He needs me."

"Nick Carney is your what?" George was listening now.

As a hard-core cycling enthusiast, George lived for the Tour and this year was even more significant. Nick Carney had become a substantial Canadian hero. He was a local boy making a gigantic splash at the Tour. George had friends who were friends of Nick. Friends who had trained and raced against him. Watching him on TV every day in yellow made George feel connected to the kid, and it gave his pursuit of cycling a sense of importance. During his recent training rides, it was as though there was a spotlight shining on him and every other cyclist in Ottawa. Motorists seemed happy to give him more space, and George concluded this was because they believed he was a cyclist with the same caliber as Nick Carney.

"Is he really your fiancé?" George asked.

"Yes, he is."

"I have friends who ride with him. Nothing but good things to say; well mannered, polite, competitive but overall a good-natured boy."

Emma giggled, "For the most part that's true, but when he's under pressure, he has his moments."

"I actually just finished watching today's stage. I saw what happened and listened to his interview. His actions are going to be all over the media. Going to be rough," said George.

"That's why I'm concerned."

George stared at her. He couldn't believe the girl he just hired was Nick Carney's fiancée. Did he win the lottery? "Listen, take two weeks and go be with Nick. It will have to be an unpaid vacation. Are you okay with that? When Nick is back in Ottawa, can he take me out for a ride?"

"Oh my god. Thank you, George. Of course, he will," shouted Emma. She was so relieved, she kissed George on his cheek. It may have been too much, but she couldn't help herself. She could be with Nick, as initially planned. Maybe now, she could bring peace to him.

Roberts Saunders was part of the media scrum interviewing Nick after stage six. He was shaking his head and thinking, who is this kid? Where does this anger come from? This was the Nick he had first met earlier in the race in the hotel lobby. His actions and comments were real and unintentional, and unquestionably beautiful.

This was what the sport needed.

CHAPTER 8

Saunders Creates Magic

Robert Saunders ran back to the media tent. Stage six had finished, and Nick Carney provided the media with a sensational soundbite. His initial story a few days ago, depicting tension between Nick and Bomber may have gone unnoticed, but he wondered if people were paying attention now. Nick informed the world that he owned the Tour. What about Jack Bomber? Where did he fit in Nick Carney's fabricated world?

Robert began writing frantically, trying to get his story completed. He wanted it syndicated, picked up and published in all the major English speaking newsprint around the world. He believed his story would create the necessary drama that made the Tour a thrilling event to watch. It would get people talking.

Robert couldn't contain his excitement. He hammered the keyboard and stuffed his face with chocolate goodies, sipping his black coffee. His writing was swift and efficient. It depicted Nick as a confident, but arrogant racer looking to dethrone his leader. Nick Carney wasn't the polite and humble stereotypical Canadian the world had come to know and accept. There was a hunger laying deep within him, screaming to come out and conquer the Tour, to make it his own.

It was over the top, but Robert was a writer. He wanted his words to create magic. He needed to ignite his readers' imaginations. He yearned for the Tour to be more than just a physical challenge among men. He grew up romanticizing the talented champions of their era. He depicted them as Gods who could overpower their humanity by enduring nature's greatest hurdles; the thin air of the mountains, the blistering heat, torrential rain and hail, and howling gusts of wind. They needed the psychological strength to prevail and dominate over the external elements and their internal limiters. And, they needed a challenger to aid in the process.

Who would be Nick Carneys?

CHAPTER 9

Camouflage

"You aren't always who others think you are"

Nick was up in his room with tears streaming from his eyes. His last interview had been twenty minutes ago. This had been the first time he'd been alone since finishing stage six. He had skipped his massage and asked Welte to go first. He'd wanted to call Emma, but couldn't find the mental strength to pick up his phone. He laid on his bed in the fetal position, wrapping his arms around his pillow. He began to scratch his injured elbow, ripping the scab off. For a moment it hurt, but it wasn't enough. There was bleeding, but he needed more. He was desperate to diffuse the anger.

His gearbox was placed beside his bed, and there were scissors in the inner pocket. He reached down and grabbed what he was looking for. The scissors were sharp. They would be the perfect instrument to punish himself, to feel relief, and to cope with the immediate situation. He rushed to jam the tip of the scissors into his injured elbow and reopen the scar. He desired sharp pain but didn't want to draw attention by cutting himself somewhere that may be visible to team staff. His wound from yesterday's crash served as the perfect camouflage.

Before meeting Emma, Nick had coped with anxiety by occasionally scratching himself until drawing blood. At times, he would use a sharp instrument and go deeper, but it would depend on the level of torment he was experiencing; how alone and empty he felt. Nick was never prepared for when the urge would strike, but it often came after a disappointing race—the catalyst, but not the origin.

The suffering Nick tolerated during training and racing should have been enough to quell his emotional demons, but his addiction to pain numbed him in a way that cycling couldn't. The scissors ripped through the scar and blood rushed out. Nick finally felt relieved, watching the stream of blood form around his elbow and make its way towards the ground; the feeling of euphoric pain put him back in control.

He grabbed his iPad and opened his Twitter account to examine the damage he'd caused. His account was littered with tweets.

Charlie Spitz @CharlieSpitz

@NickCarney Yellow has turned a shade of ugly!

#TDF #knockout #RIPCarney

Bradley Wellington @Bradington

Rough end to the Stage. @NickCarney head up. We got your back.

#TeamApex #TDF

Jack Bomber @BomberJ1

Stayed out of trouble today. @TeamApex thanks for keeping me upright. Crazy finale! #TDF

Team Apex @TeamApex

Another stage completed. A great lesson for our young riders. Bomber looks good. Carney still in yellow.

#TDF #TeamApex

Robert Saunders @SaundersRobs

The truth is yet to be discovered. What lays ahead? Carney vs. Bomber

@BomberJ1 @TeamApex @NickCarney

#TDF

There was a knocking at the door. Nick was hesitant to answer, blood remained on the floor, and the scissors lay stationed on the soft yellowish, straight grained, durable pine table beside his bed. The sterling night lamp illuminated the puddle of blood, making it project from the surface. It looked hideous, and Nick was suddenly ashamed.

He felt like a delinquent caught in a criminal act, about to be tried and sentenced. He wiped away the blood and covered up his elbow with the dirty, old bandages that moments earlier had been on his arm. Though he still felt guilty, all evidence was now gone.

At his convenience, Nick turned the doorknob to greet his visitors. It was Tom with the Team's media relations officer, Wendy Rosling. He wondered if these intruders would be able to sense what he had done. Nick wasn't expecting to see Wendy, but he should have.

"Nick, may we come in?" asked Tom

"Of course. Nice to see you, Wendy."

"Good to see you too, Nick. How are you?"

"Can't complain."

Wendy may have been diminutive in stature, but she had a mean bite, and it hurt when those teeth clamped down on her victim. Nick prepared for her attack, though he wasn't in the mood for confrontation. His cutting episode left his stomach full of butterflies, and his body feeling as if it was floating above the ground, like in some paranormal thriller. He took a few deep breathes, attempting to calm himself down. He didn't want them looking too closely at him, sensing what he had done. He forced his body to relax

"Nick, let's talk about today," said Wendy.

"Let's."

"Don't be a smart ass," asserted Tom.

"That type of shit is what brought me here," stressed Wendy.

Nick's calmness after such an out-of-character incident disturbed Tom. They weren't here to read Nick the riot act. They just wanted to help polish his image. The sponsors had an audience, and Nick wasn't catering to it.

"You can use every swear word you want and be as cocky as you want out on the road with other riders, but with the press, you have to be polished," said Wendy.

"So, I can't be myself?"

"Be yourself but be respectful. We don't want you swearing during press interviews."

"What's the big deal?"

"It wasn't just the swearing. You acted like a pissy little whiner. Your tone and body language were out of control. You looked like a deranged narcissist preaching your superiority to the world," said Wendy.

Ouch. Wendy's bite. Damn it hurt. Nick bowed his head and apologized. The message was loud and clear. He felt anything but narcissistic—a disease he knew he wasn't plagued with. There were people in his life, like his father, who could be diagnosed narcissistic, but not him. A victim of narcissism—sure, but he wasn't a narcissist.

Wendy left the room, leaving Tom to pick up the rest of the pieces. Nick was glad to see her go, but he wasn't sure what Tom had in store for him. "Listen, kid, we love your enthusiasm, and we love the fact that you're in yellow but remember you're here to gain experience. No need to let the pressure get to you."

"Thanks, Tom. Guys like Spitz bug the shit out of me."

"Nick, that's fine. Spitz is a yappy little prick at times. But a leader doesn't let stuff like that get to him. It's a waste of energy. The energy you're going to need later in the race to help Bomber."

Nick gulped. One moment, he felt like he and Tom had what he'd imagine a real father and son conversation may sound like, then it turned sour. Why did he have to mention Bomber? Nick forced a smile, but his injured elbow no longer throbbed from his earlier cut. He became sullen, bitten by spite that radiated throughout his body.

Tom felt content with their conversation and left. Nick was alone, and the scissors lured him back. The exhilaration to hurt himself was, once more, enticing. This time he'd inflict more pain. And this time, there WOULD be more joy. The guilt and the shame would all be forgotten.

CHAPTER 10

Stage Seven

Boring day at the Tour...It happens!

STAGE SEVEN hadn't contained much drama. There'd been explosive action from the start with multiple attacks until a breakaway finally formed. There had been no rider of importance on General Classification. It'd been the perfect combination of ten riders representing various teams, all looking for that elusive Tour de France Stage win. If a rider from that group had won, it would have been a career-defining moment. It would have increased their future salary substantially. Unfortunately, the break would get caught with five kilometers to go setting up the perfect sprint finish for Charlie Spitz— who would be crowned the winner.

The commentary throughout the stage had revolved around yesterday's action between Nick and Spitz. Nick was being depicted as a temperamental kid who was having difficulty bearing the responsibility of wearing the yellow jersey. To further Nick's woes, Robert Saunders' story had been picked up and published around the world. Murmurs were spreading like wildfire throughout the press room depicting a discord brewing within Team Apex. It was leaked that media relations visited Nick late in the evening to discuss his unfortunate choice of words during interviews he gave after stage six. How it was leaked, no one knew. The source had been anonymous.

It was also being reported that Jack Bomber hadn't spoken to Nick in days. Whether this was true or not really didn't matter. The only thing that mattered was whether Tom Christenson, their Belgian Manager, would be capable of handling his budding egotistical star who was challenging the reigning Tour de France champion for leadership. It appeared that Tom and the rest of the team staff had their work cut out for them.

CHAPTER 11

Stage EIGHT

The Individual Time Trial

Bomber needed to leave the area now. He shouldn't have been noticed. He was wearing a solid black jersey and shorts, instead of his team kit, but tourist and locals began gathering around him. He was lost in his thoughts thinking about his wife, Amy, and their children—Aiden and Jonathon. He barely knew his newborn son, Jonathan, who had been born in May during the Tour of Romandie. The young infant had a full head of hair and a beautiful set of pudgy, soon-to-be cycling legs, but Bomber had only held him a handful of times since birth. He had been away racing, then on a recon of the Tour stages, a training camp in Tenerife, and now he was at the Tour.

Bomber continued looking around for an escape. If he didn't get moving soon, he would be locked down for the next hour with stranger's cheeks pressed against his, forced to smile for adoring fans swinging their phones in front of his face. *Click, click...look at me, I know Jack Bomber. Facebook post, Instagram, a tweet or two, my fifteen minutes of fame.*

Earlier he'd mounted his road bike and headed down to Cite de Carcassonne to take a few pictures of the medieval fortress. Amy, a former history major at the University of Colorado, had been disappointed that Jack hadn't taken any photos the last time he was there. She had studied the Western Roman Empire, the Visigoths, the Crusaders and the Cathars; to be in the presence of 2500 years of history and not capture the moment was blasphemy. "It's not like she's never been here," grumbled Jack as he rapidly took a selfie in front of the entrance of the medieval citadel. She'd have been here today if it weren't for giving birth to Jonathon only nine weeks ago. He veered off into the crowd, searching for something.

At one point he could feel the warmth of the strangers as they moved towards him. He noticed their whispers and gawking and tried moving in the other direction. His jersey was tugged by an older gentleman in his early sixties, wearing a cycling cap with the peak tilted towards the sky. The Colnago logo was clearly visible. The man was well tanned with sinewy legs highlighted by his veins. His arms were nothing more than bone with minimal amounts of droopy flesh. His jersey and socks were wool, and his glasses resembled those that were popular in the eighties. His bike was steel, a lugged Colnago beautifully painted by the master himself, Ernesto. The old man was Italian, and no doubt a former cyclist. He was a picture of familiarity, the unnamed. He mumbled, teeth barely present. Bomber could only faintly understand what he was saying. The older man's smile and outward demeanor were pure and genuine. He was a devoted fan. He held out a pad of paper and a pen.

"Jack Bomber?" the man asked.

"Yes. I'll sign right here," replied Bomber.

He scribbled his signature, and the man patted him on the back. He mumbled some more in Bomber's ear, laughing, hugging and tugging at the pockets of Bomber's jersey, making him uneasy.

The crowd had noticed the old man and the cyclist in black. There was something familiar about the younger man's physique, his bike, the strong jaw that stuck out beneath his Oakley's. They'd gathered around for a better look. The older man had a paper in his hand, a pen, and an envelope. It was hard to know and hard to see. The envelope disappeared as quickly as the man in black would.

Time was disappearing, and Bomber's opportunity to escape was being compromised. He could feel the heat from the gathered people's bodies as they accurately targeted his position. He was like a caged animal. An hour of photos would leave him empty and hinder his performance in today's Stage. An opening at the south end of the crowd emerged, and Bomber darted for it, planning to return to the hotel for an afternoon of relaxing and reading. Who was the cyclist in black and who was the old man? What was he holding? Someone would have recorded it. Nothing went unnoticed in the twenty-first century.

Today, Limoux, a commune in the southern area of France, part of the ancient Languedoc-Roussillon region known for its Blanquette de Limoux and Winter Festival, was hosting Stage Eight of the Tour, the Individual Time Trial. This was Jack Bomber's most robust cycling discipline. He was determined to put serious time into his main competition today. The Press was doing an excellent job generating discord between himself and his young teammate, but Bomber hadn't given Nick much consideration. Jack believed wholeheartedly that the yellow jersey belonged to him, temporarily on loan to Nick until he inherited it—to display to the world on the final podium in Paris. But he was still nervous. He was a competitor, and Nick wasn't making Jack's pursuit of the yellow jersey easy.

Bomber was in good form, but the media stress the past two days had gotten to him. Tom told him to do whatever he needed to regain focus. He chose to sleep-in today instead of taking a short drive from Carcassonne to Limoux to recon the course. There was no need too. Earlier in the year, he'd visited the area with Welte and his Spanish teammates to recon today's time trial, and the next three stages in the Pyrenees. He felt he had intimate knowledge about the course. The pavement was rough, and there was a substantial hill (a kilometer in length) starting in Saint Polycarpe and climbing to Villar-Sainte-Anselme. The downhill along the D51 contained a quick stretch of road with a gusty headwind. The next challenge would be the steep hill beginning in Saint-Hilaire, traveling along the D104 to Pieusse. He knew he'd need to push out some high-power numbers to win. Bomber thought about the course and Nick's recent comments. He chuckled to himself, *I need to own every inch of this fucking time trial to win.*

BOMBER WAS ON HIS TRAINER warming up, listening to his favorite selection of hip-hop, rap, and electronic. Scientific studies were proving that listening to music before exercising could increase performance. Bomber wasn't sure, but he didn't care. He only wanted to complete his warm-up without distraction. The media and fans were within meters, and he needed to mentally prepare for the vicious effort and energy he was about to exert. To his right was Nick, dressed in yellow, warming up. Nick was consumed by his music and sweat was dripping from his brow. Bomber wondered if now would be an appropriate time to play mind games with Nick. He looked like he was working hard. Perhaps he could throw the yellow jersey off his game and play with the young kid's mind. Jack was a master at the psychological game and knew it was time.

"Hey Nick, how was the afternoon recon?"

Nick looked up at Bomber, squinting his eyes. His upper lip curled, and he shook his head. The media cameras clicked away, and Bomber noticed. If he weren't up for some mind games now, maybe he would be later. Bomber removed his hands from his handlebars and threw them up in the air, giving a "what-the-fuck" gesture for the press. The crowd loved it and started booing Nick, but he was oblivious. Bomber went one step further. He stepped off his bike, shaking his head in disgust and entered the bus. "What's up?" Tom asked.

"I just have to take a leak," replied Jack.

Tom peered through the bus windows. "The crowd is riled up about something. What's going on? Any idea?"

"None. Who knows?"

Jack returned to his trainer five minutes later. Nick noticed the cameras, the crowd, and their screaming. He looked towards Bomber, "Is it always like this when you're in yellow?"

"Always, kid. Aren't you used to it yet?"

Bomber smiled but moved his arms and hands in a fashion that portrayed an air of confrontation between the two men. He jumped back on his bike and began pedaling. Nothing more was said. That scene, along with the remainder of the warm-up, would be up for interpretation by the journalists in attendance and reported in tomorrow's papers.

WITH ONE MINUTE until his start, Bomber was sandwiched between Ryan Ellington and Nick Carney. Ellington would start a minute in front of Jack and would act as a formidable rabbit for the reigning Tour champion. While Carney would start a minute after him; making Bomber prey for his younger teammate, the man in yellow. He was worried about Ellington, the British rider, and former Tour de France winner. Champions like Bomber were blessed with an innate ability to recognize brilliance at its prime. He had been evaluating Ellington's riding style throughout the past seven stages and knew the rider had good form. He was riding at the front of the peloton every day, avoiding crashes, and positioning himself without effort.

Bomber watched intently as Ellington moved off the starting ramp, accelerating to get up to speed. He then climbed the steps with his awkward cycling cleats tapping the carpet, muddling his gait and making him almost trip. No matter how many times he'd walked in his cycling shoes when doing so in front of thousands of people, he felt inadequate, like he had something stuck up his bum.

The minute between Ellington and Bomber felt like an eternity. He felt overwhelmed with anticipation. He had time to reminisce about his day—his trip to Carcassonne, the Italian, and the crowd. He thought about his wife, his kids, and what he did to Nick earlier. He smiled for the cameras, but his face was the epitome of concentration. He was positive the TV commentators were reading his facial expression and reporting it to the world entirely wrong. With fifteen seconds to go, he tightened his grip on his handlebars and moved his body up and over his front wheel. He positioned himself to take off like a rocket. His mind was focused, and his legs burned with a desire to push the pedals. His began breathing deeply and rhythmically in preparation for the event. He looked behind at Nick, staring at the yellow jersey; convinced he would inherit it in forty-four minutes after winning the time trial.

The clock buzzed, and Bomber moved off the ramp, stomping his pedals in a fury.

"Did you see that, Carl?" asked Allan Smith.

"I most certainly did. I wonder what Jack Bomber thought when he peered at his teammate in yellow," commented Carl Thomson.

"I'll tell you what he was thinking. He peered into Nick Carney's eyes, and said, that's my jersey. Thanks for keeping it warm, but at the end of the day I'll be wearing it thank you very much."

The famous TV commentators were caught up in their storyline. Earlier, they had witnessed the awkward warm up, and like the rest of the world, they had read Robert Saunders' recent articles on the tension between the two. It now appeared to be true, and in their minds Bomber had just confirmed it.

Out on the course, Bomber could feel that something was wrong with his pedaling, unnoticeable to anyone but him. His legs were throbbing with his right producing more power than the left. The effort on the Saint-Polycarpe climb was taking a toll, tilting his body to one side. He looked ahead, but couldn't see Ellington. The sun beat down on him, as the road narrowed and twisted at the top. He rode around the corner and peered over his shoulder. He could see a glimpse of yellow just below, maybe thirty seconds behind—could it be Carney?

Bomber never worried, he hadn't since his early days when he struggled to follow his brother's wheel over the legendary passes around Colorado. Those were the days when he was carefree, enjoying the scenery and **camaraderie** of being with his brother and father. His mind was different back then. He didn't need to win, he only wanted to participate and get carried away in the pure joy of the activity. Riding a bike was a way to be free and to explore the world. That all changed when he became the skilled rider he was today. The pressure to win, to be the absolute best, to become a legend drove every ounce of joy out of his body. He had become overly disciplined with his training, ensuring he was on the bike 364 days a year. Every piece of food he put into his mouth was weighed and consumed with precision—the macronutrient, carbohydrates being his primary fuel. Every day, he would check his bike position with his measuring tape. If it were off by a millimeter, Jack could feel it. The wrong position along with a hard workout could have resulted in sore legs for days. It was a risk he wasn't willing to take. Jack's wife would often joke with her friends that you wouldn't find Jack leaving the house without a tape measure. Perhaps it was true. He had over 25 different measuring devices in his garage. He liked precision, he liked numbers, and he lived or died by the formulas he generated in his head.

Jack's only problem now was dealing with the yellow speeding blur approaching from behind. He was worried he'd gotten his number's wrong. His ear began to buzz with a familiar voice—Tom.

"Carney's already taken twenty-five seconds out of you. I know you're just pacing it out. I thought I would let you know. You're up by ten seconds on Ellington."

Jack knew he wasn't pacing anything out. He'd gotten it wrong. He was wrong about the power numbers he needed to win today, and he was wrong about Nick Carney. The kid was proving to be a formidable rival, but Jack wasn't fazed. He wouldn't give up, he was a fighter after all. He stood to accelerate, but his legs tightened, and he seemingly went nowhere. He was at his maximum, his mind wanting him to go faster but his legs not cooperating. Once he was on the flatter section to Saint-Hilaire, he powered the big gear, hoping to gain speed and time on Nick. He turned at the intersection and began the second climb. The Abbey of Saint-Hilaire was on his right, but he had no time to look. There'd be no picture for Amy and the kids now, but she'd understand, he was a bit pre-occupied.

Jack's mind started to think of reasons why it was going wrong. Perhaps he had a flat, or his wheels were rubbing the inside of his frame—making him work harder and slowing him down. He looked at his back wheel—nothing. He thought about his tires; they felt as if they were sticking to the gravel-like pavement, the rubber sinking and slowing him dramatically, but he knew nothing was technically wrong. His bike was in good working shape—it was him who wasn't.

When the cameraman on the moto chose to move closer to Jack, the racer purposely tried to tuck himself behind the motorcycle to catch the draft. The moto sped up but kept the camera focused on Bomber's face—a face that became startled when another moto whizzed by. Bomber was experienced enough to know what that meant. He took a deep breath, but anger built within him—not anger from what was about to happen, but anger at his body for betraying him today. Of all days to abandon him, his legs chose this day—the individual time trial.

As Bomber crested the top of the hill, he glanced over at the Abbey of Saint Hilaire. He knew its history from Amy: the monastery was prosperous at one time but fell victim to wars, famine, and the ravages of the black death. Jack thought about the state of his body, suffering from extensive damage—a black death of his making. He started counting his pedal revolutions, loosening up his shoulders, trying to get back in touch with his sensations. At that moment, Nick passed him at an unimaginable speed. He looked flawless; a stunning work of art moving through space. The moto dropped back so the cameraman could get a close up of Bomber's reaction. The defending champion gave nothing away. There would be no facial gesture, no panting tongue for the camera. He was in no mood to play a particular character for the cameras now. He only wanted to get down to business.

Bomber crossed the line thirty seconds after Nick; a minute and a half down on his young teammate. Nick would remain in yellow, shocking the press and fans around the world. A lesser man would have been perturbed, perhaps throwing his bike or a water bottle in frustration. Bomber simply draped his defeated body over his bike as the media probed him for answers. Tom broke up the scrum of reporters and grabbed his star, bringing him behind the barrier to the team bus. "Are you okay?" asked Tom.

"Yeah, I'm fine. I'm fine."

"Bad day?"

"Yep. Difficult day. That's all it was. I'm good. Still lots of racing ahead. Not to worry." But, Jack was worried— distraught.

Tom couldn't entirely read Jack's body language, and he wasn't sure what to do. His reigning Tour Champion was in second place, almost two minutes down on the team's young rising star. The media was reporting tension within the team—highlights were being generated of Jack Bomber staring down Nick Carney before the Time Trial. And, Bomber didn't deliver.

Tom sat in the team car, confused as hell. Cycling protocol dictated that the team ride for the yellow jersey holder. That meant Bomber shouldn't be allowed to have a free reign and the team's support. Tom was beginning to realize that if Jack wasn't on form, it put the team at risk of not winning the overall. He had to start thinking about Carney, and his ability to deliver. Perhaps it was time to give the kid the respect he deserved. At the end of the day, the team sponsors only cared about winning. It didn't matter who got the job done.

Bomber sat alone at the back of the bus. He would travel back to the hotel with the rest of the team, while Carney would be driven back later by Tom, after the stage presentation and media interviews. It was an unusual position for Bomber to be in this late into the race. He hadn't predicted this outcome before the Tour. He never would have. He lived in the moment, confident in his training, preparation and hard work. He knew if he followed everything to a tee, the result would be a victory. He'd adhered faithfully to his work ethic the past two years, and he'd been rewarded with victory.

Like all men, Jack was driven by his fears, but it wasn't the little things in life that worried him. He didn't think about the bills that had to be paid, the laundry piling up, or whether there was food in the house or not. Those details weren't important enough to make Jack anxious.

Jack got excited about winning, nothing else mattered. But now Nick Carney was threatening his story—his existence for living. Nick was pushing Jack to his limit, and he was experiencing a type of fear that was foreign to him. The only other time Jack had experienced this emotion was when he was expecting his first son. He'd known he was an overly selfish man, consumed with his training and racing, and wondered if he'd be a good enough father. Knowing he would be responsible for another human being had crippled him with anxiety. It was the first time he'd experienced that type of feeling, and he did the only thing he knew to quell it—ride his bike, ride it a lot, and ride it hard. He was confident his loving wife would pick up the parental responsibility where he could not.

Jack gathered his thoughts. It was a shitty day, nothing more, time to move on. Riding his bike more, riding it harder wouldn't be the solution to his anxiety this time. He knew there were other ways to skin a cat. Tomorrow would be another day.

CHAPTER 12

When I was Younger, I Did What?!

The morning of the Individual Time Trial, Emma called Nick to give him the good news. Clearly frantic, she was rambling, spitting out as many words as she could. She only had five minutes. Nick was doing his best to listen, but he needed her to slow down. In a split second, he had a vision, a quick flashback to a time when he was seventeen. Single, and with the cycling season over, he was in search for a company of the opposite sex—a girl who didn't bike, diet or pursue any athletic endeavors. He didn't want to be surrounded by any more conversation about calories, carbs versus protein, or how many kilometers one had ridden. If he had to listen to another person spout the benefits of whey protein, or insist he try the latest HITT protocol, he was going to puke. He'd already spent enough days on the road with such people.

He just wanted an ordinary girl. Someone he could chill with, go to the movies, and grab some Mickey D's. If there was more on the menu—fantastic—if not, no big deal. They say variety is the spice of life. The adherence to training was necessary, but monotonous, and left him mentally stale. Nick's social circle at that time was diverse.

He was just finishing high school and had plenty of friends. Trendy, funky and sophisticated, Nick was the boy who rode his bike, shaved his legs, and competed for the National Team. He had athletic talent, style, and brains. He was going places. A decade or two earlier, shaving his legs, wearing lycra, and riding a two-wheel pedal bike, would have had him seen as an outcast, but not Nick—he was a rock star—with a strong presence on Facebook, Twitter, Instagram, and Snapchat.

His curiosity and need for something exciting led him to sign up for a speed dating event. Had he shared his adventure with his close friends, his phone would have lit up with acronyms, internet slang, and jargon: an OMG, a WTF, and a few LMAOs. He would keep it, as his friends would say on the D/L. He wasn't eighteen, but he had connections—a friend who had access to fake ID's. He remembered rotating from one woman to the next, with some gibbering at lightning speed. Those were the ones that left him confused; lots of talking, which he liked, but no connection.

Now he was facing this same scenario with his soon-to-be wife, jabbering under an enforced time limit and making no sense. "Emma, slow it down. I can't understand anything you're saying."

"Baby, Baby...I'm so sorry. I'm coming. Can you believe it? I'm coming."

"Coming. Going, where? What?"

"I'm leaving for France. I'm coming to be with you. George is a cyclist. Can you believe it? You have to ride with him, but I'm coming."

Who's George and why and when do I have to ride with him? All he knew was Emma had told him she was coming. His body began to feel transformed, letting go of the stress and tension he'd battled with in the first week of the Tour. He felt free, like a kid who'd finished the school year and had a whole summer of freedom awaiting him. In fact, that feeling of liberation was the biggest reason he'd fallen in love with riding a bike—it was his way to escape his problems at home—his dad. He was introduced to riding his bike by his older brother and was immediately enthralled with the glorious places he could explore. His imagination could take the most straightforward road around Ottawa and transform it into a European cobbled pathway in the middle of Belgium or Southern France. Gatineau Parc would be turned into the Alpes, the Pyrenees or the Dolomites. He never thought about winning anything. He focused on escaping the mental torment his father inflicted upon him. And, when he rode hard up one of his imaginary mountains he didn't feel the pain in his legs, he felt weightless. The physical pain squashed his emotional distress, setting him free.

Getting into bike racing was a natural progression and became the means to an end—a way to continue to explore, and dream, and conquer his emotional demons.

When he met Emma, his desire to ride the bike changed, making him feel connected to another human being in a way he couldn't describe. Nick couldn't tell her he loved her because he wasn't sure he knew what love was. He just knew she made him feel something beyond anything he'd ever felt before. His dreams about life changed. Racing became about making enough money in the next two or three years as a professional, and then retire for life. And, then there was his dad—the man he chose to escape from every day. Emma had told him to forgive Frank as much as he could, to blame him for the bad, but also the good. With her support, Nick believed that he'd produce results on the bike that would make his dad proud, bring the two men closer, and heal Nick's heart.

Now that Emma was coming Nick knew he would own the whole fucking time trial!! It was his to dominate and win. He would make this time trial his stepping stone to his overall victory in this Tour.

CHAPTER 13

Rest Day

The Big Surprise!

He rolled up the newspaper, crinkled it into a ball and chucked it. The force behind the pitch was far more potent than its flight; the trajectory causing it to land inches away from his feet. He kicked it and hollered. "This shit belongs in the garbage. Damn you, Robert Saunders." Tom was pacing back and forth in his room, sucking in his cheeks, clenching the delicate folds of flesh with his teeth—a habit he'd developed at an early age to deal with stress. His hands were clamped together, forming fists, and his head throbbed causing his eyes to water. He entered the bathroom in search of Advil.

His toiletry was a jumbled wreck; a mixed collection of soap, body wash, toothpaste, and medication. Ten days of living in hotels and out of his suitcase had caused this mess. "I can't find anything in this fucking thing." He rubbed his anguished head, then sifted through his bag some more.

It was 5:00 am, the first rest day of the Tour, but there wouldn't be any leisure for Tom today. He found the Advil—extra strength—

grabbed two and sucked them back with little to no water. He returned to the bedroom and picked up the thick binder on his table, a work of art Tom and the team staff put together weeks before the Tour started. Bundles of paper divided by categorized tabs. Every day, every stage and every detail had been perfectly outlined. Roles within the organization were clearly defined. "This isn't going to do me any good today. Not now."

Tom was a numbers guy, a planner by nature. He was never a talented rider, not like Nick Carney, but he was disciplined and could read race tactics better than most. When he was Jack's teammate, he saw a man with an immense amount of talent and a strong work ethic. He knew Jack could go above and beyond what he'd accomplished, reaching a higher level in the sport. With a little more discipline and rest, he knew he could turn Jack Bomber into a grand tour winner, and so he did. When he spotted Nick Carney he saw a talent he'd never seen in his 15 years as a professional cyclist, and 3 years as a Team Director. The kid had it all. Physically, he was a skinny giant with long legs and a small torso and neck—a lower body that could apply massive amounts of leverage to the pedals, and an upper body that could engulf and hide his head from the wind. He liked the kid and wanted him on the team. He was surprised when Jack agreed and helped recruit the kid. He knew how competitive Jack could be and wondered if he'd be able to mentor the young man. Forget Jack's ability to mentor, now Tom wondered if he would be able to lead his protege to victory. Nick had proven a hard read throughout the year. He didn't seem to like authority and at times rebelled against direction and guidance. Tom believed it had to do with trust issues, and he worried about how the young man would deal with what would transpire today.

Hours earlier, just before attempting to go to sleep, there had been a knock on Tom's door. He was in his boxers, flip-flopping and smashing his pillow trying to get comfortable. At times he'd felt like his dog, who he'd witnessed multiple times circling around and around before lying down; a ritual one canine expert related to the wolf-like behavior of living in the wild, the need to build a nest and feel safe. It made sense given the pressure a Team Director experiences on a rest day. And now, there was this knock. He opened the door.

"Jack. Phew. You scared me. What's up?"

"We need to talk, Tom, and we need to talk NOW!"

"Is this about Carney?"

"Carney, the Tour, cycling... I want to be at the press conference tomorrow."

"Is that it, Jack?"

"No, there's more. I'm just getting started."

They chatted for the next hour. Tom should have been ready, but he could never have anticipated this. His binder, for all its diagrams, charts, and well-thought-out plans, didn't have a manuscript on how to deal with what Jack had just told him. Why hadn't he seen it? It didn't matter. He now had one more item, a potential crisis, on his agenda to deal with.

Tom texted Willie and Wendy Rosling to meet him in his room at 6:00 am. The text was vague: "We need to discuss a potential threatening announcement." He needed their help to formulate a strategy for the looming press conference scheduled for 10:00 am. If they didn't present this the right way, the shit was going to hit the fan.

The vagueness of the text caught Wendy off guard. The conference was going to revolve around Carney and the team's strategy for defending the yellow jersey. Nick would be in attendance to field reporter's questions. He had been brilliant after yesterday's time trial. He put his good looks, his charm, and education to practical use. He had the press eating out of the palm of his hand. They loved him. Wendy was no longer concerned with Nick. She figured it must have been her speech. She must have gotten through to the kid the other night. Whatever it'd been, she was convinced they wouldn't see the Nick they saw after stage six.

Wendy knew there would be questions involving leadership. Robert Saunders had done a fantastic job of painting a tale of hostility between Jack Bomber and Nick Carney. But, she was confident that if any conflict existed, Tom would be more than capable of handling it. He was a formidable Director with years of experience. In his early days, a task of this magnitude would have been beyond his capabilities, but two Tour wins had transformed him. He stood taller, walked with more assurance, and she swore even his voice was more vibrant, more expressive and loaded. He'd surely put that Saunders in his place! So why the 5:00 am text asking her for help?

Wendy and Willie arrived at Bomber's door precisely on time. He greeted them, motioning to the table, ready to sit and discuss the current predicament. "We have a serious situation here. One I wasn't prepared for."

"What is it?" Wendy asked.

"Jack wants to hold a personal press conference at nine thirty; before the team conference. He has a few things he wants to be made public."

"What for?" asked Willie.

"Absolutely not, Tom. No personal press conferences. We have Saunders fabricating a story about Bomber and Carney. And the world is listening," Wendy exclaimed.

"I understand that. This has nothing to do with Carney. Well, not directly."

Wendy couldn't help it. She was chomping at the bit. It was in her nature. She grew up with a household of boys, and she was the youngest. To get heard, she had to be aggressive.

"Listen, Tom, I don't care what the fuck it is. At this point, he's not having his own damn conference. I don't care what comes out of his mouth, it's going to be interpreted badly. Unless he's dying..."

Tom paused, looking at both. "He's not dying, but he's made the decision to retire after the Tour."

"For the season or forever?"

"Forever, Willie. No more racing."

Wendy was shaking her head. Her mind was working hard, trying to figure out how the world would interpret this. She could see tomorrow's headlines, the tweets, and the stories to follow. *The fucking nerve of this guy. Unable to handle a little internal competition Jack Bomber?* Wendy thought athletes were delicate, insecure humans with sizeable egos, *but* she realized a great athlete like Bomber must have a significant reason for making this decision, and that it went beyond her internal petty reaction.

"Okay. He gets a press conference. I'll notify the media and set it up with the race organization. Just be prepared, Tom. It won't be pretty," she said.

They discussed it further, then Tom asked them to leave. He was relieved to have this burden shared. Now he wanted thirty minutes of peace and quiet, to slump down in his chair and sit peacefully. They'd meet the press at nine thirty and Tom would have to be on, his political 'A' game intact, and ready to entertain.

Nick was down in the lobby of the hotel, enjoying a latte and reading L'Equipe. The lobby was jam-packed, and he was tucked away in the corner, on a sofa chair, trying to make it look routine. When you're in yellow, you hardly go unnoticed. He had a camera crew following him today. They were meters away, giving him instructions on where he needed to place his cup and where the paper should be in relation to his body; too high and the audience wouldn't be able to see his face, too low, and it won't look like he was reading. No other media could approach him, but they were congregating, standing nearby and watching him. He was off limits until the press conference. Guests of the hotel walked by using their phones to snap photos.

Nick and the rest of the team had been asked to be in the lobby for nine thirty. When he initially received the text, he thought Tom wanted to meet up and go over the press conference. This would be Nick's first, so it made sense—until his roommate, Welte, received the same text.

Everyone but Bomber was there. The team was making fun of Nick, and it was all being captured on video. Bradley swooped in and grabbed his latte, taking a sip while looking at the camera, "I'm the yellow jersey, I own this whole latte. In fact, I own every latte in France." The team burst into laughter. Nick sheepishly stared into the camera, his face flushed. He didn't mind a bit. It was playful, made great footage, and it didn't seem to bother him. His teammates, by default, were becoming his family. Their dedication, hard work, and sacrifice over the last nine days meant everything to Nick. Today was their day to relax and let loose.

It probably helped that he was bubbling over with anticipation. Emma would be here in about an hour and a half. He had his press conference, a quick spin with the team, then he was free to relax.

Tom, Bomber, and Wendy entered the lobby. Tom motioned to Willie to gather the rest of the team. They made their way to the room where the conference would be. It was empty, rows of chairs facing an empty table with microphones. Tom gestured for the team to gather around. "Guys. Listen up. Jack wants to say something. Jack."

"Yep. Ummm. So, this is going to be difficult. I just want to preface this by saying this has nothing to do with the last nine days of this Tour. I've been thinking about this for a year now. Being at the peak of my career, achieving my life goals, and now with the birth of my second son—who I haven't seen that much—I've decided that after the Tour I will be retiring."

"NO! But, you're too young! No," shouted his loyal lieutenant, Escartin.

Welte was the only other father on the team. He understood where Jack was coming from. Sacrificing family-time for racing, training camps, and traveling, and being away from home for over two hundred days of the year takes a toll. He extended his hand to Jack, "Congratulations. Tough decision to make, but a good one."

"Thanks, Didier."

Nick was astounded. He looked around. Everyone was smiling and shaking Bomber's hand. *This makes no sense. Wait. Is this the reason why the press conference was moved up to nine thirty? Certainly, he's not going to announce his retirement today. If he is, what's his play? Why are you doing this to me, Jack Bomber?*

He attempted to gather his thoughts as he advanced towards Bomber. He only needed to shake his leader's hand, wish him well and move on. But, he didn't always do the right thing. He stood in front of Jack, feeling damaged, hoping what he was thinking was false. "You're not telling the press today, are you, Jack?"

"I am, Nick. That's why we're here."

"What the fuck? Why?"

"It needs to be done." Bomber extended his hand, "No hard feelings."

Nick refused to shake his hand, "Well, it feels like a betrayal."

"What are you talking about, kid? You in your head again?"

Tom and Wendy witnessed the interaction. Nick was trembling, his right hand clutching his left forearm. His thumb digging into his bicep. "Tom, grab Nick before something happens. I think he may lose it," Wendy said.

But intervening wasn't necessary, Nick didn't engage any further. He looked frightened and moved away from Bomber like a child scorned by a parent. He went to an empty chair and took a seat.

In a moment, the room would be packed with journalists, photographers, and video cameras. The attention would be directed at Jack and his imminent retirement. Nick's potential role as co-leader, but once Bomber announced his impending retirement, the focus would be on Jack. It was likely most of the questions would be directed at the potential rift brewing between the two teammates. In Nick's current state of mind, he was likely to believe whatever the press conjured up. If they interpreted Bomber's retirement the way he did moments ago, he'd feed into their accusations. He wouldn't be able to control himself.

Nick was in a trance as his mind contemplated the worst. He attempted to pull himself out of the darkness, threatening to overtake his mind. *Jack is a seasoned athlete who has won the most significant sporting event twice. He has a family. He misses them. Stop thinking negatively. This has nothing to do with you.* Nick's self-pep talk was helping soothe his nerves. Then, he caught a whiff of old man stink. He knew the smell well. Polo, Drakkar Noir, and Old Spice. He turned his head. The press gathered. It's time! He moved from his seat and joined Bomber and Tom at the head table.

Shouting filled the room, echoing off the barren, grey walls. Flashbulbs exploded, blinding Nick momentarily. It's beginning. Tom took control. "Before we answer any questions, Jack has an announcement he would like to make."

Saunders squirmed in his chair. *The buggers gonna quit the race.* Other journalists were silent, more than likely speculating he was sick or injured and would be retiring from the competition.

Bomber tapped the mic, more for show than anything else. He knew how they worked. He was a seasoned expert at dealing with the media and wasn't because he'd been in the spotlight for years. Long before his cycling career, he was learning from the best on how to deal with people. His mother, a Political Science Professor at the University of Colorado, would practice her lectures in front of both him and Michael when they were younger. Had he not chosen the bike, he may have selected the office. He'd been good at public speaking, winning contests in elementary school. He enjoyed US politics and couldn't imagine who wouldn't.

His father for one, but hundreds of political books were displayed in cases at the Bomber residence. Jack's favorites were the political thought and theory manuscripts. He enjoyed reading Nietzsche, Hobbes, and took a keen liking to Machiavelli; *the end justifies the means!* He leaned into the mic, his eyes widening and looking up towards the ceiling, then sighed. "I've made the difficult decision to end my career. This will be my last Tour de France."

The media in the room erupted, and disarray of sounds and words flew through the air. All sense of order was lost. The winner would be whoever could talk the loudest and the fastest. Saunders jumped on his chair and gave a lively, screeching introduction, "Robert Saunders. North American Syndicated Press." His respective colleagues quieted themselves. Saunders had the floor. "What made you make this decision? Why now? And, what do you think of all this, Nick?"

Bomber was fixated on Saunders, his eyes never blinking. *I'm the alpha, I control this room.* "The decision was made a year ago, with close friends and family." Tom shifted away from Bomber. Not enough for anyone to notice, more of a twitch than anything else. *Where was I a year ago when Jack made this decision? We've been inseparable for the past three years. Jack was the best man at my wedding. So much for being family,* thought Tom.

"As to why now?" Bomber sighed, "The time feels right. I've got a great bunch of guys around me. We've enjoyed early success as a team with Nick. As we head towards the *real* part of the Tour, where it will be won or lost, I want the team and my fans to know that I will be leaving nothing on the table. I'm going to go full gas and give them the best Bomber they've ever seen."

"And Nick, Nick! What do you think?" shouted Saunders. He wanted all his questions answered, especially this one. Nick was slow to the mic. Today, Tom was supposed to announce that Nick would be the co-leader of the team with Bomber. They would defend the yellow jersey and do everything to retain it. Bomber won't attack Nick and Nick won't attack Bomber. The forthcoming terrain would sort out who was the strongest. But now... this announcement. How Bomber framed, it had Nick confused. He answered Saunders tentatively. "Jack can announce when he wants to retire when he feels it is the right time. He obviously feels it's the right time. The guys on the team are obviously bummed, but we're excited we're part of Jack Bomber's last Tour. It's pretty cool."

Wendy was standing by the door. A smile emerged. "Good boy, Nick. You handled that like a pro," she muttered to herself.

A journalist from the British newspaper, The Guardian, was next. "Paul Davies. The Guardian. What are your thoughts on your main rivals? What do you think of Ellington?" Bomber was quick to the mic. Nick didn't have a chance. "Ellington and Morkov are looking strong. They'll both be tough in the mountains. I'll need to keep a close eye on them. You then have Alvarez, Peraud, and Bartoli. They're all threats. The race is close."

"And Nick, your thoughts?" Davies asked.

Bomber. Without a doubt. He's my only rival, my most significant threat. At least that's what he wanted to say, but he continued being the Nick that would make Wendy and the team happy. He nodded his head, "Your man—Ellington. He's got great form. He's a picture of perfection on the bike right now. I'm not afraid to say that. He's a good friend of mine. We're here to win though. We'll seek to contain him and put him into difficulty every chance we get over the next three days."

Being a Brit, Davies loved it. He would have some kind words for Carney in his column tomorrow. He'd taken a shining to the young lad.

The press conference lasted an hour, with similar questions being asked by different journalists. There were also the typical rest day inquiries: How have the hotels and transfers been? How's your sleep? How many calories are you burning and consuming? What will you do today? What do your power numbers look like? And, as always, there was a host of interrogative journalists that had to harass Nick and Bomber about performance-enhancing substances or illegal activities.

The room cleared, and Nick looked at Tom, "May I be excused now? Emma should be arriving any minute."

"Yes. Of course. Enjoy your day, Nick. Keep your cell phone close, just in case."

Nothing was uttered between the two riders. Nick didn't want to be in the presence of JACK THE GREAT any longer. Every word out of Jack's mouth in the last hour had revolved around him. Every answer he provided was about how he'd do this or that, or how the team would help him. He was self-absorbed, not lending a supportive hand to Nick. *Could he be any more like Frank Carney?* Not one of his answers had conveyed a working relationship amongst equals. It was clear Bomber believed he was the sole leader. Nick and the team were there to serve him. Had Tom not spoken to him? Could he not see who was wearing yellow, thought Nick.

CHAPTER 14

Emma Blake

Emma arrived at the Blagnac Airport in Toulouse. She was tired from the seven-hour, transatlantic, red-eye flight but over the moon to see Nick. As she left the plane, her steps quickened. Her pace was so fast, she was almost skipping down the airport terminal towards baggage claim. Her smile was broad and radiant, and her athletic, well-defined figure captured the glances and imagination of every man she passed. She waited patiently at the baggage terminal for her luggage, switching her phone off airplane mode. She wondered what it would be like to see Nick. A month had gone by with no physical contact. All communication had been via phone, text, and email. She couldn't wait to see him, touch him and smell the man she was in love with. His smell was unique to her. No man had that sweet, comforting aroma that Nick possessed. He was in yellow now, a man of power and fame. Would he still be the boy she fell in love with?

The doubts subsided as she spotted her pink luggage. Nick was a one-of-a-kind gentle soul, committed to life, and dedicated to his loved ones. He would be no different. Emma grabbed her oversized decorative luggage. She lifted the handle and as soon as the wheels hit the ground, began making her way to the rental car counter. Nick insisted she use EuropeCar; a former sponsor of a World Tour Cycling Team. They boasted one of Nick's favorite riders, Pierre Roland. He was a tall, slim, dominant rider who had an efficient and graceful pedal stroke that Nick admired. His physical characteristics and body position on the bike mirrored those of Nick, and that's partly why he liked him so much.

Emma spotted the green and black signage and headed towards the counter. She was greeted by a young man in French. She was warned by Nick, who like Emma, spoke French, that the language in the Southern part of France was different. She would need to be prepared to listen, and perhaps struggle to capture the meaning of unknown foreign phrases. The man's accent was thick, and he added far too many zings at the end of every word. His droll was similar to people in the Southern parts of the US. She registered very little of what the man said, and as a French-Canadian, she felt inadequate. She asked politely if he would mind speaking English and he complied without hesitation. His English was far better than his French, as far as Emma was concerned, and the remainder of the interaction went smoothly.

With the keys in one hand and her pink luggage in the other, she departed the airport and headed to the car lot. Waiting for her was a metallic, effervescent, blue Peugeot. She opened the trunk, threw her luggage in, and got comfortable in the driver's seat. She looked down and to her surprise noticed the car was manual. *God damn stick.* When was the last time she'd driven a manual? It'd been her driver's test back when she was sixteen, and she was forced to use one. Her father was a driving enthusiast and refused to buy anything automatic. "You have to feel the car, connect with the machine and the road," he liked to preach. She'd spent six months before her test stalling at red lights, missing shifts and avoiding any road with an incline. As soon as she passed her driver's exam and was able to afford her first car, she chose automatic, much to her father's disappointment.

She started the car and slowly lifted her foot off the clutch, as she applied pressure to the gas. The car moved forward, and she giggled. *It was just like riding a bike.* Nick would be proud; not because she was driving a manual, but because of the cycling phrase she'd thought about. Her foot was heavy. She shifted to second then third and tore out of the airport. Within minutes she was on the AutoRoute moving towards…where? This was just like her. She had been so busy worrying about getting the car going, thinking about her past manual driving inadequacies that she neglected to set up the navigation system. She was moving at a solid hundred and thirty kilometers an hour, but cars were flying by her on the right, with the driver's giving her nasty looks. She saw a sign for her destination to Carcassonne and veered to the left to make the exit. This was too easy.

The road was a single lane of rough asphalt, winding through the French countryside. Vast vineyards and fields of sunflowers decorated the landscape. Emma knew she wasn't lost, but she wasn't entirely sure she took the correct route. She pulled over, parking the Peugeot on the side of the road as she set up the GPS. She punched in the coordinates to Nick's hotel in Carcassonne, and it quickly spit back a travel time of 1 hour and 35 minutes. Nick had told her it wouldn't take longer than an hour from the Airport.

Her phone was at the bottom of her purse. She rummaged endlessly through sheets of travel papers and receipts, throwing her lip balm, make-up kit, and hand sanitizer on the passenger seat. After a minute of frustration, she located her phone and decided to text Nick. She had misled him before leaving Ottawa, telling him she was on a later flight. She wanted to arrive early to surprise him. Now, she felt a bit stupid. She wasn't as hard on herself as Nick tended to be. He beat himself up regularly for simple things, and she was always there to bring him back, helping him heal his self-inflicted wounds. She always chalked it up to him being a type A individual, a perfectionist and hard-charging athlete, but she knew his issues went much deeper.

Nick answered quickly. "Hey, Babe. Are you on the airplane?"

She laughed. Wi-Fi had been available on the plane, to text and to call, but she was a long way from being in the air. "Nope, I'm on the road, Nick. I took an earlier flight and wanted to surprise you, but I took a wrong turn."

This was just like her. "Where are you, boo?"

"I'm on my way, but I'm taking the scenic route. I'm heading towards Castelnaudary, I think. Isn't that place famous for something?"

Nick knew this area well. In his final year as a junior, he'd raced for a small amateur team in Blagnac, traveling to small races surrounding Toulouse. Castelnaudary was known for hosting stages of the famous Women's Tour de Aude back in the '90s and early 2000s. The year Nick was in France, he'd participated in an International Individual Time Trial; a route that traversed alongside the Aude Canal in the middle of city square of Castelnaudary. Nick easily won that day and was rewarded with one hundred and fifty cans of Castelnaudary's famous cassoulet: a hearty meal of duck, sausage, and white beans packed into a can. He had lived on it for two months and made sure to bring some home for special occasions. Numerous celebrations between him and Emma had occurred over a warm plate of prepared Cassoulet a la Chef Nick. Emma was none the wiser that his acclaimed cassoulet came from a tin can!

"It's where I learned how to prepare cassoulet," said Nick.

Emma laughed. "That's right. They're famous for that dish, aren't they?"

"Yep. So, when do you think you'll make it here? I just finished up my press conference."

"The GPS is saying about an hour, but I'm getting hungry. Maybe, I'll stop in Castelnaudary and get a bite to eat."

"Perfect. I'll go for an easy spin with the boys for a couple of hours, then meet you at the hotel. The parking lot is a zoo. You may have trouble getting in. Just tell the security guard that you're my fiancée. I'll let him know you're on your way. You can wait in the lobby. And we have a room to ourselves tonight. No roommate. Tom's treat for me being in yellow all week." Emma's face turned red, not that Nick could see her. She'd been dreaming about touching and smelling her man for the past week. She could hardly contain her excitement, trying to keep her voice calm so Nick wouldn't get too excited. She knew he had to stay focused, at least for now.

"Sounds good, baby. I can't wait to see you. I miss you so much. Love you."

Nick squirmed. God, he loved Emma. She was the epitome of perfection, his everything. But he hesitated, then said what he always said. "Right back at you, babe…you know it." Emma was used to it by now. It had perturbed her long ago, at the beginning of their relationship, but she accepted it now. She knew how much he loved her by his actions and understood why he struggled to say he loved her.

When Emma arrived in Castelnaudary, her priority was finding a place to eat. France was vastly different from Canada. Starbucks, Tim Hortons, and McDonald's were not easily located on every corner. Instead, she was surrounded by opaque boulangeries and small cafes that lined the main boulevard. She walked down a populated street, peering into the shop windows at the beautiful baked goods, stacked artisan sandwiches, and baskets full of baguettes. The choices were overwhelming, and everything looked delicious. She hesitated to commit. She neared the end of the street and, as she approached the corner, she found a quaint cafe. A single white table and chair were placed in front of the shop along the walkway. There was no rhyme or reason for the staged eating area, but Emma chose to make this her stop. The sandwiches looked stunning, and the Pomme de Terre delectable. She ordered a croque monsieur with frites and picked up a coca cola. She skipped dessert for now. She took a seat on the white chair and watched people pass. She was in France for herself, as much as she was here for Nick, but she knew the longer she stayed put, the more time she would be away from Nick. She soaked in as much as she could and then headed back out onto the road.

When Emma arrived in Carcassonne, the hotels were packed with team personnel, media staff members, race organizers, and fans from all over the world. Emma pulled into Nick's hotel, La Rapiere. The parking lot was littered with team buses and mechanics scrubbing down the riders' prized possessions. Every part of their bike and the spare bike had to be in perfect working order. The lot was packed with wandering people staring at buses, doing their best to try and chat with anyone associated with a professional cycling team. Emma parked and moved towards the door. As she entered the lobby, she was stopped by a man dressed in official Tour attire.

"Mademoiselle, arrête ici. Avez-vous vos informations d'identification."

"Non. Nick Carney est mon fiancé. Je m'appelle Emma Blake."

The official looked at her with a frown, shaking his head from left to right. He gestured with his hand to have a seat in the lobby. Emma sighed in exasperation, turning on her heel and surveying the packed foyer. She was eventually able to find a quiet corner; a comfortable couch to rest her tired legs. A man in a bespoke suit strode over to Emma.

"Madame. How are you this afternoon? Are you Emma Blake? Monsieur Carney's Fiancée? May I have some identification please?" The man spoke with a thick French accent.

Emma was slightly taken aback by the request. It seemed odd. She didn't know who this man was. He looked like the staff, but she couldn't be sure.

"May I ask who you are?" She knew you could never be too careful.

The man looked down at his jacket, and a bemused smile appeared on his lips when he realized his name tag was missing. "I'm sorry Madame. I am the manager of the hotel. Nick asked me to let you into his room to wait for him. I must request identification from you, please."

Emma smiled back, more at ease, producing her license from her wallet, careful not to look at the picture herself. Why did it have to be so bad? Her hair was short, her cheeks chubbier, and her expression all business. She looked thirty instead of twenty-three even though the picture had only been taken two years ago. To Emma, it was hideous. The gentleman made a quick look and smiled. He wasn't as concerned as Emma.

"This way, Madame Blake. Follow me."

He escorted her to Nick's room and let her in to wait. A quick glance around the room was all she needed to see the whole thing; it was tinier than she expected for the rider in yellow. It had a queen-size bed, with only about two feet around it on each side, and a small table in the corner. The bathroom had just enough space for a toilet and a stand-up shower for one. Too tired to be more concerned, she flopped on the bed, resting her head on a pillow. She wanted to take a shower, but her eyes were heavy and dropped instantly. In a few minutes, she would be fast asleep.

Thirty minutes later, the door swung open and Nick entered, seeing Emma laying on his bed. The hotel manager had chased him down the corridor to notify him of Emma's arrival. The moment he was finished with his ride, he dropped his bike off to the mechanics, unhitched his boa straps to remove his shoes, and began racing to his room. He was trying to remain calm, but he was eager to see his blonde-haired beauty. He knew her green eyes would sparkle when they finally saw each other face to face after being apart for so long.

Nick crossed the small room quickly and sat where she was resting. He gently caressed her head with his hand, moving strands of her golden hair away from her face. Her pouty lips seemed to beckon his, and he didn't resist. Much like a fairytale, Nick tried to wake his sleeping princess with a kiss. Their mouths united, and Nick could feel a quick transfer of heat. His skin and bones tingled and radiated with an energy that was absorbed by every cell of his body. Emma didn't wake up. She didn't even move. Nick could only laugh, happy this wasn't a fairytale and his kiss the cure to a curse. He stood up, taking off his cycling clothes and squeezing into the shower. He didn't want to purposely wake her, but he secretly hoped the sound of running water would bring her to life.

WhenNick finished cleansing he peeked his head out of the bathroom door. Emma still appeared lifeless. Her body hadn't moved one bit, and she was making deep muffled sounds through her mouth. He wrapped a towel around his waist and snuggled into the bed behind her, making sure to spoon her perfectly. He ran the back of his hand down her arm and waist, and then slowly turned it so his palm could gently grasp her deliciously toned ass. She was wearing a thin pair of low cut booty shorts, the type Nick adored. They showcased her long, athletically sculpted legs.

He couldn't help but admire the greatest gift in the world. At times like this, he still couldn't believe she'd chose him. A fucked up, mouthy kid, who rode a bike for a living. He began to kiss her neck and nibble her ear. His excitement, among other things, grew and parts of him throbbed against her bottom. He gently kissed her.

"Mmmmm. Is that you, baby?" asked a sleepy Emma.

"Yeah, It's me. God, I missed you. I want you so bad."

Emma slowly turned her body towards him, playfully kissing him across his jawline. She looked into his eyes and giggled, "You want me?"

He kissed her some more. "I want all of you. You're my everything."

Emma tensed her shoulders and moaned. Her body was stricken with enormous amounts of searing heat. She wanted him as much as he wanted her. It had been over seven weeks since they'd last made love. "Take me, my Yellow Jersey Champion."

Nick's kisses came to a halt. "Seriously, Emma?"

She laughed. It was awkward, and she intended it to be. "Won't sex mess things up for you?"

"That's a myth. It's been proven."

"Are you sure? You're doing amazing. What if we screw..." She stopped mid-sentence, giggling again. "...you know what I mean."

"Yes. I do. We want to screw. Let's get to it." He felt the mood fading. He kissed her neck once more, trying to get her back into the right frame of mind. He knew what she liked, and with a few well-placed kisses, she wouldn't be able to control herself. She rolled on top of him and pushed him back hard, ripping the towel around his waist off, and pulling her shorts away. She straddled him with firm pressure. He squirmed, but only for a moment, yanking her bright pink shirt off. He fumbled with her white lacey bra strap, wrestling to get it off. She reached behind her back with her arms, and gently teased him. "Let me help you, amateur." The snap was immediately released, and he peeled it off, cupping her firm breast with his tender hands. There'd be no foreplay today. She extended her hand down below his waist, grabbed him and pushed him deep within her.

Twenty minutes later, they lay on the bed, half asleep stroking one another's naked bodies. For Nick, it felt as if no one in the world existed. It was just him and Emma. No Tour, no rivalry between teammates, no reporters shoving cameras and microphones in anyone's face. It was only the two of them. And for Nick, this felt perfect. Nothing could penetrate this bubble. Suddenly, there was a knock on the door. "Nick, it's Tom. You're next for a massage. Melanie is waiting for you. Let's go." Bubble burst.

Nick scrambled out of bed. "Shit. I'll be right there. Thanks, Tom."

He looked at Emma as she lay calmly on the bed, "You going to be okay for about an hour?"

Emma yawned, stretching cat-like. "Yeah. I'll go get my luggage. I've got a special bag for you."

"Okay, awesome." Nick grabbed his official team sweat suit and left the room. He had to go quickly, or he'd be tempted to get back into bed with her. He walked down the corridor and entered the masseuse's room. His legs were achy to the touch, twitching and moaning internally. He was looking forward to Melanie's strong hands stroking and kneading his muscles. His legs were his professional instruments. They needed to be handled with care, rubbed down by expert hands that could unlock knotted bundles of tissue, moving unwanted toxins towards the liver.

Emma laid in the bed for a few minutes after Nick left, before going out to the car. She grabbed her pink suitcase and headed back to the room. There were no interruptions this time. Once in the room, she unpacked a few plastic bags containing personal items for Nick. He had requested a jar of peanut butter. France is a country filled with delectable condiments in abundance, but the creamy spread wasn't one of them. Nick wasn't fond of Nutella and had reached his limit with butter and jam. She placed the jar on his pillow. It would be the first item he saw when he entered the room. She expected he'd do a happy dance, grab the Kraft-labeled-jar and give the big yellow bears a kiss.

When his massage was done Nick headed back to Emma. His mind was relaxed, and his legs were bouncy. Every step felt effortless like he had springs for legs. He pushed open his door, ready to see Emma again. She did not disappoint. He saw her long bare legs, clad only in her underwear and one of his old sweatshirts. He was about to jump on the bed to join her when he saw the peanut butter. "Get the fuck out. Yes, Yes, YES!!!"

He ran over to the jar, opened the lid, and stuck a finger in, scooping up a whopping amount. From finger to mouth, he sucked the substance for a good long time, eyes closed, savoring the moment. Emma regarded Nick apprehensively. "That's disgusting."

"Is it? God, I love this stuff."

She ruffled through the bag beside her. "There's more, Nick."

"More peanut butter?"

"No," she chuckled at his hopefulness though. "More things from home. Your mom thought you may want some of these items."

"More, more, more! Like what?" He sounded like a child on Christmas morning.

"Take a look."

Nick rummaged through the bag. There was a blanket—his lucky blanky he'd owned since he was sixteen. The fabric was coarse, with the World Championship rainbow stripe graphic proudly displayed across the center. He'd brought it with him to Italy and slept with it the night before winning the Junior Worlds. "I'll definitely need this. I'm glad Mom thought about it."

He reached for more. There were articles from his brother and sister, his neighbors, and his fellow local cycling buddies. Congratulatory cards, homemade goodies, and some small hometown wearable tokens.

"Everyone wants you to have a piece of home and make Ottawa proud."

Nick began reading the cards. He was smiling for a moment, but the grin became a pout. A tear dropped from his right eye, another formed in his left. His cheeks were quivering, and his hands became unsteady, shaking the cards. "Nothing from Frank?"

"Baby…"

He threw the cards onto the bed and raised his voice, "Anything from my dad, Emma?"

Her eyes dropped to her feet. She could no longer lay relaxed on the bed. She pulled herself upright and grabbed Nick by the shoulders. He appeared to be in a trance; streams of tears ran down his cheeks. "Nick look at me. He's a bastard. He does this on purpose to hurt you."

Nick couldn't control himself. He moved to get away from her grip. He reached for his blanky and contorted his body into the fetal position. In these moments, Emma had learned she needed to remain calm. She cuddled next to him and whispered repeatedly, "I'm here for you baby. I love you so much. I'm here for you baby. I love you so much…"

CHAPTER 15

Stage 9

The End before the Beginning

The motorcycle driver closed in so the cameraman on the back of the bike could get a better look at Nick. He steadied himself so his lens could capture Nick's facial expression—empty and lifeless. He was gulping for air, swaying back and forth. His jersey was stained white with salt, and there was dried vomit around his mouth. The first mountain stage of the Tour was coming to an end. Nick only wanted to finish. The chants from the obsessive fans, contained behind steel barriers, were pushing him upwards. Their energy helped to conceal the fatigue Nick was experiencing. Soon he would finish cresting the summit of Ax 3 Domaines, and the pain would cease. He thought he'd done enough for the day, but he wasn't sure. His eyes were blinded by the sun. He was dizzy, and he couldn't make out the clock above the line marking the end of the race. He'd removed his earpiece long ago, severing communication with Tom when the pain had become too consuming.

Journalists awaited his arrival, eager for his comments. They needed soundbites, explanations about what had happened today. They wanted his thoughts while they were fresh and raw, riddled with fatigue, no retrospection to deaden the story. A story that transpired from a moment divine in nature. It had captured the attention of the entire press, and Robert Saunders wanted to be the first to reach the young rider. As Nick made his way to the finish line, Robert accelerated ahead, his energy jolting his bones. He never could have predicted what happened today.

Before the end, there's always a beginning. Stage nine, came the day after the rest day and was the first day in the mountains. It can be a stressful day as rider's transition from flat stages, powered by big gears and absolute power, to the mountain stages, where brute force and ballerina grace was required.

The stage had begun in Limoux, home to stage eight's individual time trial. It had cost the tiny village millions of euros to host this section of the race. Cycling insiders had wondered if Limoux would be able to recoup their considerable investment. Couiza, the small village only minutes away boasted Renne-Le-Chateau; the potential burying ground of the holy grail—Jesus Christ's bones. The tiny French town was made famous in the early 2000s in Dan Brown's wildly successfully novel, The Davinci Code. Hundreds of thousands of tourists had come to the Castle to experience the magical words of Brown come to life. Now, Limoux hoped the Tour would create an enchanting experience that would lure the world to its charming doorstep.

Even before the stage, as people arrived in Limoux in hopes of grabbing autographs and selfies, the drama had been fierce. The morning papers had been covered with headlines screaming of an emerging battle boiling between Bomber and Carney; a situation they said threatened Team Apex's chance of overall victory. If either man chose to put their individual needs before the team's, there would be consequences. Paul Davies from The Guardian had written a piece describing Nick as a young rider with no boundaries, a kid who'd found himself in a place he shouldn't be in. He went on to say that Nick's new-found success would see him rise to the challenge; that Nick's demeanor exuded ambition, and his talent had no limits. Davies was bold enough to write that both Ellington and Bomber, in the context of history, would be nothing more than stepping stones, paving the way to an era that would be dominated by Nick Carney.

His article was not an isolated blurb without context. Hundreds of journalists composed remarkable news stories about Carney's physical dominance, his age, and whether it had pushed Bomber to consider retirement. The rumors and speculation wouldn't end. TV commentators were rife with conjecture; compiled facts from multiple authorities stating that Team Apex would implode. There were theories that Carney would be leaving the team next year to ride with Ellington, a known friend, and a potential ally in this year's Tour if Bomber didn't stick to the script. And, clinging to the script meant riding in support of the yellow jersey.

Eurosports sought out Robert Saunders for his sensationalized commentary, which was bordering on the absurd. He was insisting that Jack's retirement announcement was a team ploy, meant to distract the Press from the internal battle. He believed Team Apex was collapsing under the weight and force of his most recent article:

In the midst of a renowned French spectacle, a race as revered and familiar as a relative coming home for the holidays, filled with the beauty of what the human body can do when pushed to its limits, a hatchet is being driven into the back of Bomber by the hands of Carney in his rush to glory. It's a battle of North America, Canada vs. The USA, taking place on European soil, in a European dominated sport.

Unlike other journalists covering the race, Saunders didn't have a place for Ellington, Morkov, or Alvarez. He'd sensationalized his story, making it over the top to gain the attention of the people in the United States. Saunders was a pro at writing engaging tales detailing the clashes between mortals of great strength, and now he would have the chance to tell the World on television.

Eurosports anchors Carl Thompson and Allen Smith were preparing for stage nine. Saunders was sitting beside them, while the make-up artist finishing layering a small amount of foundation and blush. Robert's facial features were harsh and weathered and needed a touch-up. The quality of television today with their 4K HD properties showed everything. Wrinkles, sunspots, something awkwardly stuck in your teeth, like that small grainy poppy seed from the bread you had at breakfast, all jumped out and attacked the viewer.

Make-up was also needed to create an important and newsworthy authority; an expert on a subject matter central to the theme of the race. A persona who could articulate an event, connecting the viewers with the Network.

Robert was sitting in his chair ready for the spotlight. The cameraman stood directly in front of the trio counting down 5,4, 3, 2...1...Thompson didn't waste any time. He welcomed the audience to stage nine and began to rattle off the pivotal points in the race for that day. A red line traced the route over a green mountainous screen, so viewers had a visual cue to associate with Thompson's words. He talked about the crucial moments that would be critical for every rider, making sure to point out the mountains that would play a pivotal role in the overall contender's quest for victory. The audience needed to be informed of when the race would be explosive, the difficulty of the climbs, and when the attacks could possibly come. He turned towards Allan Smith and Saunders. "The Tour continues today, moving out of Limoux and heading toward the Pyrenees. We have Carney in yellow, with his teammate and designated leader, Bomber, trailing by a minute and a half. This is the first mountain stage of the Tour, coming directly after the rest day. We all know some rider's bodies don't respond well to this sudden change. The final is brutal with the uncategorized climbs Port de Pailhères and Ax 3 Domaines. What do you think we can expect?"

Smith piped up first, "Yes, it's a tricky stage. Incredibly difficult terrain to conquer. If one of the favorites isn't one hundred percent ready to tackle these two mountains they're going to suffer relentlessly. I think we'll see multiple attacks by many of the overall contenders. The race is still very much open."

Saunders was next to chime in, putting his unique spin on the matter. He wanted the viewers to connect to his story. "I think the day will be tough for many, but the drama is going to be between Bomber and Carney. I can't wait to see what happens on the slopes of Pailhères or Ax 3."

Carl interrupted, "Robert, you've been writing for days about Team Apex, and the tension between these two riders. You're an American, but you seem to be rooting for Nick Carney. Does this have anything to do with last year?"

Saunders sideswiped Carl's question. He was in no mood to entertain the events that transpired during last year's Tour. "I love Bomber. We all do. He's an amazing athlete. What we have here, at this year's Tour, is what this sport is all about, a real challenge. I don't believe Bomber had to deal with this type of pressure in his last two Tour de France victories. Carney is a real threat. He beat Bomber in the race of truth, Bomber's strongest discipline. And we all know Carney can climb. He's tall, lean and hungry."

The three men bantered for the next five minutes before a commercial break for BMWs halted their flow. It was the car made for the driving enthusiast, the ultimate driving machine. And the Tour, this spirited spectacle of competition filled with men who fine-tuned the engine they're born with, pushing the boundaries of their capabilities, was the perfect host for BMW to pay millions for advertisement time.

The remaining commercials ended, and the audience was returned to the broadcast studio where the three men sat in comfortable chairs behind their professional anchor news desk. The race was about to depart Limoux. The anchors were enthusiastic and thrilled to get the action started. The start would be rapid as the breakaway formed along the roads to Couiza and Quillan.

Once established, there would be a lull. While the race was never tranquil for the riders, this was the part that could leave the audience less than inspired. Thompson, Smith, and Saunders would create an extensive narrative, using background information about the riders and their palmarès, historical facts about the area, the terrain, and the castles. Every ruin, every tree-lined road, every sheep, mountain goat, and exotic bird would be discussed. It added richness and color very few sports boasts. This would be the exposition leading to the rising action, at which point the back stories would seize. The journalists would focus entirely on the race. The story would build towards the climax…

A few more labored pedal strokes and Nick crossed the finish line. He stepped off his bike, collapsing under a cloud of fatigue, the weight of the yellow jersey forcing him to the ground. Journalists hovered around him scrambling for pictures, creating a scene that looked similar to a gang of bullies hovering over a victim who was lying helplessly on the ground. One of his soigneur, Jonathon, shoved the maddening swarm of men, creating some breathing room for Nick. Willie kneeled to the ground and lifted Nicks head up, forcing him to sip water.

Nick looked at Willie and smiled, unable to describe what he was feeling. He couldn't speak and didn't want to. He wanted to relish the moment. It wasn't long before he began coughing. He titled his head and vomited. Saunders looked at Carney with sheer admiration, and when he was no longer puking held out his mic, "Can you describe what happened today out on the road? What was going through your mind?"

Nick wiped his mouth with his hand. "Well, you and the entire world saw what happened. I think you have a good idea."

On his small screen, in the press room perched on the summit of Ax 3 Domaines, Saunders had indeed witnessed the event, reporting his thoughts and feelings towards what had emerged. He'd only had a few minutes to discuss the race finale with Carl and Allen, before rushing down to Nick. He craved the thoughts of the wounded champion laying beneath his feet. His role for Eurosports now was to capture Nick's emotion and insight, so that he could confirm the created story he and his co-anchors had concocted earlier in the stage.

The Eurosport journalist's narrative had begun to take shape shortly after the tranquil beginning, they were talking about the emerging rivalry between Bomber and Carney, and where they expected the action to take place. Allen and Carl, both Brits, were hoping Team Apex would implode and open the door for Ellington.

Meanwhile, their special guest, Robert Saunders did an excellent job of expanding on his theory that Bomber's retirement announcement was nothing more than a hoax; a disguise to re-direct the press, regain stability within the team, and potentially throw off their rivals.

Then it happened!

They watched as Bomber pulled over and got off his bike. Saunders was astonished. His eyes widened, his jaw slackened and dropped towards the ground. He threw his hands up in the air. "Is this actually happening?" he shouted.

CHAPTER 16

Stage 9

The Carney Family is Watching

Frank Carney was busy in his home office, fumbling through stacks of papers scattered on his desk, racking his brain for the right words. He whipped out his highlighter, creating a yellow glow around dark lettered sentences, praying they had a purpose. It all looked foreign to him; a different language. He comprehended the words themselves, but the meaning of them? Not so much. He was formulating a speech on Cloud-Based-Systems. He had to present at a conference being held in San Francisco later in the month. He'd be treated like a rock star because he was a tech legend, an entrepreneur who'd made it big. Yet he knew nothing about this innovative technology that had emerged a few years back.

He rubbed his eyes, scratching his head before deciding it was time for a break. He was hungry and wanted a delicious snack to get refocused. As he headed downstairs to the kitchen, he could hear a commotion. Catherine, his two eldest children, and their family friends were in the living room screaming at the TV. He wished he could sneak by, go directly to the kitchen, prepare some baguette with brie, and pour himself a scotch in his personalized etched Glencairn glass. He wanted something to soothe his nerves and numb his brain; a mid-morning drink to warm his body and bring him to life.

Frank slipped by the family room, entered the kitchen and went straight to his scotch cabinet—a cabinet he had explicitly made by a local Quebec company that harvested the wood from hundred-year-old reclaimed trees from the Ottawa River. The quality of lumber was dense and contained an exotic pattern that enlivened the piece of work it was transformed into. A work of art meant to enrich the soul of its owner and make a man like Frank Carney feel smug. He reached for a bottle of 16-year-old Lagavulin, wanting some peat, then redirected his hand to the Ardbeg Corryvreckan wanting something more complex. He opened the bottle and brought it close to his nose, taking a whiff of its excellent profile. His taste buds exploded like the fourth of July in anticipation of the complex richness of this malt. Without even a single drop, he could taste the vibrant meld of peat, smoke, and sweetness.

He recorked the bottle and returned it to its dedicated resting place. With the sun barely up, his desire was for something sweeter. He reached for a bottle of 30-year-old Isle of Jura, a limited edition scotch consisting of a unique profile highlighted with hints of toffee and orange peel. Like the intriguing whiskey itself—hard to find— Frank was hoping his family wouldn't spot him in the kitchen. He had no desire to watch his son on television— being glorified for riding his bike around France.

He opted for eight ounces instead of four and poured the beautiful colored scotch into his personalized glass. After a few sips and a handful of crackers, he tip-toed out of the kitchen hoping to return to his study. An eruption of cheers from the living room caused him to tremble and wobble his glass. "Jesus Christ!" he shouted.

"Honey. Oh my god. Where have you been? You're missing this," Catherine said, turning her attention away from the TV for a moment.

"The only thing I'm missing is an ounce of Scotch. My finest whiskey is all over the floor."

"Oh, the Jura. Don't worry about it, Frank. I'll take care of it. Get over here. The race is getting good."

"Yeah, Dad. This is amazing. Nick is riding well, but that fucking Bomber," said Laura, his only daughter, his eldest, and his baby girl. It didn't matter that she was thirty, married to a hot-shot lawyer, and had two kids of her own, she was Daddy's Girl and always would be. Sitting next to her was Alex, her younger brother—Nick's older. Alex was content with watching the race. The action was increasing in intensity, and his heart was beating rapidly. He wanted to take it all in. His dad's arrival and the emerging conversation was proving distracting.

At twenty-eight, Alex was close to Laura in age but closer to Nick in spirit. The two shared a passion—cycling. It was Alex who taught Nick how to ride his first bike, took him out for long rides exploring the neighborhood in his childhood, and even got him into racing. When Nick began showing talent, winning races at 8, Alex was by his side coaching his brother. Eventually, it became his full-time job, one he still did today. He was intent on watching his protégé succeed but wasn't happy with the current situation transpiring on the roads in France. He could see and feel Nick's demeanor changing. The camera was capturing one thing, the commentators, and the audience another, and Alex was interpreting something completely different.

Nick's face looked all but vacant, expressionless, dark sunglasses hiding his eyes. His upper body was like a statue, quiet and showing no sign of movement. His hips were steady and anchored to his seat, with only his legs moving. The commentators from Eurosports were insisting he looked calm, telling their viewers that

129

Team Apex had everything under control. Nick Carney was safe, well positioned and needn't worry. Alex knew better. He could see Nick's cheeks were sunken, not because he was skinny and they're naturally concaved, but because he was pulling them inwards in frustration, biting down on them with his teeth. If the situation with Bomber wasn't resolved shortly, Alex knew that blood would leak from the corners of Nick's mouth. *Come on brother...Keep it together...Nothing to worry about.*

"I can't believe Nick's team is doing this to him. It's unbelievable," shouted Laura.

"What's going on?" asked Frank. He didn't really care, but he could see his beautiful daughter's eyes light up.

"Bomber is having difficulty. He just pulled over," said Catherine. She smiled, he was finally showing interest, and she wanted to encourage it. "Honey, tell your dad. You're so good at describing these things," she nodded towards Laura.

"The announcers have no clue what's happening. Jack Bomber is off his bike. He may be retiring from the race or getting a simple bike change. All I know for sure is that Nick's team sent everyone back for Bomber. They left him isolated. He only has one teammate with him, Welte."

Frank shook his head in confusion. His son had been competing in this sport for over ten years, but Frank was ignorant of the unique intricacies of this sport. He was never involved in Nick's life. He couldn't be. He'd tried, but it proved too difficult. There was a time when Nick was young, his cute features reminiscent of those of Catherine, melting his heart. But there was also his tongue, so harsh and violent in his early years that it repulsed him. He never knew if he wanted to connect with his son, or just ignore him. Later in life, Frank would learn how to exploit his son's emotional weakness, crushing Nick's spirit, bringing happiness and order to Frank's world.

"Son of a bitch," yelled Alex.

Good grief. It's a bunch of guys riding their bikes in spandex. Men with shaved legs and arms, toiling around France pretending their life has meaning. He wanted to shout at Alex, *Hey, dumb ass, relax, this isn't the real world. It wasn't even entertaining.* But he knew better. Alex was bigger than him and protective of his younger brother's aspirations. God knew Frank couldn't beat the spirit out of that boy with his harsh words. Not the way he could with Nick. Alex wasn't only tall and muscular, but he never backed down from a war of words. It wouldn't end well. And they had guests, close friends of the family bent on watching Nick. Frank wouldn't have wanted them privy to the intimate family dynamics of the Carneys.

"It's a simple flat. A bike change. And you send the whole damn team back. Are you fucking for real?" Alex practically screamed.

"Watch your tongue young man. We have guests," said Catherine. She apologized to George and Renée, their neighbors and close friends for the last thirty years. They adored Nick and the Carney children. Renée was always there to help Catherine babysit when needed, pick the children up from school, or take one to the doctor's office when Catherine couldn't. She genuinely cared for the family and wanted nothing but the best. It helped that she and George didn't have kids of their own.

When Nick was born, they had decorated the Carney's lawn with plastic penguins, lions, and pandas. They used their spare key to leave flowers and baskets full of goodies for Frank and Catherine. In the earliest days of Nick's birth, they sensed marital strain between the Carney's and insisted on taking the eldest children to Disney for a week. They had convinced Catherine they couldn't go to Disney without them. It's would be all wrong to get autographs from Mickey, Donald, and Goofy without children by your side insisted Renée. She'd need Laura for Princess activities, and George needed Alex for Star Wars excursions. It just made sense. Even today with the children all grown up, both she and George spent countless evenings with

Catherine when Frank was away. They'd spent many evenings drinking wine and preparing food from recipes they found on Pinterest.

Alex got up from the couch and began pacing with his arms crossed, trying not to nervously bite his thumbnail. His thoughts were with Nick and the ensuing battle taking place on the roads in France. The race was approaching the menacing Col de Pailhères, the uncategorized climb. The yellow jersey needed his team. He should've been surrounded by an endless stream of Team Apex jerseys setting the pace and protecting him from the wind. Instead, Nick was battling for position as Alexie Morkov, and Team Aqua Talon pushed the pace, trying to take advantage of Bomber's mishap. Meanwhile, six Team Apex members were a minute behind in a sea of cars guiding Jack Bomber back into the race.

"Jesus. It's taking too long. You guy's should never have sent your whole team back there," Alex exclaimed.

"Relax honey. Everything is looking better. They're back in the convoy, and it won't be long now until they're by Nick's side," said Catherine.

"Are they really by his side?" asked Alex.

"Mom, this team is so messed up. This whole race they've looked like amateurs," said Laura.

"Look like amateurs? Try raced like amateurs," sneered Alex.

"Tammy from my work, her husband, is a big cycling fan, she thinks Team Apex is corrupt and out to get Nick. Have you had a chance to speak to him Catherine?" asked Renée.

"I've spoken to him every day. With Emma's arrival yesterday, he didn't have much time to talk. There's tension between him and Jack, but you know how sensitive Nick is. I'm sure it's not that bad."

"Mom, he's having a rough time with Jack and his Director Tom. Those two are thick as thieves. I told him last year when we were looking at teams to avoid Team Apex. He was convinced he'd learn so much from Bomber, but I knew. I knew, and I didn't convince him otherwise," said Alex, his pacing growing more erratic as guilt took over.

"Do you think he would have been better riding with Ellington?" asked Laura

"Absolutely. He and Ryan have spoken a few times during the race. He told Nick multiple times that Jack isn't very supportive. He wants him to break his contract at the end of the year and join him at Team Sprint. I've been in contact with Nick's agent, and it may be possible."

"Oh? How is Alberto?" asked Catherine.

"He's good, Mom. He knows Nick is getting a raw deal now. He thinks he's handling it like a champ, well, for the most part anyways. Alberto is one of a kind. He'll figure something out. He always does. That's what makes him such a great agent."

Alex, Laura, Catherine, and Renée ceased their conversation and turned their attention back towards the race. It had been five minutes, and the race situation was no better. The one-minute gap between Bomber and the hard-charging peloton remained—his teammates desperately chasing to close the gap. Alex returned to the couch and uncrossed his arms, his fingers made their way to his mouth, and he began chewing his nails.

Moments later, screams from the women erupted, piercing the eardrum of Frank who was still standing in the doorway. "Oh, My God...Nick is falling off the back of the race!" They watched as Nick's struggled to keep pace and began to move backward, behind the main peloton.

"Is he getting dropped?" asked Renée.

The TV announcers weren't offering a conclusive assessment of the current situation. The women were anxious. Laura had both of her hands on the top of her head, twirling her long blonde locks and tugging them lightly. Catherine was horrified, her eyes were as wide as the decorative dinner plates she kept on display in their dining room. Her mouth was stretched open, lips quivering.

"What the fuck is going on?" shouted Laura.

"This is a catastrophe," sobbed Catherine, as her eyes swelled, and the tears streamed down her cheeks

"Don't cry, Mom. We still don't know exactly what's going on," said Laura, letting go of her hair and trying to stay calm.

"I know. I can't help it, baby. This shouldn't be happening. Not like this."

Alex stood again, pacing back and forth, yelling at the TV. He was fuming. It didn't matter whether Nick had a mechanical issue or whether he was getting dropped, it was poor decision making on Tom's part. A leader left stranded, without his lieutenants. How could an established Director let this happen? "Whatever this is, it's going to end in a very dark place for Nick," stated Alex.

George moved away from the ruckus and whispered to Frank, "This is crazy. I can't imagine tackling the distance these guys are doing every day. The speed is outrageous, and those mountains frightening. Throw in all this adversity…I'm so impressed with Nick. I suppose it was just a matter of time before he cracked."

Frank remained quiet. He had tuned out the room long ago, staring blankly at the screen while admiring his Sonos wireless surround sound system, a home theatre system he'd proudly purchased at a local electronics store after haggling with the salesperson. He smiled for George, but his mind was thinking about that day he bought the speakers. A young sales associate had chosen an educational approach with Frank, providing him with multiple options. He was good-looking, young, outgoing, and flirtatious. He had Catherine giggling, hanging on his every word. He'd described the system as a life-altering experience. He was a true audiophile, and it irked Frank. He made the young man pay. Every attempt to explain the features were met with a condescending comment or an unfair comparison to a system not available in the store. He was working the young man over, breaking him down slowly. Eventually, he would go in for the kill, hammering the kid on price until the salesperson's patience broke. The manager was called in, and Frank scooped up the speakers for an unprecedented thirty percent discount. The reduced price was no doubt an exit cost, a please-get-out of our store expense.

Frank focused back on his scotch. It was working brilliantly, coursing through his veins. He was steady and resilient, coping well with, as he would describe them, nonsensical people. He needed to get back to work but realized this was a critical family moment. If he left now in front of his long-time neighbors, he'd look suspicious. His phone vibrated—a simple app alert, but Frank took advantage of the situation. "If you'll excuse me. I need to make an important call. I'll take it in my study."

He slowly returned to his office, thankful to be away from the Nick-worshipping he had to endure for the last fifteen minutes. He began working on his speech. The words flowed smoothly, pen to paper. Shortly after that, the first draft was completed. He stood in front of his full-length mirror practicing his speech, evaluating his body movements and how they connected to his words. He ensured his voice was crisp and powerful, accentuating prominent material. His goal would be to dazzle the audience, and he was confident it was a feat he'd be able to accomplish. After all, he was Frank Carney.

CHAPTER 17

Stage 9

Where is Nick Carney Going?

The wind was blowing, gusting and howling like a pack of wolves. It jolted the moving peloton from side to side as they approached the deep valley before the Col de Pailhères. Rock formations drooped from the sides of the mountains, hanging over the twisty narrow road. Tiny rocks had trickled gently down from all angles of the mountain cliffs, making their home on the pavement. The Aude River that travels along the route was filled with kayakers exploring the great outdoors. Most were wearing yellow and would wait patiently until they heard the roaring thunder of the race helicopter. At which point they would bring their kayaks together, wave their paddles frantically, and hope to get some time on television.

Nick was at the front, protected by Welte, trying to keep pace with the tempo being set by Team Aqua Talon. Nick rode up to Alexie

Morkov, their team leader, looking for answers. "Alexie, what are you guys doing? You're going to blow up the whole damn race."

Morkov mumbled in his thick Russian accent, "We need rid of Bomber...now."

Nick was pissed. Why was this about Bomber? "Alexie, forget him. He's getting back on. We have our whole team with him bringing him back. You're just going to make Ax 3 Domaines a shit show."

"Shit show!? We make shit hurt now. You not strong, you don't win. Simple."

Nick shook his head and retreated behind Welte, pinching his mic to talk to Tom. "Alexie isn't backing down. His team is going full tilt. Why the fuck did we send everyone back for Bomber? What about me?"

Tom wanted to sympathize with Nick, but he was the Director, and he needed to remain in control of his riders. His tactics for the day had been clearly laid out before the stage. During the team meeting, Tom left nothing open to interpretation. Team Apex would ride the rest of the Tour with two co-leaders. If anything were to happen to either Carney or Bomber the team had strict orders to drop back and assist. Half the team would go back to the fallen leader, the other half would remain by the side of the other. When Bomber flatted, there was confusion. Tom called on three riders to fall back, but three riders had already made the decision to stop and assist Bomber.

He wasn't happy seeing his whole team out of position, working frantically to get Bomber back before the first big mountain. He was positive, based on their facial expressions, that his riders were in the red; at their physiological limit, burying themselves for Bomber. They were at their breaking point and were most likely seeing stars. Before the stage, there were journalists calling Tom one of the greatest Directors of all time. He had been described as a moderator of a team containing two egos—one a proven winner, the other an unknown entity. He was a man who had guided a rookie to yellow, a man who could possibly escort this rookie to a place in history as the youngest winner of the Tour de France in the modern era. Now he looked like a fool. He knew his blunder more than likely had the Press having a field day at his expense. He wondered what they could be thinking: *The young man under his tutelage, the current leader of the race, left on his own to battle the one-hundred-and-eighty-man strong peloton. Abandoned for their rider sitting in second place. How competent is Tom Christenson really? Does winning at the professional level no longer matter?*

Tom began to ponder his actions, his decisions and the ramifications of his error. *How could I make such a mistake?* His team was going to work as hard as they could for as long as they could, but he knew Morkov would not relent. *Shit, when the team makes it back, they'll be empty and exhausted. Even if Bomber is fresh, he won't help Nick. What if Nick can't pull through in the mountains? He's ridden well, and he's been successful in the time trials, but these are the mountains. In the end, we're only going to have Welte to assist in setting the pace for our leaders.*

He wanted to punch the glove compartment of the slowly moving team AMG driven by Willie. It was crawling behind the peloton, while the noise of the motor rumbled, shaking his body. *This is fucked up, and I'll take responsibility when the time comes, but for now, I have to keep it together for the team.* He gently tapped his mic, "Stay calm, Nick. The boys are working their way back. Everything will be fine. They're almost there."

"Almost? Almost as in where? Are they in the caravan?"

"Yes, Nick. Stay calm."

"Shit…Shit…SHIT," shouted Nick.

"I said to stay calm. Relax. They'll be there in thirty seconds."

"My chain just snapped. Tom, my fucking chain just snapped. I'm going backward and fast. I'm going to need my spare bike."

Tom looked at Willie. "Mother Fucker. When it rains, it pours. Okay, get me in position Willie. I need to grab his bike and get him back quickly. We can't screw this up."

Tom tapped his mic, "Okay guys, Nick is in trouble now. We need to do a bike change. Welte, drop back to help. Brad and Antoine, when you work your way up here, leave Bomber and the rest of the riders to assist Nick. Everyone got that?"

Tom repeated the instructions one more time. There was silence. He wasn't worried, he knew the riders were at their limits and couldn't reply.

Willie approached the back of the speeding peloton. A yellow-clad figure was dropping like a stone. He pulled the car to the side and slammed the breaks. Tom was out in a flash with Nick's spare bike.

"Let's go Tom…let's go…give me my bike," panted Nick.

"Don't panic. Brad and Antoine will be here in ten seconds. I need you to slow it down and wait for them."

Nick snapped, "Fuck that shit, Tom. I don't have time."

He removed his water bottles and GPS from his broken bike and attached them to the new bike. He clipped in, and Tom began pushing him, running to bring him back to speed.

Welte was the first to make contact with Nick. He ensured Nick was directly behind him, sheltered from the wind before he started setting the tempo.

"Welte, are they slowing down at all?" Nick asked.

"Nope. Morkov won't stop. He's on a mission today."

"I'm the fucking yellow jersey for Christ sake. Where's the etiquette?"

Welte didn't answer. He couldn't find the words to answer Nick only wanted to get on with his job. He was experienced enough to know that discussing etiquette at this point wouldn't benefit their cause.

Team cars in the convoy began honking, and Nick could hear screaming. He turned to the left and could see Team Apex lined across the road.

"Let's go, boys. Jump on," shouted Bomber.

Welte and Nick moved over, tucking in neatly behind the seven-man express train. Brad was at the front hammering hard. It wouldn't be long until they reached the back of the peloton and began moving towards the front. Nick was at ease. The pace in the pack had come down. Word of Bomber's imminent arrival had been relayed back to Morkov, and he called his boys off.

Welte was next to take the lead. He guided his men through the splintering peloton and reached the front with Nick and Bomber tucked behind him in his draft. Shortly, the road would go vertical. The early slopes of Pailhères would be brutal, averaging 9% for the first few kilometers. Bomber turned to Nick, "How are you feeling?"

"I'm pissed Jack. Fucking pissed."

"Great. That's not what I asked. How are you feeling physically? I'm going to need you in the early part of this climb. It's a real bitch. Morkov and Ellington are going to have their domestiques hitting it hard. We aren't going to have many opportunities. Most of our guys are fucked from the chase. I'm only going to have you."

If Nick felt pissed moments ago, he was now fuming; enraged beyond words. He didn't respond to Bomber. He couldn't. Not because he was out of breath, but because if he tried to speak, he was afraid he'd say something that would lead to him jumping off his bike and tackling that mother fucker, Bomber, right off his bike.

The grade began to alter its shape, shooting straight up into the sky. Riders for Team Aqua Talon and Team QCC-Quadron accelerated to the front. Nolan Thomas, Ellington's super domestique, guided his leader to the side of Morkov. Bomber was the tenth wheel, just behind the two of them. Nick was hidden, tucked within the confines of the thinning peloton. The quick turn onto the steeper slopes caught him off guard and pushed him further back. He was just out of reach of the top twenty riders. This wasn't ideal positioning, and he knew it. His Spanish teammates, the climbers, were alongside him, swaying their bikes back and forth, trying to gain momentum to reach Bomber. He latched onto their wheels. Miguel Rosas moved to the outside to avoid a rider going backyards. He stood, and stomped the pedals of his bike. The effort was dramatic, but it wasn't effective. He didn't go anywhere and was no help to Nick, who was gasping.

Nick was no longer working comfortably hard. He was beyond his physiological threshold. The lactic acid, the hydrogen ions, were infusing his blood, outstripping the ability of his oxygen-rich blood's ability to clear it. He wasn't alone. The faces of the men around him were also twisted in agony. Each in their own personal battle, trying to survive the onslaught being inflicted by Team Aqua Talon.

The only sound was that of moving bicycles and men breathing hard. Nick jumped up just behind Bomber. His peripheral vision was abandoned, and he narrowly fixated on the backs of the men in front of him. An odd but familiar sensation overtook him. The feeling reminded him of the time his father locked him in a dark closet while his mother was away. He had stepped out of bounds, and Frank punished him. Only a small amount of light crept in beneath the edges of the closet doors, and Nick clung to them for hours; the rays of light offering the young boy hope. Without them, he would have been swallowed by an inner beast of his making—his feelings and imagination running wild. Now he was in a similar position. He didn't want to be swallowed. Nope, he tried to move toward the light beyond the riders. If he could.

The sweat was streaming down Nick's forehead, dripping towards the hot asphalt and painting his yellow jersey with a salty white residue. He waited for a moment of reprieve in speed to gather himself. He prayed it would come shortly. He needed a mere thirty seconds of tranquility to gather his breath, find his legs, reposition himself, and calm his thoughts. During these intense moments of pain, the concept of time disappeared, and a battle ensued between the physical and mental spheres. Nick's one-dimensional realm was relegated to primitive attributes needed for survival. He believed that if this rapid pace continued he'd be dropped. Flashes of failure crossed his mind. That closet. That God damn closet. Hours in the dark, in silence, confined to a small, claustrophobic space. Tears had streamed down his face. His body had trembled as he fought to understand his father's actions. His Dad…Fucking Frank Carney.

Nick thought of Emma, and it restored his peripheral vision; she became the light squeezing out the darkness. The full capacity of his cognitive abilities reemerged, and he became aware of the riders around him. He became attuned to his breathing. He slowed it down to a controlled, and rhythmic action. His legs remembered they were connected to pedals and he effortlessly churned out efficient circles of power. The pace steadied and became more manageable. He looked around, and the peloton was down to fifty strong riders remaining.

Nick headed to the side of Bomber, to evaluate his condition. He studied Bomber's face for any sign of discomfort, but there was none. His teammate looked robust, calm and relaxed. He continued his ascent towards Ellington and Morkov; both were breathing hard but appeared content with the effort. Nick wanted to attack, but he knew it was far too early. He had to fight the urge to accelerate and use up valuable energy. There was no point striking your opponent when they'd yet to reach their breaking point. He steadied his emotions and contained his desire to inflict pain. Instead, he'd rely on the lesser riders, on Ellington and Morkov's team, to ride tempo; slowly draining the best rider's precious energy they'd require as they approached the end of the stage.

Nick fell back into the line of strung-out riders, just behind Bomber, and reached for a gel from his pocket. During this lull, he needed to refuel, to ensure his body's cells were topped up with the necessary sugar for the next high-intensity battle. After sucking the gooey mess from the tiny plastic packet, Nick heard a familiar voice coming from behind. "Nick, I'm right here. I'm right behind you."

The lull in pace allowed Welte to move forward. Initially dropped on the lower slopes of Pailhères, he was able to regain contact with the front group once the pace slowed. "I've got your back, Nick. Whatever you need, I'm here."

Nick nodded in appreciation, a calmness swept over him. He wasn't alone. Bomber may ride for the same team, but he wasn't here for Nick. Miguel was a few riders ahead, monitoring the men setting the pace. Nick knew Miguel was there for show, doing only what he could. He'd watched Miguel stomp on his pedals early during that last critical moment and had watched him go nowhere. He knew the Spaniard was operating on fumes.

Nonetheless, Team Apex couldn't appear weak to the other teams. They needed Miguel to ride at the front. They needed him at the head of the peloton, to make the other teams believe they had control of the race.

The middle of Col de Pailhères was rather flat, a tunnel of forested trees leading the riders out across an open barren patch of land. The wind had been predicted to be strong. Nick's earpiece began to vibrate and crackle. "Okay boys, this is it. You need to be at the front and to the left. The wind will be coming from the right. We're down to five in the main group, so we don't have a lot of options. Let the other teams set the pace and control the speed. It's out of our hands at this point. Position yourself well and expect the riders to drill it over this stretch of road before it kicks up," coached Tom.

Nick wondered who the fifth teammate was. He was hoping it was Brad or Antoine. Either one of them would ride their heart out for him when required, plus both were having strong Tours for being somewhat inexperienced. He was also confident that Welte would be there for him. Over the past week, his roommate had proven to have his back at every turn. They'd become close even though the conversation had been scarce. Welte's actions during the race and after were those of a mentor. He'd been like a father, or in Nick's case, like his older brother. At every turn, he was there watching Nick, guiding him, making suggestions on positioning, when to eat and when to drink.

The teammates that concerned him were Miguel Rosas and Joaquin Escartin. They were friendly and would help Nick if ordered to by Tom, but they wouldn't give that extra ounce of energy that could make a difference. They were loyal to Bomber, dedicated to the man who'd led their team to victory in the previous two Tours. Each Tour they'd been by his side sheltering and guiding their champion to the front of critical splits, positioning him for victory. And they'd been compensated handsomely for doing so. Bomber had leverage. The kind Nick didn't.

There was no time to think. Team Aqua Talon swarmed the front with four riders spreading themselves out across the narrow road. The remaining peloton became blocked with riders unable to move from their existing position. They were now at the mercy of Team Aqua Talon's tactics until the road widened. The canopy of trees blocked the sunlight, making navigating the tiny highway difficult. Riders bumped into one another as they jostled for position. The effort required massive concentration, but Nick felt comfortable. He was slightly frustrated by riders who were at their limit. Examining their pedal stroke revealed the strain they were enduring. Gaps began to open, but the narrowness of the road meant Nick couldn't go around them, and to try, would leave him exposed and exhausted. It was impossible.

Three riders from Ellington's team, positioned just in front of Nick, began struggling with the pace, and a gap of three to four meters opened. Nick was more concerned than ever. The difference would necessitate a massive surge of power once the road opened, an effort he would have instead saved for Ax 3 Domaines. He looked around for Welte, but couldn't see him. Bomber and Miguel were just beyond the split. The gap was widening. He pinched his mic, "Welte, where are you?" There was silence. Nothing.

"Welte...Didier...where are you? I need you."

"Nick, it's Tom. What's wrong? Do you have a mechanical?"

"No. A gap is opening up, and I'm on the wrong side of it. I need Welte. Where is he?"

"We have no visibility, Nick. He hasn't fallen back though. He's still with you."

Nick stopped playing with his mic and noticed the road opening up. As he left the shelter of the trees, he could feel the heat from the sun returning. He stood on his bike, preparing to sprint toward the lead men on the road; now three to five seconds in front of him.

"Sit down you fool!" shouted Welte. He was behind him, steadily making his way forward.

"Grab my wheel. Keep that acceleration for later. We'll steadily make our way to them. Don't worry."

Welte moved to the front, sheltering Nick from the wind, but his pace was slow, and they weren't gaining any ground. In fact, they lost a bit of time, and a couple of team cars moved around them. For the first time, Nick questioned the loyalty of Welte. *Was he doing this on purpose? Had he been playing me all along? He's been there for Bomber's victories. How could I be so stupid?* Nick pulled alongside Welte, "Didier, we haven't closed the gap at all. I need to punch it or my days in yellow are over."

"CALM DOWN NICK. TRUST ME," shouted the usually reserved Welte. The outburst was something Nick hadn't previously seen from his roommate.

Nick wasn't amused and was in no mood to listen to someone who was out to get him. Clearly, he was a man working for the enemy; sabotaging him. Nick strengthened his grip on his handlebars and forcefully moved them back and forth. He looked down on his small computerized Garmin, watching his power number skyrocket to just over a thousand. His thoughts had disappeared entirely—he was empty—with only one singular feeling prevailing; the desire to latch on to the front riders. He'd initially thought it would take no more than ten, maybe fifteen seconds to catch them, and at this power level, it would be worth it.

Nick moved through a couple of team cars, positioned between him and the front riders. He looked around, apparently disoriented, trying to figure out why there was team cars in front of him. The confusion was short lived as he worked his way past the cars. He expected to see the riders as he swept around the next turn. At that point, he would sit on the back, bring his breathing back to normal, and regain his strength. The corner came and went, so did a few riders he passed. But the front group remained dangling just in front. It wouldn't be long now. His body was screaming at him to quit.

Nick reached the last man in the strung-out line of riders. The pace was exceptionally fast. He couldn't catch his breath. His legs were full of tension. The effort was thirty seconds longer than the ten seconds he'd calculated. Nick couldn't believe he got it wrong. No wonder Welte was trying to temper his pace and contain his anxiety. Nick was now in agony, and it wouldn't subside.

The sun was in full effect; a ball of fire, illuminating the mountain terrain, but Nick couldn't feel or see it. The darkness had returned. He was once again trapped in that damn closet where the light that had seeped through, nourishing him with hope, were vanishing.

Nick wanted to move up the line of riders on the Col de Pailhères, and come alongside Bomber, Morkov, and Ellington at the head of the group. He knew his presence at the front would deter the lead riders from continuing to push the pace. So, he accelerated, going deep into the red. Every part of his body screaming at him to stop. The exertion went beyond being physically uncomfortable. His lower limbs felt disconnected from the rest of him. His upper body could barely control his bike and keep him upright. His belly and ribcage experienced a deep throbbing ache from just breathing, and his upper cheeks twinged from keeping his mouth wide-open to capture every speck of oxygen.

Nick's effort had made him feel like a wounded animal left to die on the mountainside. Part of him was hoping a kind soul would recognize his suffering and put him out of his misery. But he couldn't stop. Not now. He needed to reach the front men. Leading the Tour may have been unexpected, but now that he was in a position to win the overall, he couldn't concede to the pain.

Every moment of the last nine years had been spent dreaming of a moment like this. Nick's life and his training had been dedicated to winning the Tour someday. High School had been relegated to a hobby, and after becoming pro this year, University was put on hold. His social life outside of cycling was rather dismal. He had Emma of course, but his non-cycling friends had become used to him sacrificing their time together for training commitments. Long hours on the bike left him exhausted. When he wasn't on his bike, he was off his feet resting on the family couch. He couldn't participate in social activities—they'd only impeded his recovery. And, insufficient recovery would lead to less power, and less energy would mean less fitness.

For Nick, everything had become revolved around his pursuit to win. Even his love for food had to be broken long ago. His diet was now complex and calculated. He weighed out his portions when needed, adhering to the principals designed by the team trainers. Any emotional attachment to food had to be rejected. A necessary evil to increase his power to weight ratio; making him a formidable hill climber.

Nick's emaciated body was being propelled forward by a brain not willing to throw in the towel, despite the pain. When he reached the front, he could only regard Bomber for a moment. His eyes rolled—not in disgust—but because of the fatigue. For a moment, he thought Bomber must be laughing at him—laughing at the thought that Nick Carney's time in yellow was coming to an end. His inexperience and lack of maturity were killing him slowly, on the first critical mountain stage—the real race for Tour victory. It had started today, and Carney was proving to the world he was nothing more than a one-week side act before the real contenders came out to play. Nick realized he couldn't continue to think negatively. He'd spent hours with the team psychologist earlier in the year, testing thoughts versus power. He'd realized, with the help of sophisticated apps, how negative emotions could drastically impede his power.

Nick meditated, emptying his brain's cognitive contents. He thrust his bike forward, and he pulled in front of the leaders. He was ahead, attacking the main animators, Morkov, Ellington, and Bomber. Nick was unaware. He was merely moving his legs effortlessly in a world of his own. The road narrowed, and the switchbacks came every hundred meters now. They were quick and sharp and gained elevation quickly, but Nick didn't take notice of the changing landscape. He pounded on the pedals, working his way to the top. Five kilometers of twisting road, wrapping itself around the mountain peak, awaited the riders. The leading group was twenty strong, with some riders protecting their leaders from the massive gusts of wind. If Nick continued his solitary pursuit, he'd have to put out an insurmountable amount of power to stay away. It would be suicide.

An end to his yellow jersey!

CHAPTER 18

Stage 9

Emma's Journey

Nick's sleep before stage nine's first mountain stage was peaceful and restful. Emma's sleep, in contrast, was not. Before going to bed, she had expended a great deal of energy reassuring Nick. Receiving nothing from his father had sent Nick into emotional turmoil. Emma had to pick up the pieces and put him back together. She'd done it before, and she'd do it again. She was good at it, but it made her angry. She hated Frank Carney and his power over his son. Her anger caused her to toss and turn, keeping her awake. She even found herself sleepwalking at one point. Thankfully the size of the hotel room wasn't significant, and her night-time jaunt didn't put her at risk.

In the morning, Nick was happy and content. Not a word about the previous evening had been mentioned between him and Emma. She knew from experience not to say anything. The moment passed— perhaps forgotten. Nick had buried it deep within and was moving forward. Bringing it up would only hinder him. She knew he didn't need any additional distraction today. The Col de Pailhères followed by Ax 3 Domaines would be excruciating enough. She had seen the course profile and could only imagine the physical exertion the riders would endure.

Emma would be partaking in her own journey today. She had skipped breakfast with Nick and the team. She needed to get an early start to make it from Carcassonne to the final mountain ascent. Some of the team staff had offered to drive her rental to the next hotel so she could go with Nick's head soigneur to the top of Ax 3 Domaines. She happily declined. She wanted to explore the French countryside on her terms. A huge Dan Brown fan, she'd been hoping to grab a coffee and croissant in Couiza, then head up to Rennes-le-Château for a quick look at the famous alleged burial site of the Holy Grail. There was a constant flow of traffic out of Carcassonne, working its way toward Limoux; the start of the day's stage. She hoped it would subside once on the other side of Limoux. Then she'd be able to enjoy the sites of the bountiful and luscious vineyards. It took longer than expected, but once in the heart of the tiny village of Couiza, she stopped and parked along the main D118. She went to the small boulangerie on the corner of Route Rennes-le-Château and picked up a few croissants, a baguette, and a coffee. She would need food for later and couldn't resist the smell of freshly baked bread.

Emma jumped back into the car and took the road up to Rennes-le-Château. The road twisted and turned for an uninterrupted six kilometers before reaching the peak. She tried to take it all in as she drove cautiously from one bend to another. The beauty of red Spanish roofs caught her attention, along with the ancient ruins of a long-ago castle that decayed years ago; perched on some mountain near Alet-Les-Bains. Once she reached the top, she was greeted with narrow, steep roads, surrounded by homes that appeared to be hundreds of years old. The houses were concrete, adorned with beautiful colored wooden shutters. Some of the windows had baskets filled with vibrant flowers that brought the exterior of the houses to life. The remaining buildings were constructed entirely with colored cobblestones that matched the ancient cobbled roads that lead from one charming home to another. Emma was in awe. The scenery felt imagined, almost made up; a painting coming to life for her to witness.

The morning clouds were just about gone, but there was a slight dew in the morning air. She parked at the top, jumped out and began taking pictures of the rising sun over the mountains. Bugarach lay directly in front of her, the mountain is known for its UFO legends. She looked at the vibrant red dirt, etched with deep canyons that lined the county side, aiming her phone in every direction to capture the wondrous landscape. She turned her attention to the small castle that appeared to dangle unsupported on the mountain's edge. A beautiful almond tree swayed back and forth, showcasing its bright pink and white leaves. Every photo was magical, and Emma felt connected to the terrain, and the solitude of her surroundings. She found a spot under the tree to sit, taking a sip of her coffee and a bite from her flaky croissant. She sighed. The isolation was actually comforting.

She only had a few more moments to take it all in. She wondered if she would ever get another moment in her lifetime to experience this beautiful tiny village. She knew bits and pieces of the theories that encompassed the historic Priest François-Bérenger Saunière, his buried treasure, and Rennes-le-Château, but she wished she knew more. She could feel the magnitude of this small commune. She thought about the Davinci Code and envisioned Dan Brown sitting on the ledge writing. She highly doubted this was where he created his globally acclaimed masterpiece, but she felt inspired.

The connection to France's landscape and an appreciation of the creative arts were not lost on her. The Tour had become larger than life. Her view on Nick's achievements was developing beyond the admiration of pure athleticism; Nick was creating a heroic, adventurous story. His narrative was taking form: he was the master painter, stroking his brush against the backdrop of an ancient country rooted in deep history. Today he would lay down a work of art, stir the people's consciousness, and embed his story in the minds and hearts of the people as an everlasting masterpiece.

She walked down the hilltop to her Peugeot, jumped in the car, and drove the twisty descent back into Couiza. Once on the D118 she headed for Quillan, turned right, up into the mountains toward Puivert, then headed to Ax-Les-Thermes, home of Ax 3 Domaines —the final beast of today's stage. It was only 10:00 am, and the race started at noon, but she expected delays. The D118 may have been flowing fast and efficiently earlier, but her pit-stop at Rennes had cost her time. She only touched the outer border of the city before turning towards Puivert, but she could see crowds lining the tiny streets. Cars were scattered along the side of the main road, and the parking lots were packed.

The traffic lessened as she moved through Puivert, and she had a moment to reflect. The riders would fly through Quillan, spending only a handful of visible seconds in front of the fans. Yet, the crowd had been immense. Emma had no doubt that Ax 3 Domaines would contain ten times the amount of people. It would be an absolute zoo, a sea of fans. She'd seen enough cycling footage to realize that the mountains brought out the crazy fans. She wondered how many people would be half-naked today, wearing thongs and running alongside their heroes. Nick always got pissed when he watched footage of fans on foot, sprinting beside the riders screaming in their faces. *I'd punch those fuckers out*, he liked to say to Emma.

When Emma arrived in Ax-Les-Thermes, the traffic had built steadily. She worked her way out of the town and found a nice parking area just before the Ax 3. She planned to walk to the midpoint to cheer on Nick and the boys. Once on the slopes, she wasn't alone. Droves of people were walking and cycling up the climb to find a position to cheer on the race. They were singing and walking, while others huffed and puffed, powering their bikes with tiring legs. All were smiling, and the mood was festive.

Emma was wearing a Team Apex jersey and carrying a Canadian flag. Everyone who passed by acknowledged her with shouts of, "GO CANADA!" or "Carney, Carney!" She loved the attention and felt a sense of pride; for her country and for her fiancé. After four kilometers of walking, her legs gave out. She reached into her knapsack for some water and a snack. "Team Apex...Go...Go...Go! Let's go, Nick Carney!" Emma turned around. A group of blonde-haired women and men were approaching her. They were fair skinned and dressed in orange—the Dutch. The man heading the group looked at Emma. "Are you with Team Apex?" he asked.

"No, I'm just a fan," she replied.

"Canadian. Or just a Carney fan?"

"Both actually. I'm a Canadian and a huge fan of...Carney."

She felt strange referring to her fiancé as Carney. He's Nick, her man, her honey bear. He's not Carney.

"That Carney kid is strong. We like him a lot," said the man.

"He's adorable. You Canadians have some good-looking men," uttered one of the Dutch women.

Emma blushed. "I suppose we do."

"You're super pretty. I'm sure if Nick Carney gets a look at you while riding up this mountain you could snag the young man," the woman teased.

They all laughed out loud.

Emma couldn't contain herself. "I've already snagged him. He's my fiancé."

They looked at each other, apparently shocked at the way their joke had played out. The Dutchman who spoke to Emma first recovered quickly and introduced himself, "I'm Henrik." He began pointing to the others, "The woman who teased you is Sonia, that's Bart, John, and Jenna."

"It's wonderful to meet you all," said Emma.

"You must come further up the climb with us. We'll all cheer for Nick when he comes by. It'll be so much fun," gushed Sonia.

"I will. Absolutely!!"

Emma felt rejuvenated, the tiredness seeped out of her body, and she pushed on, inspired by the enthusiasm of her new found Dutch friends. They bounded up the mountain, cheering and chanting Nick's name. Moments ago, she'd been in Rennes-le-Château, another world, awed by the tranquility and terrain France had to offer. Now she was part of moving celebration. A sea of heartwarming fans spreading out over a colossal mountain peak.

Emma and her new friends arrived at a steeper section up the mountain, four kilometers from the finish. The Dutch insisted this would be a focal spot to watch the race. They believed this would be where the real race action would start. "Nick will attack here and drop the main contenders," insisted Henrik.

"You think?" asked Emma.

"You'll only have a small group of maybe ten guys—the main contenders. Nick will be one of them. I'm sure Jack Bomber, Rod Ellington, and Alexie Morkov will be there. Those guys are riding well, but Nick destroyed them in the time trial yesterday, so I think he's on form. How's he feeling?"

Emma paused, contemplating Hendrik's question. She wanted to provide him with a thoughtful answer, but all she could picture was the night before, Nick weeping uncontrollably. "He's doing great. He woke up looking forward to making everyone hurt today."

"We hope so," Sonia said.

"We've been reading Robert Saunders' articles, going to his blog, and listening to his commentary. Let's just say we aren't fans of Jack Bomber. There's no Dutch contender this year, so I suppose we're now supporting Nick. In your honor, of course," said John, the other Dutch gentleman.

Henrik chimed back in, "Jack Bomber is so boring. His style of racing is too precise and calculated. He's like a robot. He ruins the sport. The last two Tours have been so uneventful. This year is so much more exciting with Nick. Especially with them being on the same team. It must be tough for Nick though."

Emma thought about the internal team conflict Nick had been experiencing, the multiple calls home to her complaining about Jack, his insecurity about not receiving the support he required and deserved for being in yellow. She wanted to bellow out loud *if you only knew*. But she, of course, did not. "The team is doing well. Everyone is getting along and doing what they need to do to win the Tour. The media is making something from nothing." The words coming out of her mouth made her want to vomit. She didn't mention Jack's name on purpose. She was afraid that if she uttered his name, she'd slur one profanity after another. She didn't want to make the situation with the team worse. The last thing she wanted to see was her name in print in tomorrow's papers:

Dutch fans spend the day on Ax 3 Domaines with Nick Carney's fiancée, Emma Blake. Emma reveals the high tension between Bomber and Carney. She insists Team Apex is doing a poor job supporting Nick. Bomber hates Carney and Carney hates Bomber!

The Dutch fans didn't look convinced, but they dropped the probing. The race began, and they turned their attention to their mobile devices. Some were watching live footage, others were listening to the radio, and others were reading live tickers. Fans without mobile access were inquiring with those who did. Everyone wanted to get a feel for what was going on. "Emma, is this your first time at the Tour?" asked Sonia.

"Yes, it is."

"You're in for a treat then. In moments a race parade miles long will pass us, handing out souvenirs. The parade leaves a couple of hours before the riders and heads out along the day's route. The participants are sponsors of the Tour and the teams. Cars will be decorated in all sorts of ways to gain attention. The drivers and passengers hand out samples of their products—bike bottles, snacks, clothing, and tour paraphernalia—that you can wave at the riders when they pass by. You'll have a bag full of goodies by the end of the day. Exciting, no?" asked Sonia.

"Very. It's a lot to take in."

Emma was amazed. She had no idea there would be a procession. The atmosphere was already a celebratory one, full of energized fans conversing with one another, keeping tabs on the current race situation. Alcohol was flowing freely. Faces and bodies painted alike. Flags from various counties were waving freely, but every fan was there to support the riders regardless of their nationality. The noise of the rowdy fans had turned a serene mountain pass into a football arena. The chaos was currently manageable, but Emma envisioned more mayhem once the riders arrived. She now fully understood why crazy men ran beside the riders during the race.

Emma's thoughts turned towards Nick. Her Dutch compatriots reported that he was in the pack. His teammate Antoine Doucette was in the early breakaway, meaning Team Apex wouldn't have to put their men at the front to chase down the breakaway riders. Nick was tucked away safely in the peloton enjoying the shelter of his teammates. She felt relief that the race had finally started. Her only job now was to wait patiently for the riders to arrive. Estimated arrival time to reach her destination was three and a half to four hours. She had nothing but time, time to think about Nick and what she hoped he would accomplish today. Her stomach turned with anticipation. Last night's crying episode in response to Frank would either make him or break him. And, if it crushed him, it would happen quickly, when he was least expecting it.

CHAPTER 19

Stage 9

The Penultimate Summit

Nick was within reach of the summit of the Col de Pailhères. He was by himself now, deep in concentrated effort and pain. Only he couldn't feel the pain. He was numb. The crowd was massive, cheering the man in yellow. Their voices, loud and vibrant, echoed in the thin air of the mountain top, bouncing from one peak to another. The road dipped in the last two hundred meters, and Nick caught his breath. He only had thirty seconds to gather his thoughts. He never intended to be alone at this point in today's stage. This had not been a calculated and well-thought-out tactic. It just kind of happened. One minute he was off the back, chasing down his main competitors, and the next he was away.

If he chose to continue, he'd have to ride the descent on his own. Nick knew there'd be the possibility that he'd encounter riders from the early breakaway. The best-case scenario for Nick would be if the riders chose to work with him on the descent, but he highly doubted that would play out. He knew they'd more than likely be dead from the massive energy they expended to stay out front. Could he do it on his own? He thought about what this effort would do to him on Ax 3 Domaines and realized he wouldn't be able to maintain the race-winning power necessary to stay ahead. Morkov, Ellington, and even Bomber, now thanks to Welte, would have men sheltering them all the way to the beginning of the final mountain ascent. If Nick made it to Ax 3 Domaines, he expected it wouldn't take long before the fresh legs of Bomber and the others passed him. Not only would they catch him, but they'd also leave him for dead. Nick's overall race lead would evaporate, as the others gained minutes on him.

Nick wondered if he should ease off the gas. He figured his current lead was about thirty seconds. He knew it wasn't enough to stay away and win the stage. He had too much to lose and knew he should shut it down right here and right now. The smart decision would be to coast on the descent until Bomber, Welte and the rest of the substantial men reached him. Then he could forget this little escapade ever happened, work with his teammates and then battle it out on the slopes of Ax 3 Domaines.

He looked up and saw the barriers marking the end of the climb. He positioned himself for the final one hundred meters and began scanning the crowd for his soigneur. He needed a musette; gels and a couple of bottles with a carb solution. He spotted one of the team's soigneur's holding out a musette, swung his arm out and caught the bag. The descent began. He was on his way.

A decision needed to be made NOW!

CHAPTER 20

Stage 9

Eurosports Drama

While Nick was on the attack, Robert Saunders watched the live footage of the Tour on a small screen in front of him. His body slumped deep into his anchor chair. He awaited the questions from Carl Thompson or Allen Smith. He knew what they were thinking. His boy Carney was on a suicide mission. His attack on the penultimate climb was a clear signal to the world that Team Apex was riding for Bomber. Nick was now playing a supporting role. Saunders had seen this tactic a thousand times; send out a strong man and have your competitors work hard to bring him back. Nick was no longer an equal to Ellington, Morkov, Bomber, or Alvarez. Allen called on Saunders for a comment. "Robert, what do you think is going on with Nick Carney? Do you think his attack on the Col de Pailhères will succeed, or do you think he's conceding his attempt to win the Tour? Is he riding for Bomber now?"

"It's suicide. Carney is waving the white flag. I didn't think we'd see this. I thought he would put up a good fight until the end. In modern cycling, you can't be attacking at this point. He's going to burn matches he doesn't have. Bomber and his toughest competitors will be fresher for Ax 3 Domaines. His quest for overall victory is over."

"This must upset you, Robert. You had high hopes for the young man from Canada. We know you're not a Jack Bomber fan. Especially after what transpired between the two of you during last year's Tour," said Thompson.

"Thanks, Carl. We won't go there. What upsets me the most is that this is likely a team order. I can't see Nick wanting to initiate this attack. It's pure stupidity. I blame the man behind the wheel. The man in charge, Tom Christenson."

Carl looked at Allen. They wouldn't take the bait. They were both good friends of Tom and believed he was an exceptional Director. They had interviewed him many times throughout his career, both as a rider and a team manager. They had profound respect for him and how he'd handled his riders at this Tour. If they hadn't been pressured by their producer to include Robert Saunders today, they wouldn't have. His journalism was highly respected, but his current body of work on this year's Tour was being questioned. His colleagues wondered if it was a vendetta against Jack Bomber. Their feud during last year's Tour had been highly publicized, and Robert came out of it battered and scarred.

"Do either one of you think there is a remote chance he stays out front and wins the stage?" asked Carl.

Robert sat back in his chair, sulking as he shook his head. His arms crossed.

"There *is* a chance," piped up Allen.

"How can you say that?" asked Saunders.

"If he hooks up with some of the remnants of the early break on the downhill and they collaborate, he can get a free ride to the base of the Ax 3. He'll be fresh, with time on his side. His teammate,

Antoine Doucette is up front. I'm sure the team will call him back, tell him to wait for Carney, and provide him with assistance. This may be the plan for today. Give Carney a well-deserved mountain stage win, before the real contenders take over," stated Allen.

Saunders didn't buy what Allen was selling. He wanted to call him an idiot. The man had been a cycling broadcaster for the last three decades. He was old, but not out of touch. He could typically be counted on to provide a reliable analysis of race dynamics and strategies, but in Saunders' belief, Allen was out to lunch on this one.

"I wish that were true, Allen. I spoke with Tom earlier today before the start of the race, and he said Bomber and Carney were co-leaders. I'd be surprised if this were the plan at the beginning of the stage. Nick struggled on the early slopes of Pailhères, and I think Tom ordered him to punch it hard when he returned to the main contenders. Burn out his legs and have Bomber's competition chase. They'll be no stage victory for Carney today, and his days in yellow will end. He's no longer a contender for overall victory. It's a sad day," said Saunders.

"Let's say you're right, Robert. I'm not sure it's a sad day. The kid is twenty-three and has led the Tour from the start. If he loses the yellow, he'll more than likely retain the white jersey. Nick Carney has a long future ahead of him. I think we'll be talking about him for the next decade. He will win a grand tour," stated Carl.

Robert couldn't argue with Carl's assessment. He knew Carl was right. However, it didn't take away from the fact that Saunders' felt full of anger. Perhaps last year's incident with Bomber had affected him more than he wanted to admit. Maybe he wasn't even a Nick Carney fan really, just a Bomber detractor. He couldn't escape the misery he was feeling watching Carney descend the mountain solo. He was disappointed. Carney was supposed to put Jack Bomber in his place, and Saunders was supposed to regain his popularity with the masses. The reputation he lost last year at the hands of Bomber. He took a moment to re-evaluate his conversations with Nick. Did he see something raw and powerful in the young man? He stopped mid-thought. *Could Nick Carney be attacking on unrestrained emotion—like the great Eddie Merckx or Bernard Hinault?*

During their first interview, Robert had been intrigued with Nick's uninhabited emotion. He'd strayed from the current professional's robotic and well-rehearsed vocabulary. *Could this surprise tactic be a maneuver that propels Carney further ahead?* His mind was full of questions he couldn't answer. He felt like a journalist once more. He wished he could be in Nick's head now. While Robert couldn't be there, he could sway the audience to his biases. He realized his pessimistic message wasn't going over well with Carl and Allen, and he imagined the audience was less than thrilled. He was surely coming across as the bitter journalist that got burned last year.

Robert had been spaced out the last minute or so in deep thought. The other two men were doing the heavy lifting—keeping the dialogue and story going. Robert decided to take Allen's position, " You're right."

"About what?" asked Carl.

"Carney has a chance for the win. The team is going to call back Antoine Doucette. I'm sure they already have. We just don't have TV footage yet. The kid is doing it his way. I take back what I said earlier. I don't think it was a team order. In fact, I think it's the complete opposite. The internal strife on the team is rampant, and Nick had no choice but to attack now. He had to go when he did. If he hadn't, I'm sure Bomber would have ordered him to set the pace for him."

Carl and Allen were perplexed. They weren't sure why Saunders had suddenly changed his opinion on matters. What changed his mind? They didn't get a chance to respond. Their producer was waving at them to wrap it up—commercial break. The producer, Jonas

Blakely, a young man in his thirties, was delighted with Robert. "I love your angle, Robert. Brilliant. It's exactly what we're looking for."

Carl didn't think it was. In fact, he wished they could just report the race as it happened. There were many instances in history that proved reporters wrong. He thought about Phil Ligget and his commentary during the 2002 Tour de France—the Alpe D'euz Stage— and the iconic look. He had reported that Armstrong looked deep into the eyes of his biggest rival, Jan Ulrich, starring him down just before attacking him. It inspired the notion of greatness and cockiness. A man on a mission, staring down anyone who would challenge him, letting them know he was about to attack, then effortlessly riding away from them. Later, during a retirement interview completed by Ligget, after Armstrong's final victory in 2005, the audience would learn there was no such intent behind that look. In fact, Armstrong was merely looking down the mountain to see where the rest of the competition was positioned. It was a letdown to the millions of fans he still enjoyed at that time in his life.

"Do you think it's a bit of stretch?" asked Carl.

Allen nodded his head in agreement, "Can we not just let it play out? If Carney's attack works, great. If not, so be it."

Jonas paced back and forth looking at the various TV screens in the room. He turned back. "We get paid to speculate. We create the story. We create the riders' emotions; right or wrong. Without your voices, without your stories, you have nothing more than a bunch of men riding bikes through France. An attack doesn't even exist for the first-time viewer. All he sees is a man riding his bike faster than other men. So, let's use Robert's dialogue the best we can."

Saunders thanked Jonas for backing him up. It felt like a long time since he'd had a colleague on his side; fighting to let his voice be heard. He took a sip from his glass of water and returned to his seat. Carl and Allen followed, placing their earphones on their head. In moments, live footage of the race would return to the airwaves, and they needed to be ready.

During the commercial break, very little happened. Nick had traveled a couple of kilometers downhill while the main contenders crested the peak of Pailhères. They surveyed the video, the rider's faces, and any other footage streaming to their TV screens.

"Welcome back," greeted Carl in his thick English accent.

"If you're just tuning in, you couldn't have picked a better time. The Yellow Jersey has attacked on the penultimate climb and is putting time into his rival," stated Allen.

"What can we expect from here?" asked Carl.

Allen was quick to reply, "We'll have to wait and see. Carney is riding well. Maybe he's got a shot." There was no emotion in his voice. He was stating a fact, nothing more. It irked Saunders. He looked at the screen. The video showed Antoine Doucette from Team Apex slowing down. He was on the lower part of the descent, soft-pedaling, and letting the breakaway men, he crested Pailhères with rapidly move away. Saunders disposition went from annoyed to smug. "It looks like they've called back Doucette. Exactly what I said they would do."

Carl didn't hesitate and jumped all over Saunders' proclamation. He'd been thinking about Saunders' last statement before they'd take their break for a commercial. It seemed wrapped in a contradiction. Instead of confronting him off the air, Carl chose to give his young producer exactly what he wanted: fireworks. "Does this mean the team is working for Carney? Would you say the internal strife has ended? Is Doucette's order to slow down a potential sign of forgiveness by the team? If one is needed."

"No."

"Well, who would have given Doucette the order to slow down, and why?"

"I'm not following you, Carl. Sorry. I'd say he caught wind of Carney's approach on his radio and is choosing to slow down on his own."

"Fair enough. Before the break, you suggested the team would call Doucette back to help Carney, insisted there is internal strife, and that Carney would be ordered to help Bomber if they arrived at the foot of Ax 3 Domaines together. So, I'm just a bit confused. I'm sure the viewers would like some clarity as well."

Carl smiled at Robert. *Got you, big boy. Let's see you get out of this one.*

"Thanks, Carl. I suppose I wasn't clear on the situation. Perhaps you're right. Maybe the audience doesn't possess the clarity they need and desire."

That's an understatement, thought Carl. *I'm sitting beside you, and I barely understand whether Team Apex is supporting Nick Carney or Jack Bomber.*

"Let me paint the picture for you, Carl. The team is divided. There are those who are supporting Bomber and there or those who are supporting Carney. I have yet to determine who Tom Christenson is really supporting. Knowing that he's a good friend of Jack's, I'm going to assume his allegiance is with him. He's the boss. The order came from him directly, but he's not stupid. Every chance he gets, he'll have the team riding for Bomber, but if Carney fights hard, which he's doing, he'll back Tom into a corner. Tom will have no choice but to make a decision that appears—I repeat—*appears* to support Nick. He'd be a fool not too." Carl fidgeted in his seat.

"So, you're saying the team is supporting Bomber, unless otherwise, and, even then, it's only superficial?"

"Bingo."

Jonas was on cloud nine. His smile consuming his whole thirty-something baby face. His hands were waving up and down furiously for more. He was loving Carl versus Robert. Viewership was spiking. It may merely have been a coincidence based on what was happening in the race, but he didn't care. As a former racer, he couldn't help but watch this young kid in yellow boldly attacking the race and its seasoned veterans. As a producer, he knew the audience wasn't as keen. He envisioned the masses lying on their couches, TVs blaring in the background while they surfed the net on their tablets, occasionally looking up. He was almost sure that Robert's and Carl's dialogue had the audience firmly watching the Yellow Jersey's sensational attack.

Jonas couldn't have been more right. One family couldn't take their eyes away from their television and the heart-pounding action. The Carney family and their neighbors continued to watch the excitement. Earlier, the family and neighbors snacked on breakfast goodies. They shouted in anger when Bomber lost contact and Tom sent the whole team back to help him. Nick had been left alone and vulnerable in the pack. They cried in disbelief when Nick himself ran into mechanical issues and fell behind the peloton. Now Nick was attacking the race, putting the favorites into difficulty.

Catherine couldn't contain herself. What proud mom could? "Frank, come downstairs. Your son is winning! WINNING!"

Frank mumbled to himself. He was deep in thought, practicing and perfecting his speech. The last thing he wanted to do was interrupt his current flow to watch his son's shenanigans. He'd like to shout "I'm fucking busy, leave me alone. What don't you get? Do you think I give a shit about that little fuck?" He knew he couldn't. With George and Renée in the house, he had to be more diplomatic. "I'm a bit busy, hun. I'm sure Nick is doing great." He rolled his eyes, unable to get through that sentence without feeling he needed another scotch.

Catherine was angered by his reaction but tried not to show it. Laura picked-up on her mother's distress. "Dad come downstairs.

Come watch Nick. It's incredible. Take a break and watch the rest of the race with us. I'll make you a drink."

Frank considered his daughter's offer. He was tired, he could use a break, and he could use a drink. At least the alcohol would take the sting off from having to watch the race. "I'll be downstairs in a minute, kiddo. Scotch. Straight. You choose. I'm easy."

Frank entered the living room to no applause, no recognition. He felt slightly jaded. He showed up. He was here. Why didn't they care more than they were showing? Why did they insist on rubbing Nick in his face?

"Hey, Dad. I'll grab you your drink." Laura left the living room and headed to the kitchen bar. Frank took a seat on the couch beside Alex and Catherine. "So, he's riding well."

"Yes, honey. Extremely well. I'm glad you were able to join us. It means a lot to me."

Frank Shrugged, willing to sit through this for the sake of this wife and a stiff drink. He thought about how happy he made his wife with this simple act of watching a stupid race on TV. He could still do that at least. Laura rushed back in, handed her father his scotch and turned her attention to Alex. "Robert is getting his analysis bang on. He's on fire. Don't you think?"

"Yeah. He knows what he's talking about," Alex agreed.

Frank felt the eyes of his judgmental neighbors peering at him from the adjacent couch across the room. "Who is Robert Saunders?" he asked.

"He's a cycling author and journalist," stated Alex.

"And…what's his story?"

"He's reporting on the internal dynamics of Nick's team. He must have inside information about some of the tension between Nick and Jack Bomber."

Frank took a few minutes to listen to the television then turned his attention back to Alex. "This Robert is an expert, correct?"

"Yes, Dad."

"Is this Carl commentator an expert as well?"

"He's a cycling commentator. He has been for many years. He's a respected journalist."

"More respected than Robert Saunders?"

"Absolutely not."

"So, why argue with the expert. What a waste of time."

Alex wasn't surprised by his father's sentiment. He had the honor of living with the man for eighteen years before escaping for the dorms of an out-of-town university. He learned long ago that his father harbored extreme opinions that couldn't be reasoned with: you don't argue with a respected figure or a person of authority. If you're not important, you shut your mouth and move on. His dad liked to view himself as important, superior to others. His sense of entitlement was overwhelmingly dominant.

Alex felt like a ticking time bomb, ready to go off on his father. It would be the perfect time to lecture him on ignorance, the human dynamic, and the need for differing opinions. But he hesitated to speak. It occurred to him that his father had inadvertently taken Nick's side. In his neurotic attempt to make conversation, his argument in support of Robert lent itself to Nick. It made Alex feel a sense of warmth and glee; a satisfaction he would have gladly brought to his father's attention but knew better. His father would have felt vulnerable and humiliated and would have masterfully manipulated any dialogue thrown his way. He'd either belittle Robert Saunders, Alex or both. His sense of insecurity would be so profound their close-knit audience would witness Frank's distaste for his youngest son; a well-known fact in the Carney household. Alex's intent to enlighten the man himself, and bring out a greater sense of self-awareness, would only be lost on Frank Carney.

CHAPTER 21

Stage 9

Nick's Destiny

When Nick had crested Col de Pailhères by himself, he'd began to have severe doubts about the remaining kilometers. His legs had felt shattered from the intense effort, and his mind, which had temporarily shut off, had taken inventory of how the rest of his body was doing. He still found himself conflicted on what to do, which was a regular part of any bike race, but this was the Tour. The stakes to win were much higher, and an emotionally fueled decision could cost him everything. A crackle in his earpiece broke his introspection.

"Nick, it's Tom. Keep it rolling. You have a whopping minute on Bomber and the rest of the contenders."

Nick was shocked. He knew he had put out a solid effort of power and expected a gap, but not by this much. "The descent and the valley to Ax 3 will be too much for me on my own Tom. I don't think I can make it."

"Doucette is just ahead. We've given him orders to slow down and wait for you."

"Antoine! He's up ahead?"

"Yeah, we have him slowing to a crawl. Keep charging down the descent as fast as you can. He has orders to pull you to the base of Ax 3 Domaines and stay with you as long as he can."

Nick didn't bother to ask whether he thought the tactic would work. For the first time, he felt Tom was supporting him. He cut the corner of the switchback hard, overshot and got a magnificent view of the edge, a steep rocky cliff with no barriers. Smaller rocks lined the barren mountainside, rocks that had trickled down the vertical bluff and made their home. Nick had no intention of striking up a permanent residence here. He regained focus in pursuit of his teammate. Moments later he spotted Doucette rounding a corner at a crawl. "Antoine. I'm just behind. Come on. Move…Move…Move."

Doucette didn't hesitate. The sound of Carney's voice meant it was time to accelerate and get up to speed. He was tired but not exhausted. He'd do whatever he could to help his leader. He had what experts would consider a free ride in the break. It wasn't until Pailhères that he had to put out maximal effort to remain in contact with the lead group. Even then, he'd had strict instructions before the stage to conserve as much energy as possible and be prepared for Bomber or Nick when called upon. Now would be his moment to shine as a domestic. He knew this part of the race would be televised in its entirety, as the cameramen on motorcycles moved quickly alongside them to capture every moment of the Yellow Jersey's brave attack. His efforts would be scrutinized by the media. And the success of the day, the team, and Nick would be attributed to his labor. He could feel the pressure mounting, weighing down his shoulders like a twenty-five-hundred-pound elephant. He moved in front of Nick to block the wind, and the media mottos engulfed them.

Shortly after Nick had made contact with Doucette, Bomber had crested Pailhères with Morkov, Ellington, and the other top contenders. He was feeling good and was happy to have his teammates, Welte and Rosas, by his side. Spectators who had tuned into their televisions could see a calm and collected group of men, but were they relaxed? Bomber's pedal stroke was smooth, his cadence high and his upper body stiff as a board. His face showed no signs of stress, strain or panic. He pressed on his mic to speak with Tom. He wanted to know what the gap was to Carney. "Tom, it's Jack. What's the situation? I just heard you talking to Nick. Did you say he has a minute on us? Is Antoine waiting for him?"

"He's got just over a minute on you guys right now. Doucette is leading him down the bottom portion of the descent. There's still a group of six riders, fifty seconds in front of them. How are you feeling Jack?"

Bomber felt destroyed. The effort from the early chase to regain contact, then the overindulgent pace set by Ellington and Morkov's lieutenants on the early slopes of Pailhères, had caused him to dig extremely deep. His power output during the final five kilometers of the climb, when Nick was out front gaining substantial time, was well below his sustainable pace. He wasn't alone. The impetus in the group to invite pain upon themselves had become non-existent. Knowing everyone was in the same boat, decided to play coy, "I'm feeling great, Tom. Any idea how Nick is feeling?"

"I'm feeling great," shouted Nick into his mic. He'd been listening to the conversation as he followed Doucette's wheel around one steep corner after another. His arms and shoulder ached from having to grip the handlebars for the last thirty minutes, but he couldn't stand hearing Bomber's voice. It hurt more than the physical strain he was enduring. Even just over his earpiece, Bomber's tone irked Nick. He couldn't help but think Bomber was full of shit.

"Good Nick. Keep it up. Go as long as you can until you blow," replied Bomber.

Nick couldn't contain himself any longer. He felt he'd been respectful to Jack in every situation throughout this Tour, but in the middle of an attack, near the end of the stage, when one is overcome with fatigue and adrenaline, inhibition is weakened. "I'm going all the way until the end. Then I'll fucking blow. So, be prepared."

The radio was reduced to silence. Jack shook his head, shocked and pissed with his young teammates' arrogance. It wasn't supposed to be like this. Did he underestimate Carney's character? Tom assessed the situation, and for a moment was hesitant to supply direction. Finally, he screamed into the car's mic. "Boys just RIDE. Shut the fuck up and GO. The race is in full flight."

For the first time, Bomber was suddenly aware that Tom might not be one hundred percent on his side. He rode up to Ellington, "The race is over if you guys don't chase harder."

"Is that your tip of the day?" replied Ellington.

"No. I mean. We're riding for Carney, and he's in full flight now. He won't be slowing down."

"There's not much more we can do, Jack. I've got my men on the front chasing full tilt. Why do you want us to go harder?"

Bomber looked around. The TV moto rode up beside them, close enough to capture their facial gestures, but not close enough to hear them. Bomber put a gentle hand on Ellington's shoulder, flashed him a warm ingenious smile, and whispered, "I want you to go harder so that your lovely wife never finds out about you and that podium girl you had in your room the other night."

Ellington pushed him away in disgust, but there was fear in his eyes. He rounded the switchback and lost a few positions, slipping a few bike lengths behind the leading group. He was flustered. How did Jack Bomber know about him and Emily? He'd covered his tracks well. His Director had given him his word that the situation was contained. It wasn't his first time flirting with an attractive young girl at the Tour, but this was his first time going this far. He turned fantasy into a reality, and he couldn't rationalize why. It was entirely out of character for the family man from Manchester. If the British press were to find out, they would crucify him. His marriage would be over. His two children's family would be destroyed; split in two with only weekends spent with dad. Even then, with a training and racing schedule that consumed his entire existence, he wondered when he would see them.

He wanted to better understand Bomber's threat, and how far he planned to go. Did it end here, with Ellington pushing his men harder, as Bomber insisted, or were there future ramifications? He didn't need to know why Bomber was doing it. Ellington already knew. He, himself, was a man who had tasted victory in the Tour and knew how addictive it could be, how it could drive a man to commit unthinkable actions. Standing on the podium of the Champs Élysée and being declared the champion of the most significant cycling event in the world could change a man. And Jack Bomber's character transformed the moment he stepped on the top spot of the final podium of his first Tour victory. People could see it in his walk, sense it in his voice. The closer you got to him, the further away you wanted to get.

Ellington rode up to his two remaining lieutenants and shouted at them to drive the pace harder. Their fatigue was showing in their legs. Their increased speed was visible, but it wasn't sufficient for Bomber. He wanted more. He hadn't thought of Carney as a real threat until now. He believed Carney would crack, or at least remain loyal—as Jack's Domestique. Nick was now a loose cannon, off script and potentially writing new dialogue for this Tour.

Bomber's ear rumbled. Tom rolled out the time gap—a minute thirty. The thought of Carney with that type of gap crushed Jack. He knew, based on the current pace, power output, and his sensations, that Nick was on a good day. For whatever reason, he was having an off day, and he wasn't alone. The leading contenders surrounding him were faring no better. To be sure things didn't get out of control, he played a card he hoped he wouldn't have to use at this stage of the race. He accelerated up to Alexie and his three teammates. "Are you guys moving as fast as you can?"

"We're going as fast as we want," replied Alexie.

"Well go faster."

"We don't play your game, Jack. We do our own thing."

"Alexie you'll move faster, and you'll move now. I had a great discussion with your soigneur in Mount Tenerife. Did you forget he used to be a member of my team? Get you and your mates moving your *unnatural legs*. They should have a lot more *juice* left in them."

Morkov grumbled, ignoring Jack. He knew it was a threat, but he couldn't have cared less. His lieutenants were done. The first sign of the impending Ax 3 ascent and they'd lose contact. They were all paying for their earlier attempt to dislodge Bomber and Carney when they were off the back struggling with mechanicals.

"Did you hear me, Alexie? Most of us don't do that shit any longer. You're in the fucking minority. Do you want to lose two years of your career?"

"WE GO AS FAST AS WE CAN, JACK. WE'RE EMPTY," he shouted back.

"Get on the front and help Ellington's men."

The remaining men in the lead group with Bomber, Ellington and Morkov were in a state of uncertainty and ignorance. It made sense that Ellington and Morkov's men chase. They had the numbers. They bore the responsibility, but they didn't understand the screaming coming from Bomber. They saw him ride up to Ellington and moments later the pace of the small pack increased. Then he rode up to Alexie yelling at the Russian leader, and again the speed increased further. Like the rest of the riders in this elite group, their legs ached, and they longed for a slightly more tranquil ride before climbing the monstrous final ascent. The speed on the descent was already lightning fast and was a cause for concern for many of the exhausted riders hanging on. Going harder put every rider at risk of crashing—a potentially life-threatening incident.

Nick tucked in behind Antoine, ensuring his body was sheltered from the strong gust of wind. Tom and Willie, in the team car, drove up to the pair of men to take inventory. "How are you feeling boys?" asked Tom.

The boys smiled, "Doing great."

"Do you need anything special? How are your energy levels?"

"I could use a couple of the special chocolate gels with extra electros," said Nick.

Tom handed him a couple of packets and an additional one for the final few kilometers. He then asked Willie to grab a couple of salt pills and a few water bottles for the boys.

"Tom get me some caffeine pills. I'm losing energy fast," gasped Antoine.

Willie rummaged through the medical kit and came up with two small pills containing 200mg of caffeine, handed them to Tom, who then placed them into the hands of his weakened rider. "Anything else boys?"

"Nah, that should do it for me," said Nick.

"I'm good too," said Antoine.

Willie surveyed his laptop, which was streaming every team member's physiological data. He could instantly examine the rider's power output via their power equipped bicycles as well as their heart rate and level of oxygen— using a small sleeve, the riders wore around their biceps. Nick's numbers looked good—strong and stable. Antoine was showing elevated levels of variability with his heart rate and oxygen levels. His power output was right at his limit, and it wouldn't be long until he blew and left Nick on his own. It wouldn't matter how much caffeine and energy he ingested—when your body is done it's done.

Willie looked at Tom and pointed to the screen, highlighting the riders pending outcome. Tom kept a hand on the wheel and popped his head out the window. "Antoine, you're doing great. Keep it up. Nick needs you. You have to make it to the base of the climb. If you can ride tempo hard for the first two or three kilometers of Ax 3, it will be even better. You guys have this."

"Got it, boss."

The car pulled hard to the right, retreating behind the head commissaries car, and left the two young men on their own. Their destinies would be in their hands now.

CHAPTER 22

Stage 9

Commercials Kill the Flow

Commercials were playing for the greater audience, while Robert Saunders and his fellow journalist watched the small screens streaming the cycling footage with keen interest. Jack Bomber had just finished chatting with Ryan Ellington before moving his way to Alexie Morkov. They now had their respective teammates at the front of the chase group, pounding their pedals with vigor. They were chasing two men—specifically the one in yellow, but the gap was growing. Ellington looked visibly shaken, and Morkov appeared angered.

Robert, Carl, and Allen wanted to debate the merits of Bomber's actions, but their producer, Jonas asked them to be patient. He wanted them in full flight, prepared to battle on air. Saunders was slightly hesitant about what he should say concerning Bomber. Last year still haunted him. His actions nearly cost him his job. He, and his newspaper affiliate, still faced litigation action from Bomber and his legal team. He thought about last year and the scenario involving

Bomber that he'd reported. Within the tight-knit world of cycling, among the riders and team personnel, there'd been whispers and innuendo about Bomber and his dirty little secrets. But, nobody was willing to speak out.

The commercials ended, and the Tour was back on the air. Saunders chose to go on the offense and spoke first. "Looks like the race is really moving along now. Carney and Doucette are working well together. The young Frenchman is burying himself for his teammate."

The footage went from being live to a flashback; a slow-motion clip capturing Bomber's conversation with his top two adversaries. "This happened while we were away. Bomber was having a quick conversation with Ellington and Morkov. What do you think he said?" speculated Allen.

Robert was silent. If the rumors he reported on last year were right, he had a shrewd idea of what was said. He had no choice but to keep his mouth shut. He'd let Carl and Allen speculate. "If I had to guess, he told them the race is up ahead. Keep your men working. Nothing more than a friendly reminder that his teammate is in yellow up the road, and he, along with Welte and Rosas, wouldn't be helping," said Allen.

Carl shook his head in agreement. "Yeah, nothing more than a psychological reminder of who the Patron of the Tour is. Jack is in total control. He's acting like the boss he is," stated Carl.

"What do you think Robert?" asked Allen.

"I think you're right. You've got to keep your main competition in line. Sometimes they forgot their responsibilities and need a stern reminder."

Robert hated every word coming out of his mouth. His lips moved, and he could hear his voice, but they'd been little bubbles of lies. He didn't believe that it was an innocent prompting. Men like

Alexie Morkov and Ryan Ellington are motivated athletes who pushed their bodies to the extreme. They knew what it took to win a race and knew how to handle their teammates. They would never have needed a nudge from Jack Bomber. Never. *What had Jack said to them?*

A man like Saunders was driven to find the truth in action and meaning, report his findings to the world and do so animatedly and entertainingly. His shoulders slumped, and his chest tightened. His mind jumped to unfounded fears; *I'm having a heart attack, I'm going hyperglycemic, I'm about to have a seizure.* But, Saunders was a man of fitness and took considerable pride in staying in shape and eating healthy. The only thing he was suffering from was being inauthentic in front of millions. He had to move on, he had no choice, but he knew there was something at play here. Perhaps it was an extension to his already well-established Bomber versus Carney narrative.

CHAPTER 23

Stage 9

Vomiting has its Benefits

Stage nine continued under the heat of the afternoon sun. It baked the riders, drenching them in sweat and salt. There was a crowd of people at Ax-Les-Thermes, lined up behind hot metal gates that contain sponsored billboards. These fans had waited hours to see the race come by. A mere glimpse of their heroes awaited them.

Antoine and Carney rode under the "Ten km To Go" banner. The audience cheered and chanted, clapping their hands and waving their flags. Their smiles and enthusiasm had been caught on video, but the riders saw nothing—they had tunnel vision. Antoine was frantic to get Carney into position and ready to start the climb. Meanwhile, Morkov's and Ellington's men were desperate to bring back the man in yellow. They were charging at the front with incredible strength.

The beginning of Ax 3 Domaines had been steep, with pitches starting at eight percent, and rapidly increasing to just over nine within the first few kilometers. An abundant number of energized fans lined the smooth tarmac narrowing the rider's passage and visibility. Fans were pushed to the outer edges of the road as rumbling motorcycles raced in front of the two men, clearing a path so the riders could continue to race on. Nick momentarily thought about the significance of Ax 3 Domaines. Two of his cycling heroes had won the Tour by leaving their mark on this prominent climb. Could he emulate the great Carlos Sastre or Chris Froome? He wanted the stage victory now; he wanted to win the Tour. Five men, remnants of the break, were ahead, up on the road, but it wouldn't be long until he and Antoine overtook them.

Antoine was tiring. His leg muscles were tense, like the strings of an over-tuned guitar, ready to snap and rip apart, strand by strand. The tension was his enemy, and he needed to relax, to harness his power and guide his leader. He reached for his mic, took a deep breath and started to converse with Nick. "How you feelin'?"

Nick didn't bother to grab his mic. He didn't want anyone else on the team knowing how he was coping. He shouted from behind Doucette. "I'm good, Antoine. Keep holding this power output. I need two more kilometers from you. Just two more."

Antoine nodded to acknowledge his orders but had hoped Nick could've taken it from here. He was dizzy and wanted to throw in the towel, but he could sense panic in Nick's voice.

A man wearing nothing but a thong ran out screaming, "Allez, Allez, Allez!!" Nick wanted to tell him where he could go, go, GO!

Just before Antoine had spoken to Nick, and only shortly after the naked man came running out toward Nick—his stomach tightened, cramped and turned violent. The stomach flu can bring a man to his knees. Have him leaning over the toilet for hours, with morsels of undigested food scraping the lining of the esophagus, begging to get out. The ramifications are never pretty and typically result in a newly decorated bathroom. But, there are no pit stops during the Tour. No place to run to, to evade the cameras when nature calls, or to slip away when a cramp displays itself. Nick didn't have time to warn Antoine, his chocolate gels ingested moments before, on the descent, were making their way up and out. He could feel his throat burn, tasting bile and chocolate simultaneously. His jersey became covered with messy syrupy goo. He wiped away the remnants left on his chin with the back of his right hand, soaking his cycling glove.

He could see the cameraman just up ahead, capturing everything on video. He wondered what the world was thinking. He figured at this point, a journalist like Robert Saunders was sensationalizing every moment. How many times would they replay the footage in slow motion? He thought they'd do it at least a dozen times. No matter the truth, he knew people would label him sick. He caught a bug on the rest day. This was his last hoorah in the Yellow Jersey. This was Nick's moment to go out hard, make the other teams work, and then retire at the end of the stage.

The puking didn't stop him from pedaling and working hard. His heart rate was right around his threshold. He was calm and in control, but his earlier exertions on Col de **Pailhères** must have put too much stress on his digestive system. Part of him didn't care about the incident. He knew bike racing was a hard-man sport, and the body could turn on you in any moment. You had to be prepared, ready to suffer and fight through whatever came your way. But, he wondered if his dad was watching. He could only imagine what Frank Carney would think if he were.

There had been a time, in grade four, when Nick had caught the flu. He woke in the middle of the night, vomiting everywhere. His mother was away, tending to her sick mother, and Nick was left with his father, hoping he would provide care and tenderness. It never came. He screamed out for his dad, but there was only silence. When he entered his parent's bedroom, his father ignored his pleas, eventually shushing him and telling him to get out. Nick didn't react favorably, swearing bitterly and telling his father that he was a narcissistic alcoholic, nothing more than a failure in life. He didn't even know what narcissism was at that time, but he'd heard his older brother refer to his father as one multiple times. Nick assumed that if he pushed his dad hard enough, he'd get some help. But he got nothing.

The remainder of the night was spent in the bathroom feeling like death, using cold face clothes to help with the heat his forehead was generating. In the early morning, just before school would typically begin, Nick had finally been able to calm his stomach and find peace in the comfort of his bed when Frank charged into his room, screaming at him to wake up and get ready for school. Nick tried to reason with him but was unsuccessful. With little energy left, he was forced to struggle to get up and walk to school. Once there, his teacher knew Nick was ill. She sent him to the school's nursing station. He trod down the hall as slow as he could, feeling like he was walking to his own funeral. He knew they'd call home and he was paralyzed with fear. His dad was home, working on some sort of presentation, and you didn't interrupt Frank Carney when he was working or drinking.

Nick did his best to lie to the nurse, telling her he felt fine, he was up late, nothing more. After taking his temperature, the nurse wasn't buying his story. Nick begged her to stay so he could sleep it off. Sleep was all he wanted. Peace and sleep away from home, away from 'him.' She didn't listen to the young, sick boy. She couldn't. School protocol dictated she calls his parents to have him picked up. Five minutes after the call Frank Carney showed up at school, surprising Nick with his swiftness. Frank was all smiles, laughing and joking, charming the young secretaries in the front office. He apologized to the nurse for sending Nick to school. He hadn't realized his son was ill. *The boy hadn't said a word, such an independent little man, he was.*

When in the privacy of their home, Nick could hit his dad with a few harsh words and insults every now and then, but he would never counter his father's claims in public, no matter how untrue or ridiculous they seemed. He knew better. His father held out his hand, Nick reached for it, and the two walked out of school looking like the perfect father and son. Once in the car, there was dead silence. The drive was short, and when they reached the driveway, Frank looked at Nick. "Do you know why I came and got you?" Nick had no idea but knew it wasn't out of the goodness of his heart.

"You messed up the bathroom pretty bad last night. The smell is so bad I had to work downstairs. You need to clean it."

Nick didn't care. He was too sick to fight. The best he could muster was a "yes, sir." He kept his anger with Frank for another day—a moment in his life when he could harness it for something bigger and use it to his advantage.

With a relatively clean face, Nick looked up at the camera and smiled. He could see the naked man in the thong slipping away in disgust. He wasn't sure if the man fell victim to some projectile liquid, but Nick hoped he had. It served him right for being out here naked, distracting the riders, in his attempt to capture some air time. Nick focused on the road up ahead. He could see a slow-moving blur that looked like the remaining five riders. "Antoine, is that the break?"

"It is, Nick. I can see five guys. That's it. You're going for the stage win now. Are you okay back there? Did you just puke?"

"I'm fine now. My stomach was feeling a bit uneasy. Let's catch these guys. Let's win the stage."

CHAPTER 24

Stage 9

Losing Ground, but He's Got Love

It wasn't long before Antoine and Nick rolled past the five remaining survivors. A couple of them jumped on the back of the Antoine Doucette train, tucked behind Nick, hoping that they could keep pace. They'd been dreaming all day of potential glory, and now they were only five kilometers away from leaving their mark on this year's Tour, and in the history books. They didn't want the pain they'd endured for four long hours to go unrewarded, but they were no match for the speed of the two fresher riders. They were able to last a few hundred meters, teeth clenched tightly, and shoulders rolled forward before the steepness of the ascent caused them to surrender. As opportunist riders, they'd have more stages in this year's race to stamp their authority.

Antoine looked around. "Are they gone?" he shouted at Nick.

"Every last one of them. We're on our own. Just give me one more kilometer. We've got this," Nick shouted back.

The crowd was becoming denser the further up the climb they soared. The fans were still relatively tame, but they knew as they approached the peak, the crazier fans would come out to play. Nick was bracing himself. He kept preparing his mind for the claustrophobic tunnel of people he'd have to navigate. Going full out required the highest level of concentration, and half-naked fans running next to you shouting in a foreign language could throw you off your game. He tricked his mind with phrase after phrase. *I've got this, I've got this. People screaming at me is good. It's good. They like me. They want me to win. They like me. I've got this. I've got this.*

He was no longer thinking about his legs or his stomach. He observed Antoine's body swaying back and forth and knew it wouldn't be long now. He'd be left on his own, to bring home the win. He gathered his thoughts about Bomber and his remaining competitors. He firmly believed men like Ellington and Morkov were his competition now—Bomber would have to ride for him the remainder of the Tour. His early proclamation of the stage victory over the team radio had openly challenged Bomber, and now he had to deliver. He had to seal the overall win today. He had to exploit this moment and gain every second he could on his rivals.

Antoine pulled alongside Nick. "I'm done, champ. It's all you now. Give it. Five kilometers gets you the win." His bike came to a halt as his legs slowly turned what appeared to be a massive gear. Moments ago, his legs were spinning at over ninety revolutions per minute, and now he'd be lucky if they were registering fifteen. His head dropped begging his legs to move. The cameraman on the motto captured it on video before speeding back to the man in yellow. Antoine would be on his own now. With no energy left in his body, he'd slowly take his time cycling up the remaining kilometers getting pushed and patted on the back by fans who'd witnessed his courageous sacrifice for his leader. If he were lucky, he'd get to do this all again tomorrow.

Nick's earpiece buzzed, and it caught him off guard. It had been silent for the last few kilometers, and he enjoyed the peace. "Nick, keep it going stud. You're two minutes up on Bomber," reported Tom.

Nick squeezed his mic at his chest, "Bomber's group?" he asked.

"No, Jack is on his own. He's attacked Ellington and Morkov. They're about twenty seconds behind him. We're going to take one, two today."

Nick remained quiet. He hated hearing about Bomber, the reigning two-time Tour winner. He was a champion and a legend in Nick's eyes. But, his opinion about Bomber had changed dramatically since the beginning of the Tour. He wasn't sure if Bomber was as evil as the picture his brain was painting, but he felt that in some way Jack eerily reminded him of his father.

His father,—Frank Carney. Why was he thinking of that asshole in this critical moment? His legs began to feel heavy, and he could feel his smooth pedal strokes churn slowly as if moving through freshly poured cement. The fans became spectacles of noise and frustration, blurs of colorful obstacles blocking his line of sight; his path to victory. He didn't know if he could win now. His body felt drained. He knew puking up his liquid energy hadn't helped, but he couldn't bear the thought of taking in any food or gels at this point, in hopes of more power.

Earlier, he'd challenged Bomber, and now the man was rising to the occasion. Did he think his words wouldn't have inspired the champion? He was naive to think he had this wrapped up after his spectacular attack over the Col de Pailhères. The odds of succeeding were slim to none, but after entering Ax 3 Domaines with Antoine by his side, he believed in the possibility of victory. With his body tattered and wilting by the second, he realized he'd acted like the rookie he was. He wanted to ask Tom for an update but felt afraid. He knew he was going backward; physically and mentally.

Nick envisioned a buoyant Bomber, his body the epitome of power and prowess leaping up the mountain, gaining on the deteriorating remains of the Yellow Jersey. Nick conceded he was no longer the predator, but the prey; wounded and struggling to keep from being caught. His head dropped. He looked down at his long legs, striving to apply force to the pedals. Part of him wanted to keep his head down for the remainder of the climb. He was embarrassed and didn't want to see the joy in people's faces when he was in so much pain. His eyes caught a glimpse of names painted on the road surface. He spotted a faintly scribbled name, Froome. Probably painted way back in 2013 when Chris Froome won the Tour and demolished the competition on this climb. He then noticed a series of brighter set of names; Ellington, Bomber and his own Carney—with the number one, written beside it. He gulped with overwhelming emotion and heard a familiar voice calling his name.

Nick looked up, into the massive crowd of people and instantly caught a glimpse of Emma. Her yellow sundress, hugging the curves of her long, fit body made her stand out in a crowd of thousands. The sun bounced off her platinum blonde hair, mesmerizing Nick. As he approached, she remained quiet. His body language deterred her from being overzealous. She'd seen Nick in this state before and knew he didn't revel in positive encouragement when he was in pain. As he passed, she ran beside him, "I love you, Nick. Clear your mind, Baby. It's okay to be in pain. If you're not in pain, you're not living. Are you living, Baby?"

Nick waved her away. He wasn't in the mood to listen to her. He didn't want to hear anyone. He only wanted to escape this mountain, to be at home in the comfort of his room by himself, the lights turned off, blaring his music and dreaming of winning, of being somebody. Of being somebody? Winning? He looked up the road and saw the 'Three km To Go' sign. He could win. This could be his moment. He could be a champion. Was he in pain? Sure, but he could be suffering more. Could he be living more? Was he thoroughly entrenched in the moment? He grabbed his mic, "Update Tom. Where are we?"

"You're looking good, kid. Just hang in. You just need to get it done. Keep turning the legs."

"Yeah, yeah. Where's everyone else?"

"Bomber's only thirty-five seconds behind now, but Ellington and Morkov are a minute behind. When Jack comes up to you, I'll make sure you two ride it out together to the top, and he gives you the stage win. You had a good go the past week, kid. We're proud of you."

Nick didn't care to respond. The team had written him off, and now his body was feeling energized. He could hear the cheers of the crowd, and his legs began moving faster. He looked down at his power meter and watched his numbers rise. He cleared his head from everything— his mind empty, his every thought forgotten; only regaining a semblance of consciousness when he found himself collapsed on the ground, vomiting once more and surrounded by journalists asking questions.

CHAPTER 25

Stage 9

Feeling lost is like having your head in the clouds

Saunders was the first to question him, but Nick had no answers. He shook his head, wiped his mouth and replied, "Well, you and the entire world saw what happened. I think you have a good idea."

Saunders didn't waste any time moving on to the next question, "We saw you struggling for a kilometer or two, midway up the climb, before regaining steam and bulldozing through the crowd. Did you run out of energy? What got you moving again?"

"The need to survive. The will to live. Without the effort, the race, the people cheering for me, I have nothing."

The questions continued, and Saunders was impressed with Carney's answers. They were brilliant, and he was sure cycling fans everywhere were eating it up.

Nick could read the expressions of the journalists surrounding him. They were in awe, inspired and hanging on his every word. But Nick wasn't sure how to navigate their questions. He could only remain obtuse for so long. He needed a moment away from the frenzy to gather his thoughts and assess what transpired. His last memory was that of Emma, running alongside him asking him questions. He had been suffering, and Tom had reported that Bomber had been gaining time on him. He remembered feeling that he was going to lose it all; the stage and the Tour lead. Then it all went black.

It wasn't the first time Nick had blacked out and forgot large chunks of time. In his early years, when his father's presence became overwhelmingly menacing, his words too hurtful, Nick would retreat to his room for hours. He wouldn't fall asleep, but when he emerged, he couldn't account for the lost time. It had just disappeared without a trace. The only evidence alerting him to the problem was the clocks in the house.

He struggled to his feet and started moving away from the gathered journalists, who kept the questions firing. The race's press secretary, Nicole Darby, grabbed him and brought him to the press tent where Nick changed into a fresh kit and gathered his thoughts. Willie was just behind him with a bag filled with Nick's favorite recovery drink, sports wipes, and a towel. As they settled on the hard fold out chairs, Nick unzipped his sweat-drenched jersey and began removing it. Willie grabbed the sports wipes and started patting down Nick's neck and face. "You looked great out there, kid. Tom and I couldn't contain ourselves. I'm sorry if you had to keep listening to us screaming in your ear. We just couldn't believe where you were finding those legs."

Nick could only give him a blank expression. He wanted to ask him what happened, but he wasn't sure how Willie would interpret the question. The last thing he wanted was his team booting him out of the Tour for being psychologically unstable. Nick's brain went into overdrive trying to remember. Sitting in the finishing tent alone, with no sign of Bomber, he realized he'd won the stage. The blackness that encompassed the lost time haunted him. It had him contemplating the idea that he may have multiple personalities. He burst out laughing. His imagination was taunting him, and his hypochondriac tendencies were getting the better of him.

"What's so funny?" asked Willie.

"Nothing. I just can't remember shit. It's all a fucking blur."

"Yeah, without a doubt, Nick. You were in the zone."

They both laughed, and Nick asked him to pass one of the small portable iPads set up in the tent so he could see some race footage. The feed was live, but hopefully, he could catch a glimpse of a replay, listen to what the commentaries were reporting, and get a sense of time gaps. He needed something before he fielded official questions from the press.

Willie handed him an iPad and Nick watched small groups of his peer's trickle to the finish. Each racer looked exhausted but satisfied to be finished. The result screen popped up, and he finally had a chance to see how he did. He won, beating Bomber by a minute and three seconds, with Ellington and Morkov finishing a further twenty-five seconds back. How did he do it?

Before he'd lost track of the time, he was going backward and losing his time advantage. He'd only had thirty seconds on Jack. How had he beaten the man by a minute? He handed Willie back the iPad just in time. Nicole was leading journalists and cameramen into the media tent to gather around Nick. As an English-speaking rider, he'd be interviewed by either Robert Saunders or Pete Davies from the Guardian. He was hoping it'd be the latter, and that it would be quick. He didn't have time to go into a lot of detail. He'd given Saunders what the reporter wanted after the stage, but this would be his official post-race interview, and he knew Saunders would demand a more elaborate and colorful account.

Nick looked up and spotted Pete Davies and felt sheer relief. Saunders was nowhere to be seen. He either wasn't permitted after last year's stunt with Bomber, or he was compiling his story to ensure it syndicated globally, without haste. Nick didn't give it any further thought. Davies approached him and reached out for a fist bump.

"Congrats, Champ. You looked amazing out there today. Give us about thirty seconds, and we'll start the official interview."

"Sounds good," said Nick.

"So proud of you man. That was one hell of a show you put on out there."

Nicole looked at the cameraman. The interviews needed to begin. The world was tuning in to listen to the Yellow Jersey recount his stage victory.

Davies looked down at his mic, got the head nod from Nicole and began.

"Well Nick, we are nine stages into this Tour. You've been leading since the beginning. The underdog, here to help two-time Tour Victor Jack Bomber win his third, and you've beaten the Champion on his own terrain."

"Yeah, it was a tough stage. It was windy. Extremely windy. And guys were all over the road. I just kept asking our big man Welte to keep me safe, keep me out of the wind. Next thing you know, guys on the team are disappearing left, right, and center and our Director is screaming that Bomber has a mechanical. It was a pretty critical moment. And, like, Morkov and his team chose to take advantage of it, and..."

Davies interrupted, happy to be getting a descriptive account of the race. "It was a critical point, indeed. You and Welte were on your own. Did you feel isolated? Did you feel the team had abandoned you?"

"They were gone. We were alone. It made things more difficult. We were staying positive, and we were getting feedback from the car. We weren't worried. Then my chain broke. It just snapped. That's when the shit really hit the fan."

"Did you think it was over at that point?"

"I figured we were in a pretty big hole, and it was going to take a big effort to get back. An effort that was going to cost me, and the whole team later, but they did a solid job bringing me back to the group."

"You get onto the Col de Pailhères, and the attacks started early with Ellington and Morkov's men driving the pace. You looked in difficulty then you were gone."

"Yeah, I knew I had to pace it out after our chase to catch back up. I knew my body needed a bit to recover, before going into the red. Honestly, I didn't mean to attack. Once I got going, I just found a solid rhythm and rode away. No one came with me. I was gone."

"You made your way up to your teammate Antoine, who'd been in the early break. He helped pace you to Ax 3 before you were on your own. You seemed to struggle for a bit, before dancing up the climb. There was vomit involved?"

Nick laughed. He remembered that moment clearly—being with Antoine and vomiting a sticky chocolate substance all over a fan. "The stomach wasn't feeling that good. The gels didn't sit well. The poor guy running beside me, but yeah, I struggled a bit with my energy level, but found my rhythm and just pounded the pedals out at my own pace."

"Were you aware Bomber was just behind you at one point?"

"Yeah, I knew he was coming up."

"Did that influence you to ride harder? There was speculation that you were slowing down to help pace him. Were there any orders at any point from the team?"

Damn. Could there have been? Surely there weren't any. None that he could remember. If there had been, Willie would have mentioned something before the interview started. *Could Tom be giving an interview at this very moment that contradicts what I'm about to say? What about Bomber, what could he be telling the world? Will I find himself reprimanded later this evening? Will Tom, Willie, and Wendy scold me like a little boy? A child who rebelled against team orders and continued to bring shame to the team. Wait, no. Everyone is happy about this win. What am I worried about?* He played it safe. "No orders that I can remember. Honestly, I had to rip my earpiece out and concentrate the best I could. I was in survival mode and only wanted to finish as quickly as I could. If it looked easy, like I was dancing out there, it wasn't. I was in pure hell. It was so bad. Like, I was struggling and just wanted it over. Yeah, lots of pain. You know." He liked how it came out. It was the truth, mixed in with an abundant amount of words to describe pain and suffering.

"Thanks, Nick. Brilliant."

The interview finished. He'd be fine. No one other than Emma needed to know about his momentary amnesia. In a few minutes, he would move on to the podium stage, shake the hands of tour officials and political dignitaries, accept another yellow jersey from the podium girls, a bouquet of flowers for Emma, and the customary stuffed lion. Afterward, he would do it all over again, except this time for the stage win. He'd receive a bottle of champagne, which he would open and spray all over the crowd of spectators, as well as a small commemorative plaque highlighting his win today. Once off the stage, he would be presented with a dozen celebratory yellow jerseys that needed to be signed. These would go to charities, auctions and influential businessmen who helped sponsor the race.

Nick would be glad when it was over. He'd do a short cooldown on one of the trainer bikes lined up by the team bus, then head down the mountain to their hotel. Based on the number of fans on Ax 3 Domaines, it was estimated it would take an hour to get down. Nick was thankful for the luxurious accommodations of the bus and would remain relaxed, but he was anxious to see Emma.

After exiting the doping control center, Nick made his way to the team bus. He couldn't escape handshake after handshake, pats on the back, high fives and fist bumps. Every rider, Team Director, and team personnel wanted to congratulate the Yellow Jersey. Nick had been the talk of the Tour since day one, but today felt special. His peers were looking at him differently. He no longer felt like the warm-up act before the headliner of a concert. He was the boss of the Tour now, a commander with authority and validity. He could walk big, talk big, and people would listen. He earned it.

He stepped onto the bus, and applause broke out. Teammates rushed to his side to hug him and adorn him with kisses. Their faces were etched with huge smiles, but there was an underlying fatigue lurking. Their cheeks had become sunken and empty, making their eyes look as if they were bulging out of their skull. It was reminiscent of cartoon-like chihuahuas. Antoine wouldn't stop hugging him and hung on to him, whispering in his ear. "You did it, man. You won. I knew you would do it."

Nick was quick to correct him. "We did it. You and me. This is your win, as much as it's mine. I couldn't have done this without you. I love you, man. Thanks. Thank you."

Willie interrupted the team celebration. "Okay, guys. Let's get out there and spin the legs. They're estimating it will take ninety minutes to get off this mountain. I don't want you guys sitting here getting stiff. The soigneurs will be around with additional recovery drinks and goodies if you need them. Everything is roped off, so no talking to the media. No matter how much they pester, not a word. Understood?" Everyone shook their head, moaned, and complied. They couldn't have cared less about talking. The struggle would be to get back on the bike after having spent the last five hours suffering on it. And to sit there on a trainer for thirty minutes going nowhere. At least it beat sitting on a bus…going nowhere.

Nick peeked across the bus. He made his way to his to seat to grab his cooldown kit to get dressed. He stopped Willie. "Where's Tom and Jack?"

"Tom is finishing up some interviews with Eurosport. He'll be driving the car down with some of our sponsors. The CEO of Apex was here today. He is thrilled with your victory. Tom wants to entertain him. You know, corporate stuff. Keep him happy. Jack is with them. He's already cooled down. He's ready to go. Alright champ, let's get going."

Nick wasn't happy. So much for thinking he was the boss.

CHAPTER 26

Jack Bomber is Machiavellian

The car that was supposed to contain Bomber, Tom, and the CEO was winding its way slowly down the mountainside, except the CEO, Paul Corrinder wasn't present. The Executive Officer of Apex chose to use his personal helicopter to get him off the mountain peak quicker. With money comes privilege, and there was no way he was going to subject himself to an hour and a half of idle time. This left Bomber alone with Tom, which is what Bomber wanted.

The tinted windows were dark enough to protect Bomber from being recognized, but the team signage along the side of the car incurred long stares from adoring fans hoping that it may be Nick Carney. It could be their chance to get an autograph or a picture with the rising star. Others were just happy to be making their way down through the traffic, after spending the better half of the day waiting to see their cycling gladiators fight it out on the final climb.

Bomber and Tom sat in silence for fifteen minutes. Neither one acknowledged the deep sighs of the other. Bomber wanted Tom to feel uncomfortable. Today was a complete fuck up, and he knew the silence was making Tom uneasy. Bomber finally turned to Tom, "What the fuck happened out there today?"

"Relax, Jack. It was a tough day. A lot of things didn't go our way, then they did. We won, and we're sitting pretty as a team."

"We won. But the wrong guy on the team won. The team captain got left behind. I looked like a complete fuck up, second rate."

"Nick was on a good day. I have to give him the chance to be co-leader Jack. He's riding well, and his numbers look good. He's recovering and getting stronger every day."

"Who gives a fuck? He's a rookie. We brought him here to support me, Tom. I helped recruit him, remember. I've been rather blasé this whole time, but today was a pivotal stage. To walk away like he did. I was going full gas, and I couldn't catch him. Fuck retiring at the end of the year. I'm more than happy to retire tonight."

"Relax, Jack. Calm down. Don't be hasty. I understand where you're coming from, but I have the press, and now the CEO of Apex throwing their support behind the kid. He's getting huge media exposure. I need to support him."

"This is about business?" asked Bomber.

"Come on, Jack. Don't act naive. At this level, you know the only thing that matters is winning, and how much money the sponsors can generate from media exposure. Right now, the cards are in his favor."

"So, what your best guy is put out to pasture? See you the fuck later? Thanks for the past two Tour wins, but you're not good enough anymore."

There was a solid thump on the roof of the car from a few spectators, causing the two men to jump in their seats. Tom slammed the brakes. His eyes had been locked on Jack for far too long. He almost took out a group of orange-clad Basque fans. The traffic was now jammed, and the car sat idle. Tom chose to turn it off to fully concentrate on how to best handle Bomber's ego. His stomach was churning, but it could have been the tuna sandwich he and Willie had for lunch. While he wished it was the sandwich causing his distress, he knew it was the pressure he was feeling from Jack.

"You're the best I've ever worked with Jack. You're the reigning Tour Champion, and this is your race. We still have a week left. You know better than anyone how quickly things can change. You have my full support and always will, but I need to support Nick as well. He's earned it."

Jack huffed, crossed his arms and leaned deep into his seat like a spoiled child.

"He's earned shit. He's so fucking green, Tom. Splitting the team like this to support both of us is a mistake. Look what happened today. If we go into tomorrow and into the Alpes next week with the team divided neither one of us is going to win. And, and, well fuck it. I'm in second, but I'm over four minutes down. This little shit may win this fucking Tour. I'm going home. You did this Tom. You fucked it all up."

Bomber reached for the door and pulled the handle. Tom reached over to stop him, his eyes wide open I disbelief, glaring at Bomber's erratic action. "What are you doing?! You can't go out there. You'll get mobbed!"

"I told you, I'm done."

"Jack, sit down. I've never seen you like this before. It was a grueling day. You're not thinking right. You've got my support. Let me figure something out. We can make this work. You want to win, let's get you the win."

"You mean that, Tom?"

"Yeah, of course, I do. The race is far from finished. Let's work on a plan."

Jack let go of the door handle, feeling lighter and freer than he had moments ago. "Planning is good Tom. I've already started the process. I'm working on Ellington and Morkov. They should be strong allies the rest of the Tour."

The remnants of Tom's sandwich was now burning the back of his throat. He felt disgusted and trapped, confined to a cage, and being taunted and played with by a prey much more prominent than he. He couldn't find the right words to respond to Bomber. In fact, he couldn't find any words at all for a very long time. Finally, he nodded and smiled before finally blurting out, "Tell me more."

CHAPTER 27

TRANSITION

Stage 10

Coping with the Aftermath!
Nothing is as it Seems!

The Tour had ended four months ago, but the events that transpired in the final week were caught in a time loop in Nick's head. Like the movie Groundhog Day, he kept re-living one scene after another, trying his best to get it right; to make it happen the way it should have. He had memorized every second of every stage, every minute of every interaction with teammates, with Emma, with the media—anything that bore meaning or significance. It kept him trapped on the couch, wrapped up in blankets, wearing nothing more than his boxers and an old ripped T-shirt. His face was peppered with a beautiful coat of scruff, and his hair was longer and greasier than usual.

He reached for the remote and his glass of Bourbon. It was only ten in the morning, but it was a cold rainy day in Ottawa. There was no need to train, no need to be strict with the diet. He flipped to a music channel so he could watch videos. He was hoping for a full array of hip-hop videos so he could watch half-naked women shaking their oversized booties.

A full box of double stuffed Oreos laid to his left. He grabbed the first, twisted the top off and slowly licked the white delicious cream. He savored the sweetness, the sugar dancing across his taste buds. A sip of bourbon would follow, the sugar of the Oreo acted as a precursor to bringing out the flavor of the strong alcohol. The crunchy portion of the famous cookie would be discarded, and Nick would move on to the next cookie. By the end of the day, the box of Oreos and the bottle of bourbon would be finished.

After the tenth cookie, Nick's stomach protested ever so slightly. He looked out the window of his Westboro condo, and his gaze caught the harsh rain pounding the pavement. The booze couldn't numb what came next. His mind conjured up negative thoughts and images about the Tour.

He'd had an insurmountable lead over his teammate Jack Bomber, and thought he had the Tour wrapped up. Isn't that what the media had said? He recalled listening to Robert Saunders on the team bus's radio as it slowly wound down the densely packed Mountain of Ax 3 Domaines after he conquered the mountain and increased his lead. Robert had said the Tour was over, and it wasn't just his opinion. Carl and Allen, both highly respected and experienced journalist, agreed. Even journalists who were staunch supporters of Bomber agreed; a four-minute deficit in the modern Tour was too big to overcome. A casual spectator could be forgiven for believing that a race with a thousand kilometers and four difficult mountain stages could wipe away 4 measly minutes, but experienced observers knew better. The display of power and dominance by Nick Carney meant it was game over, notwithstanding a crash or a major meltdown.

It didn't matter if he was a rookie and only twenty-three. He was a professional and was riding for one of the best teams in the world. He was surrounded by experienced riders who would keep him protected so that he used as little energy as possible, sparing it for the decisive moments that counted.

When off the bike, he would be catered to like a king. His meals would be prepared by an experienced chef who would ensure he had the precise amount of carbohydrates to fuel his muscles. Protein would be added to smoothies, and his supper would contain lean cuts of meat or fatty fish. He needed iron to repair destroyed red blood cells and healthy fat to combat inflammation. Food was fuel, and without the right combination, he might as well be a Ferrari trying to run on non-synthetic oil.

But the Tour is not won until you cross the finish line, and Nick couldn't stop his mind from thinking about that god damn second day in the mountains. He wished he could forget the pain he'd endured. Unfortunately, there was no memory loss to conceal the hatred building within him. How could he have been so stupid? It would be his explosive, heroic act the day before on the Col de Pailhères and Ax 3 Domaines that lead him to difficulty the on the steep slopes of the Hautacam. That day The weather had been grey and bleak, much like today. Heavy rains had exploded from the sky, pounding the rider's bodies with a mixture of massive raindrops and tiny ice pellets. Before the stage, the riders had clamored to their team cars and buses seeking shelter. Even though they were adorned with expensive Gore-Tex wind and rain protective gear, they still used wool blankets and blasted the heat from the cars to stay warm. Most needed to be coaxed to the start line, and no one was prepared to attack and get going. Nick couldn't recall if there'd been any early attacks, but if there were, it was based on pure survival, and the need to stay warm.

He remembered his body shaking uncontrollably. His hands going numb, his legs freezing and his bones aching. Emma had decided to stay at the start line to comfort Nick. She'd wrapped her arms around his frozen body, and despite the cameras and the fans, she graced him with multiple kisses. She reminded him that he was the Champion, the man to beat and that he 'd be up to the challenge.

As a Canadian, Nick had faced worse weather conditions, but he still tried to find courage in a memory: At sixteen, his father had ignored Nick's pleas to pick him up when he became stranded on a training ride. He was caught, eighty kilometers away from home, in a snowstorm that broke through the early spring clouds. His father refused to drive out and get him, even though Nick begged, cried and bargained for a ride. With no other options, Nick endured close to three hours of riding—no surviving—in freezing temperatures, as a late-season winter storm blanketed the ground with a foot of snow. His hands were bare, his legs exposed, and he suffered frostbite on the tips of his fingers. Nick knew he overcame adversity that day and he wanted to believe he'd do it again. But, he was cold—freezing, and he sensed his body failing him.

Nick had welcomed the warmth of Emma's body and her positive encouragement before the start of that day. But it wouldn't be enough. Nothing would be. Had he known what was in store for him, he may have decided to stay in the arms of his lover.

Nick's phone rang, vibrating the glass table containing his bourbon and Oreos. His mind momentarily jumped out of the past to focus on his call display. Emma was calling from work to check in. The awful weather and the time of year, being offseason, had set Nick's mind free, wandering to the past and dwelling heavily on the Tour. It hadn't escaped Emma's notice.

Nick had shown signs of diversion and obsessive thought tendencies in the early weeks after the Tour ended, but it had become progressively worse as his time on the bike decreased. The atrocious rain day after day had left Emma picking up empty bottles of scotch, bourbon, and vodka scattered on their coffee table.

Multiple times she'd come home to find Nick intoxicated, lying wrapped in blankets on the couch or asleep in a half-filled bathtub. The questioning didn't get her anywhere, but she was happy to give him some leeway. It was the offseason, right? The strict life and diet of a pro athlete were all-consuming, and she needed to give him the time he deserved to relax. In a few weeks, he'd be attending his first team camp and getting ready for next season. He'd be surrounded by teammates and staff and would bike the alcohol and last year's Tour out of his system.

Nick groaned. Picking up the phone meant abandoning his thoughts. It felt like quitting. It felt like that freezing, frigid day on the slope of Hautacam when in the heat of the moment he dropped his head and surrendered to the pain. He had a choice that day, didn't he? And he quit. Not the race, but he resigned at that moment. He rode up the final three kilometers trailing Bomber, Morkov, and Ellington. He got passed by lesser men and cursed violently under his breath.

Nick pressed the green button of his iPhone to accept her call but remained silent. "Hey, Babe. How's it going? How are you doing with all this rain?" asked Emma.

He wanted to continue to ignore her badgering. "I'm doing great. I'm good."

"Are you sure? Do you need me to bring you home anything?"

"Nope. I've got everything I neeeeeds," he slurred, the alcohol affecting his speech.

"How much have you drunk today?"

"Just a…a…a bit. Washing it down with some Oreos."

She hesitated, her insecurity getting the better of her. Part of her thought it was her fault. Perhaps, she hadn't done enough for the man she loves. She refused to cry, knowing that it would only upset Nick further.

"Okay, well I love you. I just wanted to say, hi. I'll see you when I get home."

"Same, Bae. See you later."

He hung up the phone, tears welling up in his eyes. He wished he could have said more to her. It was a simple conversation, and even though he knew she wasn't interrogating him, he couldn't stop himself from being defensive with her. He felt nothing but unconditional, unequivocal love for her, but there was a numbness that had taken over his cognitive capacities, like a vine that strangled the life out of a beautiful flower.

Nick felt the need to fill the emptiness within, and he reached for more bourbon. A sip or two would definitely have him feeling *something*. Once the alcohol touched his lips, he remembered the excitement and optimism he and his teammates had felt after his victory on Ax 3 Domaines. Tom had allowed the team and staff to toast his success with an honorary glass of champagne. They sat around the table shooting the shit. It was still early in the race, but there were talks of overall victory. Bomber may have been distant and silent, even leaving early, but most of the other guys were full of enthusiasm and optimism.

After supper, Nick had a few one-on-one interviews with journalists, but nothing that overwhelmed him. They were quick, concise and allowed him to spend much of his evening with Emma. He spoke to her at length about his achievement and his memory loss. She reassured him that his ability to focus was an exceptional gift, endowed upon a man who could push himself to his limit. It calmed his nerves and allowed him to relax and rest his body. He loved having her there. His soulmate sharing in his glory, their glory. He shared with her what his achievement would bring to them. It would bump up his status in the cycling world, his pay grade, and their life together would benefit from his success. His dream was now hers as well, and he knew it was up to him to take care of her. On more than one occasion, she'd picked up the pieces of his entangled and shattered soul. Now it was his turn to repay her. But that day, that fucking stupid freezing cold, rainy day on Hautacam ruined everything, or at least that's how Nick felt at the time.

Nick couldn't stop the memories of that day flooding his brain. "Leave me the fuck alone!" he screamed out loud. "It was one shitty moment, get the fuck out of my head!" But that moment had been pivotal. At least he thought so. At that moment he'd quit, and it changed everything. The dynamic of the race, the team's support, even the journalist, who'd supported his quest for victory the previous evening, seemed to abandon him.

He breathed deeply, grabbed another Oreo, and for the second time in less than an hour began vividly thinking about Hautacam, and the moment he dropped his head. *I quit. I quit right there and then. I had them on the ropes, and my legs gave out. They went heavy, and my mind became consumed with doubt. It should never have happened. It was all Tom's fucking fault. Him and the team's physiologist, Paul, placed that doubt in my god damn head.*

When Nick woke the morning of Hautacam, he had gone for his early morning checkup with Paul; a series of medical tests to assess his physiological readiness. It went badly. Really badly. Paul had tried to hide his concern, but Nick read his body language with the astuteness of a detective. Paul left the room in haste, refusing to speak with Nick alone. Moments later Tom appeared. He tried to sugarcoat the situation, but Nick broke him, badgering him repeatedly for the results—ALL RED. His body was in shambles from the day before. Tom made it clear that it wasn't a matter of *if* he would crack, but *when.*

And Nick did. He CRACKED!

Fuck, he lost it big time. When he had the guys on the rope, suffering, gasping for air in his draft, Tom and Paul's voice grew from a whisper to a roar. Their insistence that everything was in the red, that he would crack, started to have an impact on him. One moment his legs were supple and sturdy, with a mind that was clear and focused on execution, and the next their premonition of cracking devoured his consciousness. His legs went heavy, and he yielded. He began to break.

Nick snapped out of the past and took another look outside. Still raining. Still grey, cold and miserable. He was trapped. Alone and confined to his house. Being mind-fucked by his thoughts. It wasn't only Tom that had irked him that day. Bomber had made comments before the start. Everyone had been shivering, cold and bundled up, but Bomber singled him out as the team rode to the start line. He recalled Bomber stating that he looked like he was pedaling squares. Medical information should've been kept private, but Nick was confident that Bomber learned of his diagnosed condition from Paul that morning. What was Bomber's part in all of this?

The pivotal moment during the stage when Nick had Bomber and the rest of the top riders trailing his Yellow Jersey, hanging on for dear life, he was confident he heard Bomber mumble, "Don't crack, kid." Fans had been only inches away, screaming in his ears, but he knew what he'd heard. And at that moment, his legs went weak. His heart rate skyrocketed, his body wobbled, and he went dizzy. It felt like an eternity, everything was moving slowly as Bomber, Morkov, and Ellington forced their bikes around him, advancing ahead.

The overhead helicopter captured the three riders leaving Carney behind. His bike and body were swaying back and forth like a teeter totter out of control. A bird's eye view was telling, and the widening gap between the men and the boy in yellow was revealing. A flood of fans on the mountainside opened a pathway for the leaders. People were running hysterically beside Nick, waving their hands and shouting. Some were tapping him on the shoulders, while other's tried to give him a push. He furiously waved them off. He was cracking. The leader was going backward losing time—this could be the moment he lost the Tour. It may not happen today, but this could be the catalyst, and if it was, people wanted to be part of it.

Back in the present, Nick took a deep breath and slammed his fist down on the table beside him. *I owned those mother fuckers. My power was beyond good. When I lost my form, they should've as well. We all should've slowed down. I don't give a shit about what Tom and Paul said. They were wrong. Could it have been something in my last bottle? Who handed it to me from the car? Tom, yeah, it was Tom. What did he do to me?*

Nick had the right to be concerned. After receiving his medical report before the stage, he'd called his brother, his coach, Alex. They spoke about his data and his effort the day before. Alex assured him that while he went deep, he appeared to be recovered. He needed to take care of himself during the stage because of the terrain, it's length and his accumulated fatigue. Yet, his body betrayed him, left him for dead in a critical moment. *Why did it happen? Why? It cost me so much...*

Nick's head began spinning. The alcohol confusing his thoughts further and further. He grabbed the remote and turned the television on again. Like a good, but obsessed, detective he prepared to research his newest theory. He pressed guide on the remote, locating the recording of stage twelve to Hautacam. Soon enough he'd have his answers. He fast forwarded over five hours of the recorded video until he reached footage of the flat terrain before the climb to Hautacam. He watched as Nick on the TV grabbed a bottle from the lead car as Tom smiled and handed it over slowly. *It was Tom. Did he drug me? No, he wouldn't do that. It would be too risky. The liquid in the bottle was sweet. Perhaps too sweet. Did I go hypoglycemic?*

Another Oreo found its way to Nick's mouth, and he gingerly licked the white sugar filling until it was all gone. The actual cookie was discarded again, and he took a swig of bourbon straight from the bottle. At this point, he no longer cared to carefully measure out his portions into his glass. He fast forwarded the video again. This time, stopping the video at the base of the climb. He needed to listen to the Eurosport commentators and their race analysis one more time.

Since the time the race had ended, Nick had reviewed this stage a thousand times, but with his new found evidence he wanted to listen intently, to see if any of the journalists knew what was coming. He conjured up what he believed to be an accurate memory; Robert Saunders lurking around Tom and Bomber before the stage. *Had they given him a heads up about what was coming? They knew he was a big supporter of mine. Did they share the team's medical finding? Did they want to tell him that I would be cracking? It could have been an "I told you so moment" for Tom and Jack.*

He turned up the volume so that Carl, Allen, and Saunders' voices drowned out the pounding rain on the window. He stared and listened. His team moved to the front, ready to put their plan into action. The first rider to set the pace for Team Apex was Bradley. He looked strong. His thin, gangly upper body remained still and silent, as his legs turned over the gears smoothly. His eyes remained hidden behind his Oakley glasses, hiding the tears that formed as the pain slowly took over his body. He showed no sign he was hurting. His facial muscles appeared relaxed, ensuring his mouth remained only slightly open. He was breathing deeply, expanding his diaphragm in a controlled manner, 1, 2, 3, 4, breath in, 1, 2, breathe out. Carl was the first to comment on the current situation, "With Bradley putting on the pressure so early into the climb, and the rest of Team Apex together in tow, it means Carney is feeling good and may be looking to do something. We know he put out a lot of energy yesterday, but he's young and should have recovered well enough to go at it again."

"It may be difficult, no matter how badly he wants it. Heck, it's what we all want, but he put on a grand spectacle for the world yesterday. I just really hope he's recovered well and has the legs to stay at the front. I suppose we'll find out in a few minutes," said Saunders.

Nick stopped the recording, rewound and played back Saunders' statement a few more times. It sounded like the bastard knew. *He fucking knew. I knew it.* He let the video resume. Allen had been optimistic about Carney's chances of staying out front, so why wasn't Saunders? Saunders was predicting Carney's demise, while Allen focused on the race and the riders—calling out the names of the riders struggling and going out the back. "There goes the World Champion Peter Denich, he's not a climber and that's expected. Is that Tommy Celtic from the US? And wow, there goes Denebourgh from Belgium. Pinot, Madach, Delridge, Thomson, that's unexpected. It's raining, but it must feel like an inferno out there. There are plenty of riders unable to keep pace as Bradley drills it hard."

Nick kept watching as a dozen or so riders, unable to cope with Bradley's pace were dropped and left behind; there would be plenty more as Welte, the big Belgian moved forward to take over. Small groups of four to six riders would get dropped every fifty to a hundred meters, and each time the commentators identified the victim's world-class resumes. The group of men Nick had gone into battle with during the month of July were nothing short of superhuman specimens; their genetic, physical make-up and their ability to dominate their sport were naked to the blind eye. A basketball player's physical makeup could be identified by his height, an NFL lineman by his overall size, but a cyclist's genetics were hidden. Most people thought a cyclist's physical aptitude was the result of only hard training, or worse, induced by drugs. But it wasn't. Nick took a moment and smiled. He chose to be kind to himself for a brief moment and admire his fellow cyclist in action.

He watched as Welte finished his pull, and the leading group was whittled down to the top contenders. Nick's Spanish teammates and Bomber were still with him, along with Morkov and Ellington. Roberto and Jose had strict orders to ride full gas until the five-kilometer mark. Before the stage, the team had figured out that the Spanish rider's tempo would put everyone into the red—suffering. Only the strongest men would be left standing. If things went to plan, Tom believed that only Nick, Bomber, Morkov and Ellington would remain.

Once Jose was done with his pull, Nick put the video into slow motion. This section had become a concern to him in recent months. He watched as Bomber, who was just behind him, waves to Ellington and Morkov to come through and provide him with additional shelter. He still couldn't figure out why Bomber did this, and more importantly, why the other two men agreed. Even the commentators seemed confused. He rewound the video and turned his attention to the commentary.

"Are we seeing Bomber on a bad day, or a perfect day?" asked Carl.

"I think we're seeing the Bomber of old. Look at Carney slowing and moving side to side. I think Bomber's realized Carney may not be feeling good today. He's got the other two men marking Nick, helping to pull, while he plays dead. He is such a tactician. This man never fails to impress me," stated Allen in awe.

"I think you guys are both right. We're seeing a stronger Bomber today. I'm confused why Ellington and Morkov aren't sitting back. You'd think they were amateurs the way they so easily complied to Bomber's demands when he flicked his elbow," said Saunders.

"Let me ask you something, Robert. Are we seeing Carney in trouble here? Could he be having a difficult day?" asked Carl.

"Yeah. It won't cost him the Tour. He's too far ahead, but it will eat into his lead. Look at his body language. It doesn't look good."

Allen piped up, "If you think Carney is in trouble and done for the day tweet us your answers to Eurosport #Carneyisdone."

"Mother Fucker…fuck…fuck…fuck" yelled Nick at the TV. He took an Oreo out of the package and chucked it at the television. *That's pure bullshit. At that moment in the race, I was feeling awesome. My legs were relaxed, and I thought I had everything under control. Where in the hell did Robert Saunders come up with the idea that I was suffering? How could he anticipate I would crack when I was at the front leading the race. How, Robert Saunders!?*

It didn't matter to Nick that Eurosport had received over a hundred responses from fans tweeting that they believed he was in trouble, that he looked terrible. Nick didn't buy it. He thought they saw what Saunders, Allen, and Carl were selling. He hated the fact that minutes later he would genuinely lose it. But there was no way at that moment that anyone should have been saying he was done or cracking. It was media propaganda reported by Eurosport, specifically Robert Saunders. And now, Nick believed he knew who perpetuated it; Tom and Bomber, via Saunders.

He took a deep breath, restlessly moving around on the couch, desperate to get comfortable. There was no need for more bourbon or Oreos. This was the part of the race he was waiting for, the part that consumed his every thought. His eyes burned, glazing over from the concentration of staring at the TV screen, his mouth pulled thin with tension. The TV blared.

"He's cracking. The Yellow Jersey is slipping away, going backward!" yelled Carl.

"Is this the beginning of the end?" questioned Allen.

"He's in real difficulty, and there's no doubt that Jack Bomber will take advantage of his condition," stated Saunders.

Nick leaned in, elbows on his knees, trying to get as close to the screen as possible. Morkov has been the first to move around him and surge. Ellington followed, with Bomber in tow, sheltering him from the strong gusts of wind. "He looks bad. Really bad. He's not having a good day. Every rider has an off day at the Tour, and it appears that Carney is having his. We'll have to see how he handles it and how much time he loses. He has a four-minute lead over Bomber, six and a half over Ellington and seven minutes on Morkov. He'll lose time today, but not the jersey," said Carl.

"Yeah. You're absolutely right. He just needs to pedal and keep some momentum, but he's looking like he's in bad shape. Perhaps he's been hit with the hunger knock," Allen said.

Saunders agreed, "He's gone. This is bad. He's suffering and struggling to even stay on his bike. He's hit a wall and looks like he's going to tip over."

Nick continued watching the footage as it went back and forth between his desperate attempt to survive and the three leaders riding away. Bomber would go on to win the stage, raise his arms in victory with his left hand displaying three fingers. Bomber was like a dog marking his territory, signaling to the world that he was in pursuit of his third Tour victory. It was Ellington and Morkov who had delivered Bomber to this victory, allowing him to remain sheltered from the wind until the final meters.

Nick shook his head, lowering it in confusion, placing his forehead in his hands. Why the fuck did they do nothing? He knew why. He'd heard stories when he was younger. Riders who were paid to lose races; superstars who always needed just one more win to add to their palmarès. Some men were competitive at all costs. Their psychology was so deeply entrenched with winning that they put their victories above all else in life. Friends, family, and wealth couldn't fulfill their ego the way crossing the line first could. Jack Bomber was one of those men. A man who would ride next to you and offer you a few grand for the win. If you denied him, he would up the offer until he found your breaking point. With a salary of four million euros a year, he wasn't struggling to put food on the table. What had he offered Morkov and Ellington, thought Nick?

Nick looked up at the TV and watched fans patting his back and giving him a push, doing everything they could to encourage him to keep fighting. It looked helpful, but Nick remembered how it felt. In that moment of suffering the hands touching him were torture; it had felt like being punished at the hands of Frank Carney. It had only happened once, but he'd pushed his father, and Frank, intoxicated, pushed back. He came at him, cornered him into a small space in the family home and pummeled him with his fists. It took his older brother, Alex, to pry Frank off, and calm him down.

Nick loathed the fact he crumbled on that climb. He hated the fans for touching him; physically paralyzing him and costing him two minutes to Bomber that day. What he disliked the most at this point was not knowing whether it was the effort the day before that lead to his collapse, or was it the team working against him? Did Tom spike his bottle? Why did Morkov and Ellington appear to work for Bomber? And, how did Eurosports anticipate that he would crack before he even knew it was coming? He looked too strong at that point for them to come to that conclusion on their own—unless it was planted there by team insiders who were going to make sure Nick lost the Tour.

Who could Nick trust on the team?

CHAPTER 28

Waking up after the Conspiracy Theory

Nick woke from his slumber, with sunshine beating upon his face. His cheeks were warm and flushed, and the heat from the sun warmed his exposed body. His head was pounding, sending a jarring pain down his neck and into his shoulders. His ears were ringing, but he could hear movement nearby. He rubbed his tired eyes and looked over to find Emma in the kitchen, preparing food. "What time is it, Babe? What's for supper?"

"Supper? Try breakfast, honey. You were out cold last night. I didn't want to wake you."

"Shit. Really, eh? I'm sorry, Babe. I was going out of my mind yesterday. It was the rain."

"Just the rain, eh, babe? And nothing to do with your friend, Makers Mark Bourbon?"

Nick laughed, uneasily. "Yeah, he may have played a role in it. I'm glad to see the sun's out though. Should be a good day."

She waved him over, insisting he get off the couch and give her a kiss. She needed some love and affection. He moved slowly but eventually made his way over. He wrapped his arms around her waist, pulled her close and gave her a simple kiss. "Coffee ready?"

"Yes, Nick. I made you an egg white omelet, and there is some toast on the table with jam. Sit down and eat. You're welcome."

He thanked her, and the two sat. He became consumed with her beauty, as the sun accentuated her silky skin and her blonde hair, making her glow. She was a strong, beautiful woman stuck with a broken man. He could see the love in her eyes but sensed anger and disappointment lurking deep beneath. "I didn't mean to drink yesterday. At least not the whole bottle. I'm sorry I let myself get that way."

She reached out and took his hand, rubbing it slowly. "It's fine, Nick. Do you want to talk about it?"

He laughed out loud, shaking his head. "Same story, different day. I was back to thinking the team had conspired against me on the stage to Hautacam. I guess I can't let it go. A little OCD, wouldn't you say."

"Well, I suppose you have your reasons."

"Yeah, I do. The press and social media can really fuck you up these days, but I think I was off the wall yesterday. I wasn't even making sense to myself at some points." He laughed again, and Emma could tell he was feeling good today. He was making fun of himself and seemed in good spirits. She hadn't seen this Nick often since the Tour and wanted to cherish and hold on to every moment. She held his hand tighter and reached below the table with her other. She rubbed his inner thigh, working her hand to the inside of his shorts, grinning suggestively. Nick responded immediately, and smiled, "Do you have time before work?"

"I can be late. Let's go upstairs."

CHAPTER 29

Zwift Island Alias

Once Emma went off to work, Nick was left alone. He grabbed an Advil and hit the shower. A good, cold shower would wake him up, get his blood flowing and have him moving in the right direction. The day couldn't get much better. In thirty minutes, he'd had breakfast and made love to the woman of his dreams. He thought about everything he had. An exquisite, luxurious condo in Westboro, a BMW M3, a gorgeous, intelligent fiancée, and a seven-figure salary. At twenty-three what more could a boy want?

But sometimes, it ate away at him. Did he really want all this? Before the Tour, he thought he did, but now, he wasn't sure. Besides Emma, everything else seemed superficial. He couldn't even find the value in his cycling success. *I ride a bike for Christ sake, and I have more than the average person. Why am I not happy? It's not fair.*

He could feel them coming; pessimistic thoughts threatening his good mood and trying to take hold. He knew he needed the bike, but he didn't want to go outside. The sun was shining, but the air was crisp, cold and uninviting. Dressing in multiple layers of clothing didn't appeal to him. He decided it would be a day on the indoor trainer.

His favorite software was Zwift. A virtual world populated by cyclists hooked up on their indoor trainers. Nick would be able to get in a good workout and catch up on some gossip using discord channels, where cyclists could speak to one another while out on the virtual road. He would use his secondary profile, Andrew Boyde. He didn't want to sign in as himself. If he did, he'd have every cyclist on Zwift Island trying to ride with him. Worst, they'd all want to hound him about last year's Tour. It's not something he wanted. He yearned to be invisible; just another cyclist looking for a relaxed, spirited ride with some good people who didn't know he was Nick Carney, the pro cyclist.

He mounted his bike on the trainer and turned on his iPad to sign in. Once he was at settings, he chose the virtual bike and the gear he wanted to ride today. He was excited to ride the Tron bike, the fastest bike on Zwift Island. He put in some solid miles last winter on Zwift to earn the bike, and now he wanted to ride it to glory. He joined a coffee ride that would last two hours, clipped in his earpiece and ensured his iPad mic was on. Cyclists were already chatting about how many watts they should ride at, their current physical condition, and asking questions about training.

Andrew Boyde was not shy, freely sharing training advice. The ride commenced, and Nick settled in, twirling his legs gently. The pressure on the pedals was minimal. He relaxed, and the conversation flowed freely. A rider from the US started chirping about professional racers, and drug abuse in the sport. The discussion became heated, and Nick wasn't afraid to share his opinion. In a matter of minutes, everyone believed Andrew Boyde was either a new rider, naive, or stupid. He couldn't honestly think that riders who raced in the Tour were clean. Pro riders were entertainers who would do whatever necessary to win and keep their corporate sponsor and fans happy.

Nick felt perturbed and was ready to leave the group when the conversation suddenly changed. "Forget drugs. Who cares? Jack Bomber literally came out of retirement a minute ago. He signed with a new World Tour Team. He just tweeted," piped a rider.

If people were disappointed with Andrew Boyde's reaction to professionals and their possible drug use, they were about to get an earful of profanities from the young man.

"What the Fuck?!" shouted Nick.

Riders began mumbling and talking over one another, displaying an abundant amount of feverish excitement.

"Wow, he's so hot. I'm glad he's back," exclaimed one of the female riders.

"Looks like the big bad American is coming back for another shot at victory," declared a rider from Canada.

"Canadian, eh? Must be a Carney fan, and Bomber hater," shouted an American.

The moderator of the group stepped in warning everyone to be civil. "Don't turn this into a hate ride. If you get too rowdy, I'll disconnect you and throw you out of the group."

Nick scrambled for his phone laying on the nearby desk. He didn't believe the online rider and needed to check his twitter account. The sweat on his hands made it impossible for him to use his thumbprint to unlock his phone. "Fuck. Shit. Mother fucker. FUCK!!!!!"

"Andrew Boyde, you've been warned. I'm going to ask you to leave the ride," shouted the moderator.

Nick didn't protest. As far as he was concerned his ride was over, his day ruined. He came to a stop, manually punched in his password to his phone and checked his twitter account. Bomber's tweet was the most recent on his feed, followed by a flurry of comments, and re-tweets. Nick was shocked. The bastard was coming out of retirement. What did this mean? What about last year during the Tour? Did he play us? Was he as bad as Robert Saunders reported? The reporter had hinted at something like this happening. Nick's head swelled with questions and a ringing that didn't seem to want to stop.

CHAPTER 30

Everything can be confirmed on Twitter

NO FAKE NEWS!

Next year's Tour route had been announced three weeks ago, and December's training camps were just around the corner. Jack Bomber made the decision to come out of retirement. He called a press conference, inviting the most prominent cycling reporters, with the notable exception of Robert Saunders. He didn't want to be bombarded with any innuendo of cheating using blackmail and bullying.

The past two seasons he'd been faced with accusations by Saunders. The first year they were fleeting, and Bomber did an excellent job of making them go away. He had tainted Robert's reputation and turned him into a conspiracy-spewing imbecile. Saunders was ill-prepared, and his source, a former teammate of Bomber's, backed out at the last moment, frightened he may have betrayed the cycling omertà. The risk of losing his position in the pro peloton was a risk he wasn't willing to take.

Saunders may have lost round one, but during last year's Tour, he'd hit Bomber hard. First, through Nick Carney. Saunders played with the young rider's bullish state of mind, creating discord between the two riders, where no such conflict may have existed— in the beginning. Next, during the final week of the Tour, he repeatedly questioned why Ellington and Morkov appeared to be working for Bomber, to the detriment of his teammate, Nick Carney.

In newsprint and during the open air broadcast, Saunders flung around accusations like the kid who cried wolf. But, in all his years as a reporter, he'd never witnessed riders racing the way they were. Their tactics made no sense. There was something behind the way Ellington and Morkov were racing, and Saunders needed to know why.

Bomber had logged into his twitter account moments before strolling up to the press table to make his announcement. He sent out a quick tweet announcing his comeback. He took a moment to reflect on the last few months. He may have been coming back, but he wasn't sure he was ever really gone. There wasn't a day since the Tour ended that he hadn't been on his bike training. He may have written off the rest of the season, choosing not to race, upsetting team management and his loyal fans, but he still had a passion for riding. Why wouldn't he continue to race while still young?

He knew in his heart he couldn't end it all and move on. He wasn't ready to become an ex-rider sitting on the couch and watching the most significant sporting event on TV every July. He didn't want to become that ex-race who struggled to be engaged in the present moment, always living in his past, reminiscing about his former glory and achievements. He loathed the idea of telling long-winded stories glorifying himself. Stories that would sneak their way into every conversation. No, he couldn't become an ex-rider. Not now. It was too soon. To save his friends, family and new riders the grief of listening to cycling war stories from the past, he knew he had to compete until the drive and passion diminished entirely. He had to create one more story that would add to his legacy.

Jack moved closer to the microphone sitting on the table. The flashes of light went on and off, as the press took photos. There was no sign of panic on his face, no sign of hesitation or second thoughts. "I'm announcing my comeback to the sport I love, the sport I grew up participating in and the sport I will compete in for the next two years. My retirement announcement in July, along with my five-month absence from active racing, means I have effectively terminated my contract with Team Apex. This allows me to look for another team. As such, I have formed a partnership with a new World Tour Team. I know there's been speculation as to which team, but at this moment I cannot announce the details until the New Year. I felt it was prudent to make this announcement now, before training camps begin, rather than later. However, I will not take any questions at this moment. Thank you, and I appreciate all who have attended."

Jack was back.

CHAPTER 31

The Tour de France

The Transitional Stages

Nick hadn't been the only one shocked and disappointed with Bomber's announcement. Tom watched the live feed of Jack's press conference via YouTube, from the comfort of his home office. He never saw it coming. "That bastard, he played us," his first instinct was to call Jack and shout every expletive known to man at him, call bullshit on everything. His retirement announcement, his absence from racing at the end of the year, and his comeback were all calculated with the precision of a watchmaker tinkering with the gears that formulated time.

Tom may have been led along in the initial phase of Jack's charades during the Tour, but it didn't last long. He saw a side of Jack he hadn't seen before, and it disturbed him. It was out of character for the calculated, reserved, and confident man who had won two Tours. Or was it?

When Jack had announced his retirement on the first rest day, it shocked Tom and the team, but he felt that Jack was putting pressure on himself to perform; to go out on top with three Tour wins. Tom believed it was an emotional, spur-of-the-moment, irrational decision that could have been sparked by the rawness and youthful jubilance of Nick Carney; his teammate who was putting pressure on him to elevate his game. He liked seeing Jack react to the stress with passion and vulnerability. It made him somehow more human, approachable and caring. Tom felt closer to the man he considered his best friend in the sport, but it would come undone as the Tour approached its final stages in the Alpes.

The four days transitioning from the Pyrenees to the Alpes had been uneventful for the general classification leaders. There'd been a second rest day consisting of press conferences, photo-ops, and of course plenty of rest. And, the other three days consisted of stages with rolling terrain, where fans were treated to watching riders who were far down on general classification, battle one another for the glory of winning a stage.

Nick Carney had still led the Tour, but his disastrous day on Hautacam meant his sizeable lead had diminished, propelling his teammate and leader Jack Bomber firmly into second, ahead of Alexie Morkov and Ron Ellington. The momentum seemed to be with Bomber, the rightful leader of the team. A betting man, a fan with years of love for this sport, would have predicted Carney would slide down the General Classification, support his leader, and retain the white jersey for best rider under twenty-five. Everything would finally be going to plan for Team Apex. The first part of the Tour may have contained a few twists and turns, the ending would finish the way it was intended, with Jack Bomber winning and gracing the top step in Paris for the third time.

Tom was happy. He had the team under control. Nick was relaxed. Having Emma by his side had kept him in good spirits.

Bomber was quiet, but not withdrawn. Every night, he and Tom discussed the impending two stages in the Alpes. Tom had assured him that Nick's physiological data didn't look right. "He's on the rivet, Jack. The mountains will reveal his declining form and leave you firmly in control. You're going to win your third Tour. I can assure you of it. Like I said, on our drive down Ax 3 Domaines."

Jack never seemed appreciative of Tom's support, and had threatened to quit again if he didn't get the full support of the team. The night before the first stage in the Alpes, Tom and Jack approached Carney in his room. Emma, who was sitting and cuddling with Nick, was asked politely to leave. She got up and slowly left the room. Before opening the door and exiting, she looked back at her man and gave him a wink and a smile. A look that said, "You'll be okay honey, I'm here for you know matter what."

Tom moved forward and near Nick on the bed. He put his arm gently around Nick's shoulder, "Kid, you've done fantastic. I'm so proud of you. The team is proud of you. No one expected you to come out and battle this way, but your physical form is deteriorating. We're not sure you're going to get through the mountains in yellow. I know you deserve the support of the team, and you know we've been one hundred percent behind you the past week, but this won't be your Tour. Jack's form is coming along. His data is good. I need the full support of the team. I'm not asking for your support. We want you to win the white jersey and get the most of this Tour. So, I want you to push it to your limit and ride for yourself. No one is asking you to ride for Jack, but the rest of the team will be ordered to. It's his last Tour. You'll have many more to come, and the team will be right there, supporting you in the years to come. You have my word."

Nick chose to feel nothing at that moment. He could have acted out in anger, yelled and whined about fairness. Shit, Nick could have pretended to be speechless, and bewildered, but Tom's words had no effect on him. The only thing he heard was he could ride for himself; he didn't need to ride for Jack. "Sounds good, boss," answered Nick, with a grin that spanned the width of his face.

Bomber was surprised. Jack knew if he'd been in Nick's position early in his career, he wouldn't have been so cooperative. There would have been no smile and no agreement. His competitiveness was too fierce. He would have spat in his Director's face, letting him know he was the talent. He would have stared down his leader, his Jack Bomber, this man competing for his Yellow Jersey and let him know he'd be keeping it, thank you very much. If you want it old man, come and get it. If his Director had been pissed, well, fuck it, he was Jack Bomber for Christ sake. He'd curl his fingers together and form the massive fists he's now known for. The fists that have seen the flesh of multiple cyclists who have crossed him in recent years. His Director would have come away unscathed of course, but the adjacent wall would have had a new sizeable hole.

But Nick appeared to be a different animal, and Bomber couldn't get a firm grasp on what he was thinking. He wanted inside Nick's head, but he couldn't seem to get there. His only option was to hold out his hand, "You're a good kid, Nick. One hell of a rider. It's been a real pleasure riding my last Tour with you." The two men shook hands.

"The pleasure's all mine, Champ."

The two men got up off the bed and headed towards the door. Tom looked down the hall and spotted Emma with her head down, her left hand placed on her cheek, pacing through the hallway. He called out to her, catching her off guard. "He's all yours, Emma."

She quickened her stride towards the door, and as the two men passed her, Bomber reached out and gently grabbed her arm. "He's a good kid. Take care of him tonight."

Emma didn't know what to think or even say. She merely nodded and reached for the door, letting herself back in. "Everything okay, Nick?"

"Yeah. As good as it's going to get."

"What does that mean?"

"It means, the team is no longer supporting me in this Tour. Tom wants them riding for Bomber. I can ride for myself and go for the young rider classification, but I'm getting zero support."

"Oh my god, those fucking assholes. I don't get it. You're still the leader of this race. What am I missing?"

Nick beckoned her to his side on the bed and wrapped his arm around her. Emma's eyes were watery, and tears were beginning to flow down her face. He wanted to feel upset like Emma, but he felt nothing, he was numb. At that moment he would've done anything to feel something. He wanted anger or sadness to overtake him; thoughts of pounding the pillow, or punching the wall, or even warm tears streaming down his cheeks. Those emotions bubbled beneath his skin, but couldn't make their way up and out. He was drowning in an abyss of nothingness.

"I'll be fine," he whispered in her ear.

"Will you, Nick?"

"I get to ride for myself. That's all that matters. I don't have to work for Bomber. I don't know what will happen, but I get to ride for myself...ride for myself...ride for myself."

CHAPTER 32

The Legendary Alpe D'Heuz

Four weeks had passed since Jack Bomber announced his comeback to the world. The rainy, gloomy days of November had been replaced with the snow and sunshine of December. The blistering freezing air had forced many cyclists into their basements, mounting their trainers for winter training. It also marked the beginning of cycling training camps in beautiful weather for the top professional teams. Nick was on his way to San Diego to meet up with the rest of his teammates. He was looking forward to escaping the harsh weather in Ottawa and leaving behind the Nick Carney who had been getting drunk and passing out on couches. He had a new layer of fat he had to contend with, but he knew after this week most of it would be gone.

The first camp was always relaxed, and a time for bonding. New equipment and clothing would be distributed. Bike fittings and physiological testing would commence. Nutritional and diet counseling would take place. There would be an initiation for the new members of the team. Nick wasn't sure what it would be this year, but he was glad he wouldn't have to go through it again. Last year, it caused him a lot of anxiety leading up to the camp. He had heard stories about the famous initiation, and negative thoughts had overwhelmed him for most of camp. Although in the end, it was rather harmless and quite fun.

The itinerary would be passed out the first day by Tom and the rest of the Directors. It would likely consist of a lot of base riding for Nick, some mountain biking, and lots of testing. He knew he'd be on the Tour team, so this camp wouldn't consist of a lot of structure and intensity. With the Tour still over six months away, Nick and the Tour team needed to ease their way into the long cycling season. Intensive training in December would only lead to mental burnout and mediocre performance come July.

Nick stared solemnly out of the window as the plane left the icy Ottawa tarmac. *Good riddance*, he thought. *I need this camp for so many reasons.* He'd been in a phase, a funk of sorts since Tom and Bomber had stopped by his room during the Tour, and Tom told him the team would stop working for him. When they left his room, he had momentarily felt alone—alone and abandoned, like when he was younger. He knew this feeling had stemmed from when his brother and sister had left the family home for school, and he was left to fend for himself. His mother was healthy, but the years of living with a man like Frank Carney had distorted her reality. She could show signs of strength when needed, but otherwise, she was a victim like her kids. When Frank would come home from his month-long speaking engagements, the house would go from relaxed and fun, to walking on eggshells.

While Frank was away, Nick found himself connecting with his mother like when he was a very young child. They would go to movies, walk around the neighborhood, and talk for hours. He could confide in her his deepest fears, his dreams, and they would speak openly and honestly about everything. His opinions were valued, debated, and challenged in a fun and refreshing way that allowed him to grow. He loved his mother, but every time his father returned home, the second he walked through the doors of the Carney residence, it all changed. His mother would disappear, not physically, but she would no longer be present. Their conversations became robotic, routine and centered around Frank; his appearances, his engagements, his life, his success. If the conversation deviated from the Frank Carney script, it wouldn't be long until there was dead silence, and awkwardness. A grown man could be seen huffing and puffing and slurring profanities under his breath.

When not the center of attention, Frank would sit silently, watching his family squirm uncomfortably. He was confident that they would eventually return their attention to him, and if they didn't he would find a way. Most of the time this would involve picking on a family member and calling out their insecurities. A bully always feels more relaxed when they have the upper hand. Nick knew that when it was just him and his mom at home, he would have to bare his father's wrath. *Why do you continue to ride that damn bike? Where do you think you're going in life on two wheels? Did you win your last race? Why not? I'll tell you why not: you're not a champion.*

The belittling could go on for a solid hour, without Nick getting a chance to speak. It was as if his father thought he was running for president, and this, his prolific speech that would garner him the victory. When Frank wasn't going off on Nick, his other would be to ignore him for hours—a tactic to demean. And this was when Nick would go numb.

It was no wonder he had become emotionless when Tom and Bomber told him his form was gone, and that he'd no longer have the support of the team. For Nick, it wasn't a logical or tactical decision being explained to him. It was a person of authority telling him he wasn't good enough; asking him who he thought he was, and did he think he was special because he had a colored jersey on his back. It was a, *hey kid, you've done okay, but don't ever think you'll be as good as Jack Bomber. Where do you think you're going? Let me tell you, nowhere. Now move over and let the man of the hour Jack Bomber take his rightful place of honor.* And, Bomber's smile at the end of their conversation, when he extended his hand towards Nick, it was his father saying, "You piece of pathetic shit, you really believe you're someone, don't you? Now, fuck off!" And fuck off he did until Emma entered the room. He may not have been able to feel the way she felt, but he was able to get inside his head—to motivate himself with his imagination.

Tomorrow, he'd be so fucking intense. Hell, he would ride his mother fucking brains out. He'd stomp his legs as hard as they could go. If they screamed out for him to submit, he'd yell, fuck you over and over until they got the message they weren't allowed to quit. It would be the most significant day of his life A day he had imagined so many times when he would get on his bike, leave his Rockcliffe mansion, and his abusive father, and create a world filled with dreams of becoming a professional cyclist. A world where he competed in the greatest bicycle races. There were so many times in his dreams that he would be leading the Tour de France. Sometimes, his legs and mind seemed handicapped, and it felt like the world was against him, but his legs always found a way to emerge at the right time. His mind never failed him, and he would find clarity in pain, allowing his legs to pump and push flawlessly. But, Nick's dreams had always been under his control, unlike his reality, unlike the Tour, and unlike the decisions, his Team Director had just made.

As Emma entered the room that night, he remembered one thing he could control. Tom had told him, "ride for yourself, kid." *Yeah, better fucking believe I'm gonna ride for myself. In my dreams, I'm always riding for myself. I'm riding away from him, from the life I hate, from the person I must pretend to be when he's around. When I'm on the bike, I'm free, and the pain I inflict upon myself is a reminder that I'm alive, I'm living, and I'm free from this illness. There's no emotional torture, no questioning of my being, no disconnection. I'm connected to everything and everyone. I can feel, smell, and taste, understand the desire, passion, and love.*

Nick knew that if he could become the Nick in his dreams, it would be a special day in the mountains. Unfortunately, he never expected to learn that his parents would be showing up overnight, and Emma would be dragging them up the final climb, the legendary Alpe D'Huez. He'd found out shortly after their embrace that night when she wept in his arms, and he chose to feel nothing, wanting only to whisper in her ear, "I'll ride for myself. They say I can."

Then Emma told him.

Later that night he'd tossed and turned, looking for a comfortable position. He was excited to see his mother, brother, and sister, but he couldn't believe Frank had agreed to come. He didn't want to focus on his dad's arrival. Frank had garnered enough of Nick's attention over the years, and he didn't want it robbing him of his time in the limelight. His mind raced fervently, and his anxiety increased as he tried to fall asleep. He was fully aware that he was on edge and needed deep, restful sleep to perform, to prove to his team, his Director and to Bomber that he deserved more than just the white jersey. He earned it all. Hadn't he showed it?

Nick remembered waking up tired the following day, rubbing his eyes and watching Emma head out the door. She'd left him a note, insisting that everything would be fine. She wished him luck and told him he would conquer the stage, that he was unstoppable and at the end of the day, she and the rest of the family would be there with open arms to welcome the leader of the Tour on top of Alpe D'Huez. Nick loved her enthusiasm. Joy overtook him; his legs felt springy, supple and recovered.

A few hours later he lined up at the start of the penultimate difficult stage of the Tour. As the leader, he had multiple responsibilities to reporters, fans and the team, but he felt no responsibility today. It had all disappeared the previous night. Officially, he was no longer the leader of the team. For the first time in over a week, he felt free. His only concern was seeing his father. He knew what even the sight of that man could do to him. He prayed Emma would take the wrong turn, get lost on her way to the final climb, or just blend into the crowd enough that Nick wouldn't see them when he went by. Maybe, just maybe, she'd gotten it all wrong, and Frank had decided to stay away.

Halfway up the historical climb of Alpe D'Huez, the twenty-one hairpin turns were having a significant impact on the peloton. The race had been fast since the beginning. Attacks had been plentiful, causing a massive split on the penultimate climb. No favorites were caught out, but it did see some of the healthy men on Team Apex get dropped. One of the Spanish climbers and Welte couldn't keep pace and were the first to go. Bomber still had Bradley, Antoine, and Rosas pacing him and keeping him protected. Nick was riding behind Bomber, safely tucked in his draft, while the other favorites, Morkov and Ellington rode further back. Nick estimated that there were only fifteen guys left at this point. He was too frightened to ease up, ride down the line of favorite's and scope out who was left. If he were feeling stronger, he'd be capable of doing this. He could do a quick recon, observe his competition, look them in the eye, and listen for heavy breathing and groaning. He couldn't though. His springy legs were gone. *It's happening*, he thought to himself. *They were right. My form is garbage.*

Just in front of Nick was Bomber, spinning his legs smoothly. It looked effortless. Bradley was at the front, tapping out a stable, sustainable pace. It was fast, but Nick felt he shouldn't have been hurting. He may not have been riding for Bomber, but the team's plan at the beginning of the day was to ride tempo until they reached the last five kilometers of the stage. At that point, Rosas would take over the duties of leading the race, then go full gas for three to five minutes. The team had anticipated this would drop many favorites, keeping only Bomber, Ellington, Morkov and hopefully Nick in tow.

With two kilometers to go Bomber would launch his signature attack. It had been anticipated by the team that if Nick could stay with Bomber up until this point, then this would be when he would lose contact. The physiologist on the team didn't think Nick would have the ability to use his upper threshold effectively. Nor did they believe Ellington or Morkov would be able to match Bomber's explosiveness. Nick had strict orders not to work with either rider once dropped. If the software were to be believed, Nick would lose a minute, putting Bomber only fifteen seconds behind him in the overall classification.

When the race approached the finish, Nick could feel the weight of the last three weeks on his shoulders. He'd had difficult moments in this Tour, but he didn't want to lose. Not now, not to Jack Bomber. His imaginary cycling world he'd created when he was younger had never hurt this much. If only Bradley could slow down a notch or two. If only Nick could have a moment to catch his breath, relax his arms, and gather his thoughts. Just one moment was needed; to recoup, refocus and move forward. He knew he wasn't going to get it. Any moment now, Rosas would take over, and this shit would get real.

Bradley slowed down and pulled over to the side of the mountain, losing himself within the crowd of fans. His foot went down to ensure he wouldn't topple over. His heart pounded rapidly, moving his chest up and down, gasping for air. If he could let himself topple over and lay down, he would. His job was done. It had been his moment to shine, to lead the way for the Spanish climber. Now, it would be his chance to recover. In a few minutes, he'd have to remount and pedal slowly to the finish.

Nick wasn't looking forward to what was about to happen. Rosas took up where Bradley left off, exploding out of the saddle and applying massive pressure on the group. Nick was ready. He diligently followed Bomber but wished he were somewhere else, anywhere else. His physical sensations didn't feel normal, they felt insane.

Nick knew he wouldn't be able to rely solely on positive emotions, the crowd's energy, or seeing the faces of his loved ones to get the job done. His body felt like it had been injected with a harmful toxin that was causing his body to stiffen. His arms felt like they were weighted slabs of steel moving back and forth, trying to propel his lightweight body. The stiffness of his neck caused his shoulders to tighten, sending painful throbbing aches to his head. His vision became blurry, and he started to lose his form. In a mere second, he lost contact and watched as Rosas rode away with the other favorites in tow.

Emma and the Carney family were waiting for Nick to pass by. They had their Canadian Flags waving proudly, anticipating the Yellow Jersey riding by, leading the pack of favorites. When Rosas passed them with Bomber, Ellington, and Morkov, Emma felt deflated. Emma wondered if she had done enough for Nick last night. She looked over at Alex for reassurance. "He'll minimize his losses. Nothing to worry about, Em. He's strong mentally, stronger than you think, and he'll know how to pace himself in this situation," he told her.

Thirty seconds later, Nick approached where the Carney family stood, watching. He was alone, with his head down. He looked up when he heard his name being called. He wished the sight of Emma would give him the strength to fight on, but he felt nothing. He looked at Frank, who was grinning widely—a grin that said, *see I told you, you were nothing.* But anger couldn't propel him forward. He was lost, really lost, for the first time in his life. The pain he thought he owned and knew, was replaced by a stranger. And this intruder was unforgiving. His grip on Nick's mind was compelling and overwhelming. He was worst than Frank Carney!

Nick had started the day feeling light and free, and now he felt like he was wearing a weighted vest as he rode his bike uphill. He may have had a two-minute advantage on Jack Bomber at the beginning of the stage, but he wasn't sure it'd be enough to keep his lead by the end of the day. Worse, he didn't know if he actually cared. The pain was doing an excellent job of wrapping itself around every part of Nick's physical body, squeezing him so that he struggled to deliver oxygen to his working muscles and brain.

He'd alternated between conscious thought—delivering pressure to the pedals to minimize his time gap—and then to the abyss— darkness where the cheers of the thousands of fans were muted. He awakened fully when he crossed the line. The sound of people pushing and shoving one another to get to him. He'd tell reporters that it was nothing more than a hunger knock—inexperience on such an epic climb. In reality, it'd been the worst moment he'd ever had on a bike.

His team soigneur screamed this name. Nick had wondered where he finished. Had he kept his lead? Was he still in yellow? He lay on the ground looking up at all the faces looking back at him, and he wondered, what did today mean? What did any of this mean?

Today, on his way to the team camp, as he looked out the small window of the plane, he thought he might finally have the answer.

CHAPTER 33

Ventoux and Blackmail

Riders and staff from Team Apex clamored into the small hotel conference room, where a dozen reporters and photographers waited patiently to take their pictures. With fresh new black and white kits, every journalist wanted to be the first to capture this moment. Nick, like many of his teammates, was tired from a busy week of training and bonding. This was the last day before he boarded a plane back home for Christmas. He stood patiently, smiling for the group photo, but thinking only of Emma and home. He knew he had a hard season ahead of him, and this camp only represented a small portion of the work that would be required of him for the new season.

In mere moments, he anticipated he'd be sitting down one-on-one with every journalist. Wendy had prepared him all week, with responses and phrases she was sure would whet the appetite of every journalist. Robert Saunders was here. Unlike Jack Bomber's come back conference, Saunders was still an authority on cycling and welcomed by all at the Team Apex camp. Nick was hesitant, apprehensive to speak to him. Last year was still fresh in his memory.

Christ, right before coming to the camp he'd watched Tour race footage repeatedly.

He slowly walked up to Saunders' table and took a seat. "Robert. How are you?"

"I'm doing great, Nick. Yourself?"

"Yeah, good. Happy to be here."

Robert smiled. "Were you told to say that?"

Nick smiled back and shook his head, "You know it."

Robert took out his pad of paper, along with a recorder. "I'm going to ask you a series of standard questions. I'm sure you went through them with some of the other journalists already. All on the record. And then, if you don't mind, I want to speak to you off the record."

"I'm not sure, Robert. Let's get through the standard questions and see how comfortable I am."

Robert agreed and began asking him about last year's race, his duel with Jack Bomber, the outcome and what he expected to achieve this year. Nick did his best to stay in line with the team's wishes. Everything was answered according to Wendy's pre-defined script. Saunders knew it wasn't the kid's true feelings, but he was happy to take it all down. Most of it was bullshit-scripted nonsense that would be published by every English-speaking internet site and blog.

Once done with the formalities, Saunders clicked his recorder off and didn't waste a second. "Did you know Jack had Ellington and Morkov in his pocket?"

Nick looked at Robert like he was just told that a family member betrayed his trust. "What are you talking about?"

"Did you not think it was funny, that the two of them seemed to be riding for Jack at times during the Tour? Did you never question, why they didn't attack the second to last day up Ventoux?"

"No, not really. Should I have?" Nick played dumb, but he'd been asked that question from friends since the Tour ended. Ventoux was a pivotal stage, with the Tour up for grabs.

Nick went into a trance, trying to remember that day. There had only been fifteen seconds separating him from Bomber. While he faltered on Alpe D'Huez the day before, he'd managed to stay in the race lead—in yellow. In fact, his fifteen seconds over Bomber was precisely what the software had predicted. It also predicted Ventoux would be where Nick lost his yellow jersey.

Mont Ventoux, the Beast of Provence, the Giant, The Bald Mountain; a legendary Col situated in the Provence region of Southern France. At 1,912m, the Beast was prone to wind speeds over ninety kilometers per hour and wind gusts over three hundred kilometers per hour. The mountain was unrelenting, gaining 1617 meters over 21.8 kilometers from Bedouin, a small French village that hosted cyclist throughout the year looking to take on The Bald Mountain. They came from around the world to conquer the mountain and cross it off their bucket list. Most would complete it between an hour and a half to three hours. Professionals could do it under an hour, with Iban Mayo completing it in an astonishing 55 min and 51 seconds in the 2004 Dauphine Libere.

The gruesomeness and cruelty of this mountain pass meant that in the past some cyclists had sought pharmacological products to conquer it. Tom Simpson, the British cyclist, collapsed to his death in the final 2.3 kilometers to the summit in the 1967 Tour. While the exact cause of his death was unknown, the heat, the altitude and the amphetamines found in his bloodstream and jersey pocket, more than likely all played a role. A shrine for the British Champion now sat prominently in the last mile of the summit and was visited daily by cyclists who left bottles and other cycling paraphernalia in his memory.

Simpson wasn't the only Professional cyclist associated with the climb. In 1970 the great Eddy Merckx, on his way to winning the stage up Mont Ventoux almost collapsed and needed to be treated with oxygen post-stage. There was also Eros Poli, one of the tallest and heaviest cyclist of all time, not a climber in any right; he won the Ventoux Stage in 1994 after building an insurmountable lead right from the beginning of the stage. The controversial Lance Armstrong gifted the legendary Marco Pantani the Summit victory in the 2001 Tour and was later criticized openly over and over by the Italian Champion, who believed he'd won it fair and square. And, the mountain would always be remembered for showcasing Chris Froome's running ability in the 2016 Tour. Up until this year, those had been the most memorable exploits the mountain was best known for, but the battle between Carney and Bomber changed everything.

Nick remember that once the darkness of the tree-lined mountain opened itself to the moonscape peak, the wind took no mercy, and the front group of riders splintered like a powerful tsunami, leaving only a few survivors. He was an unfortunate victim and watched as Ellington and Morkov rode away, sheltering Bomber. The wind had Nick swaying back and forth, holding onto the bars as tight as he could so he wouldn't fall over. He watched his excellent friend Ellington pacing Bomber up the mountain. He felt out of sorts, angry, but also not. He was told by the team he would lose his lead today. He had to accept the facts.

Robert snapped his fingers in front of Nick, bringing the young man out of his trance and back to the present. "Where are you, kid? Did I lose you?"

"No, No. I'm just, you know, trying to think about that day."

"Do you remember now? Do you remember what happened?"

Nick shook his head back and forth, "Robert, to move forward, I can't look back. What good does looking back do? History is history."

"I thought you said you would speak to me candidly. This sounds rather rehearsed, Nick."

There was truth to Nick's response. He had spent the last few months getting intoxicated and watching footage of the Tour and everything he did wrong. He reviewed the Ax 3 Domaines stage dozens of times, analyzing his pedal stroke, his sudden loss of form, and the journalist's commentary as it unfolded, questioning it all and hoping for a different outcome. But the Ventoux stage had been different. He could remember bits and pieces, but there was an emotional void jumbled in with fragmented memories. It was like a puzzle of scattered pieces that Nick couldn't seem to put together. It was another bout of amnesia that masked what truly transpired. He'd watched the footage, but he couldn't emotionally connect to the events that'd happened, nor did he care to. From what he could tell, he executed his game plan the best he could that day, given the circumstances.

"Fine," said Nick. "Maybe, it's not about looking back. I have some difficulty remembering everything that happened that day."

"What? How could you forget a day like that? How could you forget what went down?"

Robert wanted to press the issue. He could tell Nick wasn't lying. He observed the real Nick at the beginning of the Tour and could tell when he was speaking the truth, and when his words were chosen for him by the Team Media Coordinator. "What about Ellington? Why haven't you spoken to him since the Tour?" asked Saunders.

"I'm not exactly sure. We're competitors, friendly to one another, but still competitors and on different teams, living on different continents. I haven't felt the need to connect with him."

"He says you won't return his call or emails. He told me that he has tried multiple time since the Tour ended."

"He can say what he wants, but I've been busy. I think we both know that."

"Are you sure it's not because he and Morkov rode away from you on Ventoux, sheltering Jack from the wind? He told me why he did it, off the record of course."

Nick sat upright and leaned in. At first, Saunders thought he sparked the boy's curiosity and expected Nick to ask him what he meant, but he didn't say a word. He stared at Saunders. No, instead, he looked straight through him. "Come on, Nick, you know what they did to you wasn't proper," pressed Saunders.

"Robert, I'm not sure what you're getting at. At that moment in the race, I was dropped. So, they worked with Bomber. They all had something to gain."

"There was more to it than just that moment Nick, and you know it."

Nick got up from the table. He'd had enough of Robert Saunders. He was tired of reminiscing about last year's Tour. It was over, let it be done. For a moment he thought, maybe Jack Bomber had it right, maybe Robert Saunders was a menace. As Nick tried to leave Saunders grabbed Nick's wrist, "Bomber blackmailed Morkov and Ellington. Morkov won't speak to me, but Ellington did. Now sit down. You need to hear this."

Nick's put his dislike for Saunders aside, his hatred for Bomber was far more significant. "Bomber caught Ellington with a younger woman after the rest day. He threatened to expose him to the media if Ellington didn't help him. Like I said, I'm not sure what he threatened Morkov with, but I'm sure he did."

Nick didn't flinch, he didn't hesitate. He didn't appear shocked or surprised, and it honestly had Saunders feeling a bit squeamish. He couldn't understand how Carney looked so unaffected. He thought he'd dropped a bomb on the kid, and that Carney would show him some of that raw anger he'd displayed in their very first meeting during the early days of the Tour. Nick hadn't responded because Saunders' story had felt like the shit he'd told the world the year before. The same shit, which had caused Bomber to hate is fucking guts. Part of Nick wanted to blurt this out and bring it to Saunders attention, but a more prominent part of him believed every word the reporter was telling him.

He knew Bomber was a win-at-all-costs type of man, the ends justifying the means. In fact, Nick had come to believe Robert Saunders' recently published article about Bomber's supposed retirement. Saunders had speculated during the Tour that Jack Bomber's retirement was all an elaborate ploy. After Bomber announced his comeback, Saunders had his story: *Bomber's retirement announcement during the Tour was indeed a ploy, and his return to the sport was premeditated—a long con. It was done to throw Nick Carney off his game, to gain the support of the team, and to eventually leave Team Apex to join a new team.*

Nick remained astute, "Do you have any proof, or is it Ellington's word against Bomber's?" Saunders dug into his carrying case, pulled out an envelope, and handed it to Nick. "Open it. Take a peek."

Nick reached in and grabbed a handful of paper. Most were photocopies of pictures depicting a man with a young woman. They looked like crappy shots a hotel camera would capture. They were mediocre quality, but it was Ellington, and the woman he was with was not his wife. At the bottom of the pile was a letter addressed to Ryan Ellington. It was a thank you letter for all his hard work. A letter from Jack Bomber.

Nick was distraught and uncomfortable with what he'd just seen. He couldn't understand how this could be going on in the sport he loved. How could Bomber be so conniving? "Where did Bomber even get this shit?" asked Nick.

"Apparently, he got it from an old Italian security guard from the hotel in Carcassonne. He probably got it on the rest day," replied Saunders.

Nick didn't justify Ellington's action. He couldn't imagine cheating on Emma. Infidelity was beneath him, he couldn't do it. Even the thought of cheating would cause him heartache and guilt. He wouldn't be able to live with himself. He was angry with Ellington, but Bomber's blackmail was outright despicable. "Get this shit away from me. I can't handle it, man." He pushed the photos away from him.

Saunders was confident he could see tears forming in Carney's eyes. He was still a journalist at heart, and he knew now was the time to get what he wanted.

"Nick, may I ask you a few more question on the record?"

"Yeah, let's go back on the record. I don't want to see any more of that shit."

"Perfect...perfect." Saunders clicked his small recorder back on. "Nick, at any point during the Tour did you think Ellington and Morkov were working for Jack Bomber?"

"Yes."

"What makes you believe that the two men were working for him?"

"Well, we all saw it multiple times throughout the race, did we not. They never attacked, they seemed to block him from the wind like loyal lieutenants. And that last stage on Ventoux. Come on now, what the fuck were they doing? When Bomber started to falter and drop back like a stone, and I began to recover and make up ground...why did those two go back to stay with him? They rode Bomber off their wheels, looked back, slowed down and went back to him? Those mother fuckers!!!"

With that, Robert Saunders had one more story to tell.

CHAPTER 34

Christmas

A Happy Time of Year

A couple of weeks had passed since Robert Saunders published his tell-all story about Jack Bomber. It was his second exposé on the former Tour Champion since Jack Bomber decided to come out of retirement. Tales of blackmail, as well as bullying and manipulation within his own team during the Tour, were corroborated by fellow riders and staff. No names were mentioned in the article except one—his prominent, former teammate Nick Carney was quoted throughout.

Initially, tweets were rampant, with fans and fellow cyclist calling Bomber disgraceful. Headlines around the world, referred to him as the fallen hero, pleading with him to go back into retirement. While their concerns were prominent, Jack Bomber's fans were louder and more boisterous. They picked the young Canadian cyclist apart. They called him soft, fragile, and unlikely to do anything in the sport beyond what he did this year. Carney had the support of Canada and most of Europe, while Bomber had the support of the USA.

The tweets kept coming as Christmas quickly approached. Tomorrow, presents would be opened, the turkey would be eaten, and copious amounts of dessert would be consumed to the point of discomfort. Despite the negative media towards him, Nick was looking forward to Christmas. Since getting back from the training camp, he'd been feeling good. There hadn't been a training day he missed, despite having to ride his bike indoors. Emma noticed the change and was happy to have her Nick back. After months of worry, she was excited to see his passion for training return. She wasn't entirely sure what happened at the camp, but she knew Robert Saunders' article had somehow freed him. He was finally content and seemingly able to accept what happened last year. He could finally appreciate what he did, and how he accomplished it.

It was early morning, and Emma couldn't contain her excitement. She turned over and kissed the back of Nick's neck. "Baby, are you up?"

"I am now."

"It's Christmas," she shouted, like an excited child, kicking the blankets off, "get up, get up, get up!"

Nick grumbled, grabbing at the blankets to wrap himself up tightly and go back to bed. Emma was having none of it. She was a Christmas fanatic. As soon as the leaves began to change color in the fall, Emma went into full Christmas mode. Shopping lists were made, plans and events were scheduled and confirmed, and the Christmas decorations began to adorn their condo. Much to the chagrin of Nick. He liked Christmas, sure, but who loved it this much?

Nick knew if he didn't get up now, he would disappoint her. She had a whole breakfast planned for the two of them, followed by opening gifts and watching Christmas movies, before heading over to the Carney residence for supper.

She couldn't help but stare at her man, his lanky frame exposed. Those long muscular legs, his six-pack stomach, his dark hair. She believed she couldn't have done any better than Nick Carney—he was her soulmate. She thought about their pending marriage, and how in a few months she would be Mrs. Carney. *I'm the luckiest girl alive,* she gushed. "Come on sleepy head," she moaned, "gifts need to be opened."

Emma eventually coaxed him out of bed, and they headed down for breakfast. As they approached the living room, Nick could see presents scattered beneath their tree. Gifts that hadn't been there the night before.

"It looks like Santa paid us a visit," Emma said, with a wink.

Nick smiled, picked her up and gave her a big kiss. "Looks like it," he agreed.

"Do we open up gifts before we eat or after?"

"Don't be stupid, sweetheart. You know I won't let you open up any gifts before breakfast."

"Come on, Em," he moaned, "just one."

"Breakfast, boo-bear. You have coffee duty. Think you can handle it, champ?"

Nick dropped his shoulders, and pouted, all in a playful manner. He knew he wouldn't be able to break Emma's Christmas traditions, but thought he would give it a go. He went to the coffee maker, grabbed the coffee beans and dumped them into the grinder. The aroma of the French roast was strong, and Nick took a deep breath. He wanted to enjoy every morsel of its delectable scent. Today was special—everything had to be perfect. The breakfast, the presents, the movies, and his family supper would have to be impeccable. It wasn't just for Emma, Nick needed this day to go seamlessly, picture perfect, for him.

He was treading on thin ice, and he knew it.

CHAPTER 35

Rush to Glory

The Last Supper

There is a time in everyone's life when they want to feel free and live in the moment. Nick was enjoying every moment of this Christmas day, but he wasn't looking forward to supper at his parents' house. He'd be happy to see his mother, brother and sister, and of course his nieces and nephew, but he didn't want to see his father. Why bother? The bastard hadn't spoken to him since the Tour had ended. Sure, when Nick had crossed the finish line on Champs Élysée, Frank made sure to stand by his son and smile for the cameras. Not for Nick, but for himself. He had to make the world believe that Frank Carney was a supportive, proud father.

When the camera's stopped, when they were no longer in the spotlight, Frank could barely say a word to his son. Nick knew he hadn't done enough at the Tour to impress his father. Nick could win over the world, but not Frank Fucking Carney. Nothing ever would. If he hadn't realized it during the Tour while in the lead and wearing yellow, he certainly knew it for sure once the Tour had ended. The evening of the final stage Team Apex threw a massive party with friends and family. Bomber was invited, and to Nick's surprise the man showed up. Nick felt respected and even thought that perhaps, for the very first time, his dad would embrace him and tell him he was proud to be the boy's father.

That moment never came, but what did come were tears. An intoxicated Frank Carney had made a scene. He let loose and belittled his son in front of hundreds of people who came to celebrate the team's success. And Nick was a huge part of that. It got to a point where some of Nick's teammates took it upon themselves to remove the drunk. He was tossed out into the streets of France and left to his own devices.

As young and as brash as Nick could be, his father's attack left him in turmoil. It may have been a combination of fatigue, alcohol, and relief, but Nick couldn't control the tears that streamed down his face. He sobbed for close to an hour, shaking, cursing and being consoled by Emma.

It was a scene Nick had no plans on reliving tonight, but he knew it was a possibility. It was Christmas and Frank would be drinking—not that he'd ever needed an excuse to crack open a bottle of alcohol. Nick hadn't seen the man or spoken to him since July but knew Frank blamed him for being kicked out of the after-party. Nick assumed his father's inner dialogue since that party went something like this, *the poor kid is weak. It's not my fault he can't handle the truth. If I'd raised him the right way, he'd have a set of balls!*

Nick anticipated that with a little alcohol Frank would be spewing this shit all night, and he wasn't sure he could manage a second verbal attack. July may have been five months ago, but it was too soon for Nick.

It was getting close to when Nick's mom would be serving dinner and Emma was getting antsy. Nick wouldn't allow them to arrive any earlier than needed. The less time they spent with Frank, the better it would be. He'd spend the next day with his brother, doing their annual boxing day sale hunting. Nick had already gone through multiple flyers and had his eye on a new 90-inch flat screen TV. It would go well on their new feature wall, or at least that's what he told Emma to get her on board.

The young couple arrived at the Carney residence, and Catherine opened the door, "Why did you guys knock?!" she exclaimed and embraced the two of them. Nick and Emma were welcomed by the rest of the family with hugs and kisses. The kids jumped all over Nick, barely allowing him to move beyond the front door. Frank embraced Emma, and she tentatively hugged him back. She was extremely cautious around the man. Emma didn't want to upset Nick. She looked over to see if Nick noticed, but the children were doing a fantastic job bringing out the big kid in him. He was smiling and laughing, and Emma was content, believing his anxiety had likely disappeared for the time being. He'd be fine for the rest of the evening, she thought.

If only it had been correct. Nick had caught the interaction between Emma and his father. He started to have difficulty swallowing and breathing. He felt as if he'd suddenly got something caught in his throat. His chest tightened, squeezing his heart, and causing it to beat rapidly. He felt trapped and alone, and as the children joked and jumped on him, he did his best to hide his feelings. He didn't need Emma knowing he'd seen her hug Frank and it was killing him inside—breaking his fragile state of mind. He knew she was polite, but he felt jaded nonetheless.

At first, supper would go smoothly. The turkey was beautifully smoked, the mashed potatoes were oozing with butter and cream, and the stuffing was on point. People were laughing and having a wonderful time. Nick cheerfully unbuttoned his jeans, "I think I need a little extra room." Everyone at the table, but Frank, laughed. In fact, Frank's only reaction was to stare uncomfortably at Nick for a solid minute before piping up, "Getting a bit fat there, Nick? You better be careful, you don't want to be dragging that roll of fat up those mountains in the Tour next year. It'd put an end to your pathetic dreams."

It was a vicious and unwarranted statement, making everyone uncomfortable. No one at the dinner table knew how to handle it appropriately. Nick was once again his father's punching bag. He squirmed in his chair, biting down on his tongue hard, hoping the physical pain he was inflicting would take away his emotional hurt. Nick wanted to remain calm. He didn't want to ruin Christmas Dinner. An argument with Frank wasn't on his agenda tonight, but he was beginning to have a sick feeling in his stomach that a confrontation with Nick may be on his father's. He reached under the table for Emma's hand and squeezed it gently. She knew this was their cue. Dessert would be served then it would be time to leave.

Emma didn't get a chance to save Nick. As dessert was being served, Frank started his rant. Nick was the subject of most of his rampage, and with every insult and degrading comment, Nick weakened. He found himself wilting like a flower that had been deprived of water. The man didn't possess the capability of love, at least not for Nick. Emma knew they needed to get out of there and fast. She tried to politely excuse them, but Frank began yelling. She grabbed Nick's hands and pulled him up. Alex started to shout at his father, and all chaos broke out. She couldn't wait any longer. Nick was visibly shaken, and Emma knew she had to remove him from the situation and fast. She reached for their coats as Catherine apologized profusely, pleading for them to stay. "He's drunk. You know how he gets. This will be over in a few minutes. He needs to get it out of his system. Then he'll shut up."

Emma didn't care. She was tired of all the weak excuses. She was frantic but tried to sound composed, "Catherine, Nick can't take it. You know the way he is. Look at him. I'm taking him home."

He looked comatose, thought Emma. She was driving carefully through the slippery streets heading home, while Nick was lost in his head. She'd ask him questions, try to get him to focus, but he would only give her one-word responses. Emma would watch his lips move as if he were speaking, and he was, but only to himself. He wasn't willing to talk to her. He couldn't explain his current state. He felt numb.

There had been times in the Tour when he'd felt elation or devastation, success or failure. He could get deep into a zone where he felt nothing but could feel everything all at the same time. And then there was Ventoux. What happened on Ventoux? He knew how he'd finished. That day had decided the outcome of the race, but he couldn't remember how he felt. Was he happy, sad, or angry? What did he think? Nick knew it honestly didn't matter anymore, because at this very moment he felt hollow. Frank made him think this way. And, not just today, but for his whole life.

Emma pulled into the driveway. "Babe, we're home. Talk to me, please. Are you okay?" Nick turned in her direction, and for the first time since getting in the car made eye contact. He gently grabbed her neck and brought her closer, giving her a soft kiss on her delicate lips. "I'm fine, Babe," he said, almost gleefully, "Happy to be back home."

Emma found herself almost in tears but used all her energy to stay strong. "Oh honey, I'm so sorry for what your father said. He's a total asshole. I love you so much. Everyone does. I'm here for you no matter what. We'll get through this, I promise."

"Babe, it threw me for a bit of a loop, but I'm back. I'm not sure where I went, but you have nothing to worry about," he tried to sound as convincing as he could. "If you don't mind I'm going to go down to the den for a few minutes. Cool?"

Emma didn't hesitate or try to stop him. "Of course, honey." He was smiling now, and she knew this was where Nick needed to be when he felt beat up. The den contained all his cycling memorabilia, trophies, and jerseys. He would spend as much time alone as needed until he was ready to talk. Even then, Emma didn't expect much talking from him. He'd more than likely go to sleep and wake up tomorrow as if nothing happened.

Nick slowly made his way to the den dragging his feet. He couldn't understand what he was feeling. In fact, he wasn't sure he'd ever been able to. He just wanted something tangible—something of importance that said Nick Carney was significant—to look at and admire. He was looking forward to gazing at his trophies and photos knowing they'd help him heal.

Before entering the main foyer of the basement, Nick stopped in the bathroom. His head was aching, and he needed some Advil. Nick splashed cold water on his face hoping to feel more awake and alive. The bottle of Advil was almost impossible to get open, but he finally got the stubborn cap off after the third try. He reached for a couple of pills and then decided a handful would do. His head wasn't only hurting, it was throbbing, and he wanted to feel no unnecessary pain.

After a few minutes of looking at his reflection in the mirror Nick's head began to feel better. It'd been a long time since he'd looked at himself and he was shocked to see such a good-looking young man in the mirror. He had the look of a man who could grace the cover of GQ magazine or People. Yet, it wasn't how he felt or saw himself most of the time. All he could ever see was an awkward, tall, skinny boy who was weak and pathetic. A kid who got lucky when it came to catching the attention of Emma Blake. How did he get her?

Nick couldn't take anymore introspection. He slowly strolled through the alley of his basement looking at cycling pictures of him from his early days all the way up until this year's Tour. Nick had multiple shadow boxes containing jerseys from various races, but there was one he had trouble looking at. He never put it up. It was Emma who prominently displayed it. He never felt he deserved it, but she couldn't imagine not including it on his wall of fame. The shadow box contained the final jersey he wore on the last stage of the Tour.

Nick looked up at the wall but saw nothing. He couldn't recall which jersey sat in that box. Was it the white jersey or the yellow jersey? It didn't matter any longer. No jersey ever brought him glory. No jersey brought him closer to his father. And, no jersey would. It was all so clear to him now. He had all the facts he needed and realized the very thing he was looking for would never come to fruition. It was hopeless. He had everything a person could ask for, success, a beautiful and kind woman, wealth and popularity. But, he wasn't happy. He couldn't express his feelings and love for Emma because his father bullied and abused him. He was a delicate human being, easily broken by the simplicity and reality of life. He didn't deserve Emma, and she didn't deserve a fraud.

Nick grabbed some pen and paper and brought his work stool closer to the middle of the basement. He wanted to try to express himself for the first time in his life. Nick needed to write down his feelings and love for Emma, and it had to be perfect. He knew he hadn't done an outstanding job being open with her throughout their relationship. He could've been more intimate, more caring and affectionate. He could've let her see how vulnerable and insecure he was, but he was always too scared. He knew she understood him, but he wasn't sure she knew exactly who he was. He wanted to strip away everything and expose his real soul so she would understand.

Nick finished writing, sighed with relief, and for the first time in a long time felt at peace. He'd given it his all. Nick had bared his soul to the love of his life and felt free. He was ready now, prepared to move forward and conquer the unknown. He let the paper slip out of his hands and float downwards towards the ground.

Moments later Nick picked up a large rope that lay by his side. He didn't remember when he'd bought the rope, or why he'd decided to purchase one. It could've been shortly after the Tour, or months later when Nick was feeling alone and drunk. It didn't matter because at some point he'd made a loop out of the thick knotted rope and located the strongest beam in the basement.

He reached up with his hand, throwing the rope over the beam. He didn't want to hesitate. This wouldn't be some cry for help.

Like every other moment in his life, he made the decision then moved swiftly. He propped himself on the stool, reached for the rope and wrapped the loop around his neck. His hands reached for the back of the rope, and he tightened it, giving it a good yank. It was now or never. There would be no glory in taking his own life, but there was also no glory in leading a life when you felt like this. He kicked the stool out beneath him; the rope tightened as he closed his eyes. He could feel every ounce of pain as the air slowly seeped out of his body. His legs swung side to side as he struggled against what was happening—instinct—and his eyes opened widely. He stared at his final Tour jersey for a singular moment, and as his eyes closed for the last time, he was blinded by the bright, warm color resonating from the box.

About the Author

Lawrence Brooks is a part-time writer who has spent the last 27 years racing his bike. From junior to elite, and then pro and now masters; he hasn't lost his passion for racing a bicycle. He grew up reading stories of the greatest cyclist in the world and envisioned himself the next Greg Lemond or Steve Bauer—his childhood heroes. Lawrence fell in love with their stories, but his imagination wanted something that went beyond non-fiction. After years of searching, he still couldn't find a fictional novel that had it all—a riveting story that brought the reader into the fantastic world of cycling, into a race, and into the racer's mind.

Lawrence hopes that you'll fall in love with this fictional world of cycling he created, fall in love with the main characters; hate them, cheer for them, and turn each page in suspense. Like the Tour de France itself, Lawrence tries to capture the essence of the race—a rider racing it, a family watching it a continent away, fans on the mountainside, unconditional love—it's all here. The reader will move slowly through the beginning, before coming to the peak of the story, but it doesn't stop, and won't until the very end. A race isn't over until you reach the finish line and The Road To Glory is no different.

REVIEWS

If you enjoyed this Novel, please share your reviews on Amazon and Goodreads. Spread the word!!!

Rush to Glory Publishing House Presents:

Tom Danielson: ALL IN with Lawrence Brooks

You live or die by what type of process you have in place.
You're either all in and entirely committed, or you're lying to

yourself and everyone around you. Do you want to know what it's like living with one foot in and the other foot out? It's failure of the worst kind.

Over the last few months, I have started to publicly share my gruesome failures, as well as my extraordinary successes. I never imagined in a million years that my far-from-perfect life could provide an abundant amount of tools to inspire others. I am excited to announce a new book project documenting my journey. I want to share my story about surviving colossal failure/disappointment, struggling to attain success, and most importantly, to help people change their lives. I want you living your dreams every day.

The journey to write this book is going to be raw, challenging and incredibly emotional, but my story needs to be told. I know my why now, and I'm motivated to share with you how to become ALL IN.

I love you guys, here we go...

Made in the USA
San Bernardino, CA
05 August 2020